Love's Embers
Canon City Series

Lauren Marie

Excerpt from Love's Embers

Charlie stood up so fast from his seat he almost stumbled on the hearth. He went to the other side of the room and crossed his arms. "You were supposed to wait for me. You promised to wait," he shouted at her.

Lark stood up with her fists clenched. "How long was I supposed to wait, Charlie? Five years, ten? Christ, was I supposed to become Miss Havisham and wear my wedding dress until I died? How long, Charlie? I was only fifteen. When we were eighteen years old and you didn't come back, what was I supposed to do?" She saw a new expression on his face. "Let me guess, you never read Great Expectations? Figures. I thought we'd be able to once and for all put the past away, but even though you were counseled it would seem you're still angry. I'm still angry. I guess it would be better to wait until tomorrow." She turned and started out of the living room.

Charlie followed behind her and in the hallway, grabbed her arm. She looked up at him, shocked. He spun her around and pushed her against the front door. They were both breathing hard and Lark could feel tears start to burn her eyes. She kept telling herself this was not June and Charlie wasn't one of those men.

Look for Other Stories by Lauren Marie
Love's Touch - Then and Now
Going to Another Place
One touch at Cob's Bar and Grill

DEDICATION
Love's Embers is for my cousin Chip Davis. He started it. Thanks
for the great idea, Cuz.

ACKNOWLEDGEMENTS:

Thanks go to Jennifer Conner and the folks at Books to Go, Now,
for the opportunity. It's so great to be working with you.
Thank you to Marilyn Miles for the great editing. Had and Was are
the biggest pains in the behind.
I must thank Mary Allen at American Gramaphone for all the
crazy email questions and answers. I appreciate all the help.
Mannheim Steamroller still rocks.
For copies of Going to Another Place see
www.mannheimsteamroller.com.
Thank you to my friends and family for their love and support, too.
Thanks, as always, to my reader, Elizabeth Ainsley, your help is
always appreciated.
I, also, want to thank Justin at Love's Travel Stop on Highway 25
in Colorado. He answered a very important question for me.

ISBN-13:978-1505666212

ISBN-10:150566621X

"Love truly happens once in life,
as it did between us.
I will find you,
and we will flame again, forever."

Chapter One

Thirteen years ago

Sleep started to whisk Lark off to dreamland when she heard her window slide open and felt the bed move. She knew it was Charlie who crawled in beside her, but he lay on his back. She could hear him breathe hard and she sat up.

"Ducky, what's wrong?" She moved to turn on the light.

Charlie reached over and stopped her. "Don't turn the light on, Lou," he whispered and called her by the nickname he used.

She lay back down and reached over to him. Lark could feel him shake and thought he might be crying.

"Oh Ducky, what happened?" She scooted nearer to him and put her arm across his chest.

It took a little while for Charlie to settle down, and he finally turned on his side. He held her hand. "I don't understand, Lou. I don't think I'll ever understand what I did that makes them hate me so much."

"You mean your parents?"

"Yeah."

"Is you dad drinking tonight?" She put both her hands around his.

"Yeah."

"Did he hit you?" Charlie didn't answer, which gave Lark the answer. "You know, Gran wants to report them for hitting you."

"I know. I begged her not to do that."

"Why?"

"If social services got involved they'd take me away from my parents. I'd never get to see you or Gran again." He was quiet for a time and then squeezed both of her hands with his. "Lou, can I ask you a question?"

"Sure."

"Why do you like me?"

Lark sat up and looked down at him. "Ducky, you're my best friend in the whole world. You're my hero."

He rolled onto his back. "I'm not talking about alien invasion, Lou."

"I know. Charlie Stone, I love you. I'll always love you. You're one of the good guys and I'm being serious."

Present Day -

Charlie remembered so many conversations with Lark. He looked at the house and heard screams from his past. He wished it had burned to the ground and thought about doing just that. The sounds of slaps and furniture crashing rang in his head. He wanted the noises to go away. He wanted to be free from his past. He tried to remember the days he spent with Lark. The last time he saw her was the best day he'd ever lived. They'd gone on a picnic out in a field and played an extended game of War. Her hair was up in a ponytail and it bounced every time she laughed. Lark saved him so many times.

As he glanced at the house he'd lived in until he was fifteen years old, he felt the ache of loneliness in his chest. He thought the only way to get rid of the ghosts was to face them head-on. He'd spent the last thirteen years alone and didn't want that anymore. Would he be able to find her?

He'd saved up every penny he could earn over the last thirteen years. He smirked and thought, *Thirteen. Unlucky number*. He'd finally made enough to buy the old...what? He couldn't think of what to call this place. It wasn't a home. It wouldn't ever be his home. He hated to look at it and thought he was nuts to spend money on such a waste. The price was low, and it looked like a mausoleum where only the dead walked. Would she accept him after what he'd done?

There were so many times over the last years when he thought he should join the dead. His life turned into an endless road to nowhere. He owned nothing except his truck. He wanted to find life and love, again. He wanted...

He heard a low growl and turned to look at his gray wolf, Breaker. The wolf held its head low and his fur was raised on his back.

"Breaker, what have you got, boy?" he said. He looked toward the end of the driveway and saw an older woman by the mailbox.

"Can I help you, mister? I live next door," she said and pulled her coat tighter around her body. "Nobody has lived in there for a long time. Are you looking for someone?"

He felt a bit of warmth touch his iced-over heart. "Hey, Aurora." He looked at her and saw her stare at the wolf. "Breaker, to me."

The sleek blond and silver wolf snarled and moved to his master, and sat by his feet.

"I'm sorry, sir, but do I know you?" The woman took a couple of steps forward and stopped again. She looked at him and finally smiled. "Charlie, is that you?"

"Yes, ma'am."

"My Lord, but you have gotten tall." She laughed.

These days he called himself Chuck. He'd forgotten everyone in Canon City called him Charlie.

Aurora walked closer to him. "I saw the lights from your truck. The house has sat empty for a couple of years. I thought I should be a nosy neighbor and make sure we weren't getting squatters." She took her glove off and held her hand out to him.

Charlie took off his glove, too and shook hands with her. It almost caused his throat to tighten. He felt so happy someone remembered him.

"How have you been, Charlie?" She grinned up at him and her eyes crinkled. She pulled him forward and gave him a grandmotherly hug. "When did you get so tall?"

Aurora Metcalfe lived next door ever since he was born. Charlie could see she'd grayed a little more, but still had that sparkle in her eyes. She'd always welcomed him into her home and the best part was during the winter, when she made hot chocolate with marshmallows. He'd never been able to find any that tasted as good.

"I can't complain much. Things have been pretty good. I had a growth spurt when I turned seventeen, which I don't think stopped until I turned twenty-one." He smiled and thought, *Except for all the crap from the past, I have no reason to complain. Why do I feel so empty?*

She nodded. "What brings you back?"

"Well." He laughed. "I bought the house. It surprised me how low the price was, but I saved up some money and bought it flat out. I'm going to start veterinary school next fall in Fort Collins. I felt I needed a home base." He looked at the house over his shoulder. "It looks as though there's a lot of work to do."

She looked up at the house and shook her head. "Some folks moved in a few years back, but they ran out of money for repairs and mortgage and then the bank foreclosed. You plan to live here and drive all the way to Fort Collins? That's over three-hundred miles round trip."

"Yeah, I'm going to sell my truck," he pointed at the Peterbilt semi. "I'll get something way smaller and with better gas mileage. Hopefully, it will have a sleeper. I can drive up to Fort Collins on Monday, go to classes during the week and come back here on Friday night."

"So, you're going to veterinary school in Fort Collins?"

He smiled. "'Bout time, don't you think?"

"I remember how you took care of all those wounded animals. I'm glad you're going to finally do it. Listen, it's cold out here. Why don't you and your pup come over and have a cup of coffee?" She wrapped her coat tighter again and blew on her hands. "The weather man says we'll have another couple of storms move through in the next two weeks. There's a possibility of a blizzard, but he wasn't certain. It could move east and hit the mid-west more than here."

Charlie looked up at the house. "How about in a half hour? I need to go in there and see if I can find a place to crash overnight."

"You're not thinking about sleeping in there? You'll freeze."

"I've got a great sleeping bag and this fella." He leaned over and rubbed Breaker's ears. "He's a natural heat source better than an electric blanket." The wolf looked up at Charlie and woofed. "Aurora, coffee would be okay, but what I'd really go for this cold evening would be a cup of your hot chocolate. That's something I've wanted for a long time." He grinned at her.

"You got it. I bet you want marshmallows, too?"

"You know it." Charlie watched her turn and start back down the drive. "Hey, Aurora?"

She turned around quickly and put her hands on her hips. "Charlie Stone, when did you start calling me Aurora? You used to always call me Gran."

His eyebrows arched up and he puffed out a breath. "I used to call you Aurora when I was a kid and, also, Mrs. Metcalfe, too."

"Well, I'm not sure I can get used to you calling me Aurora. What was your question?"

"I just wondered if Lark is still around?" He hoped he didn't sound as desperate as he felt.

"Sure, she still lives with me, for now, anyway. She went up to Denver on Monday for some business meetings and other stuff. She'll be back tomorrow."

"Okay, I'll see you in a bit." He watched her turn the corner at the end of the drive and put his head down. *Other stuff in Denver? What does that mean?* he wondered.

He remembered a hot summer day when he and Lark were twelve or thirteen. They sat by the Arkansas River and threw rocks into the water. That morning there'd been a terrific rain storm, but the sun came out and it warmed up. They'd spent the day running through the trees and both were soaked.

"Hey Ducky, look at that," Lark said and pointed down the river.

He looked where she pointed and saw a complete rainbow stretched from one side of the canyon to the other. The colors were so vibrant. "Do you suppose if we followed it we'd find a pot of gold and some leprechauns?"

She leaned against his shoulder. "I don't know, but it would be fun to do with you. Will you always be my friend?"

He'd moved his arm around her shoulders and put his cheek against the top of her head. "Of course, I will. You're stuck with me, Lou."

They'd watched that crazy rainbow for sometime before it finally disappeared. Charlie remembered those as the best days of his life. He hoped he would be able to re-establish that friendship with Lark. She'd been so good to him.

He looked down at the wolf. "Come on Breaker. Let's see what messes we've got to take care of in our new home," he said with sarcasm in his voice. Charlie opened the door of his truck and pulled a flashlight off the seat, then turned and headed to the house.

Chapter Two

Charlie sat down on his sleeping bag and watched the flames dance in the fireplace. He'd collected some wood from a stack in the back of the house and felt grateful it was dry enough to burn. The house was cold, dark and smelled as though a family of field mice, at some time in the past, made a home somewhere in the walls or basement. He'd have a lot to clean out.

When he'd first opened the front door and stood in the entrance, he'd used the flashlight to look around. Breaker charged past him, but stopped and turned. The wolf whined and looked back at Charlie.

"It's okay, boy. Go snoop around," he said and turned the flashlight to the left and then to the right. The left used to be the dining room. His family never ate any meals there, but he remembered his father sat at the table with his post office buddies, drinking beer and playing poker. He could still smell the cigar smoke and hear the men laugh and tell nasty jokes.

Straight ahead, down the hallway was the living room and when he looked at the fireplace he almost threw up. He could hear the voices scream all around him and he wanted to back out of the house. Something deep in the pit of his heart said *you need to do this. Just get it over with.*

When he looked into the dining room again, he could see his mother bent over backwards on the table. His father leaned over her with his hands around her neck. He screamed at her incoherently, as she struggled against him.

He saw his fifteen-year-old self run up to his father, trying to get him to stop. He pulled at his father's arm and tried to stop him from choking his mother. Finally he ran into the living room and picked up the poker next to the fireplace. He walked up to the older man, swung the poker and hit him on the back.

His father let go of his wife's neck and straightened up. He turned, sneered at his son and swore he'd kill Charlie. He'd had it with this brat's bullshit. As the older man moved toward him, the poker swung up again and hit his father on the side of the head. He went down hard and then Charlie dialed 9-1-1. The police came and...

He started to cough and couldn't catch his breath. His chest felt tight and he thought it would be just great if he was struck with a heart attack on his first night home. It took a few moments to shake the memory from his mind. He'd gone from room to room and found memories around every corner. He'd gone upstairs and found his old room. Looking out the window in his bedroom, he saw the Metcalfe's house next door and smiled. There were better memories over there.

After he unloaded his duffle bag, sleeping gear and Breaker's bowls into the house, they'd traipsed next door and found Gran ready for them. She'd even set out a bowl of water and bits of people food out for Breaker.

They'd sat in her warm kitchen and got reacquainted. She told him things that happened in Canon City in the last ten years or so. There was nothing too earth-shattering to report. After three cups of hot chocolate, two grilled ham and cheese sandwiches on rye and potato salad, she tempted him with a piece of apple pie.

"Gran, I don't think I could eat another bite." He sat back and rubbed his stomach.

"Well, I'll send a piece with you. It's cold enough in that house you shouldn't have to worry about it going bad." She asked if he wanted another cup of cocoa, but he said no. She sat at the table and smiled at him. "So, Charlie Stone, where have you been all these years?"

"Lord, everywhere, pretty much. I was trained to drive a truck in detention and drove for a couple of different companies for a few years. After I saved enough money, I got my own truck. Then the money got better and I didn't have to share it with the bosses. I have a pretty good reputation on the road and I'm considered reliable." He folded his hands on the table and stared at them. "A few years ago, I got a laptop computer. It took me about six months to figure out how to use the stupid thing and after I got bored playing Solitaire all the time, I learned about this wireless business and started taking on-line college courses. I actually got my degree a year ago and started to send out applications for colleges with veterinary schools. I wanted to go to Washington State University in Pullman. They have one of the top schools in the country, but they turned my application down. I was accepted at Fort Collins and since it's not that far down the road, I figured it might be a good time to come back home."

"Do you have plans to stay in the area in your play book?" Gran asked and arched an eyebrow.

"For a while. The school takes four years and then there's an externship for a couple of months. I really want to study hard for this. I'm tired of being on the road all the time. It's not really fun anymore."

"It's a good thing, Charlie. I know you always wanted to work with animals. I remember you and Lark bringing home some poor injured creature..." she stopped when she saw the look on his face change. She put her hand over his. "Charlie, I never understood what happened between you and Lark, but I will say for a long time she missed you, very much."

"That was a long time ago, Gran. I'm sure she's gotten over it."

"It wasn't so long ago and I think you might be surprised. She still snarls at me if I mention your name. The first couple of years she had terrible nightmares and woke up crying. You were her best friend." Gran shook her head and put her hand by her mouth. "A couple of months ago, something happened to her. She won't talk about it, but she's been in a foul temper every since." She sat up straight. "I'm just giving you advance warning, if she snarls at you."

He stared at the flames and still heard the words Gran said. Breaker walked over and sat next to him. Charlie scratched the wolf's ears and back. Finally, Breaker lay down and put his head on Charlie's lap. He looked up at his master with sad, dark eyes and woofed.

"It's all right, boy. This will be our home base for a while. We both have some new things to get used to. I think I better get a couch and some plates," he said to the wolf.

He looked back at the flames in the fireplace and thought about what he'd learned from Gran. He found out his horse, Fox, was taken by Mr. Bickens, who had a dude ranch up at Royal Gorge. As soon as he made arrangements to sell his semi-truck and got a better means of travel, he'd head over to the ranch and get re-acquainted with Fox. Next to Lark, the horse was once his best friend. Gran said that Lark paid Mr. Bickens the monthly fees to board and care for the horse. She'd go out there at least once a month to ride the trails around the ranch. The rest of the time, Fox was rented out for day or overnight trips.

Then there was Lark. He felt nervous to see her again. They were best friends when they were kids. She'd supported him and helped keep him safe when his dad was on one of his many drunken sprees. They'd spent their summers having adventures in the valley by the river that ran by their homes. They'd fished that river, but never caught much to crow about. She'd helped him with English and he'd gotten her through eighth grade algebra.

They'd shared their first kiss at the age of fifteen on a picnic in the valley and then his world crashed in on him. When he'd gone to juvenile detention in Pueblo, she'd written him tons of letters and they began to make him angry at her. Charlie couldn't remember why he'd gotten so mad and now, Gran said Lark was engaged to another man and supposed to get married over New Year's. It was just another sign. Thirteen was an unlucky number and he looked forward to focusing on school.

He looked at Breaker and continued to rub the wolf's ears. "We better try to get some sleep. At least we'll have power and water tomorrow." He glanced out the window and saw it was snowing again. "Great. I hope they get the roads cleared."

Charlie pushed Breaker off the sleeping bag, removed his boots and scrunched down into the warmth. Breaker stretched out next to him with his head across Charlie's leg.

Chapter Three

The snow stopped when the red Ford Bronco turned onto Highway 50 headed west to Canon City. The drive usually took about two and a half hours, but today, from Denver, it took six. The weather was dicey, but Lark didn't want to stay another night away from home. She missed her grandmother. She needed to apologize for her behavior over the last couple of months. She'd been to hell and finally found her way back.

She drove below the speed limit and gripped the steering wheel hard the whole way. She looked forward to a warm bath and good dinner.

Lark and her business partner, Nancy Frye, were in meetings all week with suppliers for Mile High Bread Company. They specialized in mixes from local cooks for breads, soups, pasta and rice dishes and - a favorite - her grandmother's secret hot chocolate powder. The businesses books were in the black for the year and all seemed to be going well. Most of their sales were online from the website, but the shop they had in Canon City did a good local base. Sales were better in the spring, summer and fall, but this year

Thanksgiving and Christmas sales were up, too. It made them feel confident that next year would be prosperous.

The meetings in Denver were a challenge though. It was a long week and they were both exhausted.

"Did you feel anything strange in the air when we met with Frank and that other group?" Nancy asked and broke the silence. She sat up in her seat and stretched as far as she could.

Lark watched her friend run her hands through her short blonde hair, and felt grateful to have someone to share the tension with. "I just thought it was weird that they wouldn't make more of an effort to restock us. Christmas is only three weeks away," Lark said, and peered through the front window, watching the road. "This was a long week. We'll regroup on Monday and see what the damages will be. I think there will be a few things missing and we'll need to send out a few apology emails."

"So, any plans this weekend?"

"Not really. Gran wants to get the Christmas tree up and decorated. We're supposed to see what we can find tomorrow. If I know Gran, though, she'll want another blue spruce. They are pretty, and make less of a mess. There's supposed to be a broom ball game at Jay Hager's rink tomorrow evening, but I'm not sure I'll make it this time. What about you and the kidlings?"

"Probably the same. Jim wants to head up into the hills and do the cut-our-own tree thing, again. He had a great time doing it last year and the kids loved getting out of the house. We are doing the broom ball game. Jim has it in for Jay and his bud, Frank Donnelly, for the last game." Lark saw Nancy glance at her out of the corner of her eye. "Are you upset you didn't get to go do your fitting?"

Lark let out a breath. "Not really. We have too much to get done before Christmas. I can't really think about the wedding right now."

"Are you starting to have second thoughts?" When Lark didn't answer, Nancy patted her shoulder. "Is that the reason you wouldn't let me do a bridal shower?"

"Nance, I've got a whole lot of crap to think about. I don't know whether I'm coming or going with Thomas. He's insisted I move to Denver, but I don't really want to be that far away from Canon."

"Is that why you stayed at the inn this week, instead of the condo?"

"He'd just make me crazy and we didn't have time for that this week." She smiled and

pulled her Bronco into Nancy's driveway. "Get some rest and have a good weekend."

"Thanks. You, too." Nancy opened her door and stepped out. She grabbed her bag off the back seat. "See you Monday or maybe tomorrow night." She closed the door.

After Nancy got into her house, Lark backed the Bronco down the drive and headed back toward Main Street.

The weatherman called for another six to eight inches of snow today and she felt relieved they'd gotten back to town before the sun went down and the storm hit. Fortunately, she only had two more miles to go and the main road was cleared.

She turned onto Pine Ridge Road and found it hadn't been cleared. She drove slow and tried to dodge potholes in the ice and snow. She finally saw her home on the left. As she got ready to turn into the drive she noticed a big, fire-engine red semi-truck parked in front of the house next door. There were a few lights on in the house and she could see the path that led to the front door was cleared of snow.

Great, new neighbors, with a monster truck, just great, she thought. She parked the Bronco next to her Gran's car and turned hers off. She slipped out and got her suitcase out of the back. She slammed the car door, then turned to the house and made her way to the front door. As she closed the door behind her, she peeled off her boots and coat.

"Hey Gran. I'm home," she called and put on the pair of slippers that waited for her by the door.

"Thank the Lord. Hi honey," Gran said and walked out of the pantry. "I was beginning to worry. It's been off and on snow all day." She hugged Lark.

"Something smells heavenly. What's for dinner?" Lark asked. She believed her grandmother was one of the best cooks in the state of Colorado. When she came home from work every evening, the smells that came from the kitchen made her mouth water.

"I threw together a pot of chili and in a bit I'll put some of that good old Mile High cornbread into the oven."

Lark grinned. "I'm going to hire you to do our ad campaign." They walked into the kitchen arm in arm.

"Do you want some tea or coffee to warm up, sweetie?"

"No, I'm going to take a bath and try to relax. The drive was tough today." She leaned over the kitchen table and looked out the window toward next door. "Who's the new neighbor?"

Gran turned to the stove and started to stir the chili. "Charlie's home."

Lark stood up straight; she felt sure she hadn't heard what her grandmother said correctly. "Pardon me?"

"Yep, Charlie's home." Gran said and turned to face Lark. "He went with me to get the Christmas tree this morning and we got some groceries for him. I guess it's pretty hard to take a semi truck grocery shopping."

Lark looked at her Gran. "We were going to get the tree tomorrow."

"I know, but now we don't have to worry about the getting and can start the decorating in the morning."

"I suppose Charlie will come and help, now that he's been accepted back into the family again," she snarled and looked back out the window.

"Lark, it's been a very long time..."

"Thirteen years, Gran and he turned us away, remember?"

"Sweetheart, I invited him over for dinner tonight. I felt like I owed him a decent meal for all his help getting the tree set up. I want you to remember there comes a time you have to forgive. He's always been a very nice boy and I think you need to give him a chance."

Lark stood stock still and stared at the older woman. She couldn't find words to say. "Gran, he's twenty-eight years old, just like me. I think he's past the *boy* stage. Why is he here? Why did he come back?"

"He's been accepted to the veterinary college in Fort Collins and is going to make this his home base for a few years."

"Did he explain what happened to him years ago?"

"No, not really. He's been driving a truck around the country and saved every penny he could to go back to school. Charlie got his bachelor's degree on the computer. I didn't know you could do that."

Lark couldn't believe what she heard. She kept reminding herself to breathe. "Why did you invite him for dinner tonight? I just got home."

"Sweetheart, I know you still have unanswered questions for him; I do expect you to be civil tonight. He went through a lot and we'll just have to be patient."

"Gran, I'm always civil, but I'm exhausted. It's been a long week and a really long drive. I think I may have to pass on dinner," she said and turned to leave the kitchen.

"Larkspur Louise Metcalfe, go upstairs, take a nap or bath and get your head together. Please, stop whining. We're having company tonight and I don't want you to act surly." Gran pursed her lips and raised an eyebrow at her. It was the - *I might become very unhappy with you* - look that Lark knew all too well. "You've been angry about something for the last couple of months and I hope you'll tell me what the problem is or get over it."

"Great, just great," she mumbled, stomped up the stairs and threw her suitcase in her room. Then she went up to her attic office and sat at her desk. She hit the Go button on her computer and waited for it to warm up. She leaned back in her chair and brought her feet up to the edge of the desk. She'd planned to apologize to Gran for her behavior since last June, but she hadn't said anything yet. She felt guilt wrap around her stomach and stab her.

Lark looked up at the ceiling, and was flooded with memories of times past.

She saw herself as the little girl who'd lost her parents at the age of eight. It was in the spring and she'd explored her grandmother's back yard by herself. She'd gone down a little incline and then walked toward the river. Lark felt lonely in those days. Gran welcomed her with open arms and she knew she'd stay at her grandmother's for a long time, but she wasn't in school yet and didn't have any friends.

Lark liked to sit by the river and watch the people on rafts float by. She'd stood up on the riverbank and stared at the water when she heard a voice say "Little girls shouldn't be down here by themselves."

She'd turned around and saw a boy standing on a tree limb. His hair was dark and he wore torn jeans. She put her hand on her hip and stared at him.

He smiled. "Little girls by themselves could get attacked by a pack of wild dogs or alien invaders," he said.

Lark bent over and picked up a rock. With precision she threw the rock at the kid and hit him square in the chest. "Little boys in trees should watch out. I throw rocks and never miss," she said and turned away to continue down to the river's edge.

"Hey, wait a minute. How'd you do that?" The boy jumped down from the tree and ran up behind her.

"That was really cool. Where'd you learn to throw like that?"

She kept walking and ignored the kid. She didn't have any friends yet and felt a little shy. She'd seen this kid ride his bike around the neighborhood and knew he lived next door to her grandmother. She supposed she would need to make friends with him at some point.

The boy moved in front of her and blocked her way. "I'm Charlie. I live next door to Mrs. Metcalfe. Did you move in with her?" he chattered on.

Lark stopped in her tracks and put her hands on her hips. "I'm better with my slingshot, but my Gran won't let me have it. She thinks I'll shoot at birds or break a window." She walked around him and saw a tree stump. She walked over to it, sat down and retied the laces on her sneakers. "My daddy used to say I had natural aim talent. I'm really good at knocking cans off a fence."

"That's really cool. Can you teach me how to do it?"

"Sure."

"Why did you hit me when I was in the tree?" he asked, flopped down and sat Indian- style on the ground.

"You could have been trouble. I didn't know you. My daddy said I shouldn't talk to strangers."

"What's your name?"

"Lark."

"You mean like a bird?"

"No, it's short for Larkspur. My mom named me after the flower. She always said they were the prettiest flowers that bloomed in the spring."

"Are your mom and dad going to come and get you sometime?" Charlie retied his sneakers.

Lark didn't answer him and felt as though she was going to start to cry. She put her head down, closed her eyes and wished the tears away.

"Hey, I'm sorry. I didn't mean to make you cry," Charlie said. "Where are they?"

She sniffed and opened her eyes. She looked at the boy and saw he wasn't all that bad. His dark hair was messed up, but he had pretty blue eyes. "They died in a car crash. It was snowing and icy," she said quietly.

"Gosh, I'm sorry. Is that why you're living with Mrs. Metcalfe?"

She nodded and then heard her grandmother call to her. "I have to go in." She stood up and started back to the incline.

Charlie followed her. "You know, it's Saturday."

"So?"

"On Saturday, your grandmother makes cookies and she lets me come over and have some with a big glass of cold milk. It's really cool. I like your Gran. She's really nice." He walked next to Lark up the incline.

She stopped at the top. "Charlie, if I teach you how to throw rocks, can I ride your bike? I saw you from the window riding in the street."

"Sure, that would be cool. Do you know how to ride a bike?"

"Yeah, I can ride," she said. "You know, you say 'cool' a lot?"

"Yeah, I tried a curse word once and my dad didn't like it. I got spanked pretty hard for that. Now I just say *cool* all the time. "

"Lark, wake up."

Her foot fell off the edge of the desk and hit the floor. She didn't realize she'd fallen asleep. She opened her eyes and looked up at her Gran.

"Sweetheart, you've been up here for over an hour. Our company is downstairs. Comb your hair and come down. Dinner's ready," Gran huffed and turned to leave the room.

Lark shook her head and tried to clear out the cobwebs. "Great, just freakin' great."

Chapter Four

Lark stood in the hallway outside the kitchen and listened to her grandmother and Charlie talk.

"Were you able to find a new hot water tank?" her Gran asked.

"Yeah, I had to get a plumber to come out and he brought a new one all ready to put into place. I'm going to have to get the downstairs re-piped, though. At some point, the pipes froze and busted. At least the bathroom upstairs works and I can take a shower. Its crazy getting water from upstairs and bringing it down to the kitchen just so I can make coffee; I'm starting to think I should just take the pot upstairs. The plumber will be back on Monday."

"That's good," Gran replied.

Lark heard tension in her grandmother's voice. Guilt stabbed at Lark and she knew she might have put the older woman into an uncomfortable situation. She just wanted to run upstairs and lock herself in her bedroom. She looked down and saw a set of light amber eyes stare up at her. It was a huge dog and she felt the wall press against her back. The dog woofed at her and wagged its tail. It seemed to wear a grin on its face.

"Breaker, to me," she heard Charlie call. The dog turned around and went back into the kitchen. She let out a breath and pushed away from the wall. She pulled her thermal shirt down and turned into the kitchen. A man sat at the table. He looked down at the dog and rubbed its ears. He glanced up at her and stood up, moving the chair back. He was tall, very tall, with dark hair hanging down around his shoulders. She recognized the blue eyes. They sparkled in the light that hung from the ceiling.

"Lark, you remember Charlie," Gran said and pulled a pan of cornbread out of the oven.

"Sure, hi," she said and turned to the refrigerator. When she opened the door, she heard him say hi back. She pulled a bottle of juice out and closed the door. She sat across the table from him and watched as he folded himself back into the chair.

Gran cut the cornbread and set the pan in the middle of the table. "Well, isn't this nice? It's been a long time since we were together and I'm very thankful to have you both here." She smiled at Lark.

"That's Thanksgiving, Gran," Lark said and focused on her bowl. She felt very warm and looked up to see Charlie stare at her. "What?"

"Nothing. Sorry," he mumbled and picked up his spoon.

Lark found it difficult to eat. She didn't have much of an appetite. She poked at the chili and counted the minutes until she'd feel it was okay to excuse herself.

"Breaker is a gray wolf, Lark," she heard her grandmother say.

"What?"

"Breaker is a gray wolf," Gran repeated.

"Who's Breaker?"

"Charlie's gray wolf. You met him in the hallway," Gran said and finished her cornbread.

Lark felt confused. She wasn't sure what Gran meant and shrugged. Then she remembered the big dog that found her hidden in the hallway. "Oh, you mean the dog," she said

and put her spoon down.

"Breakers not a dog, he's a gray wolf," Charlie said and frowned.

Lark looked across the table at him and instantly wanted out of the room. "Yeah, Gran said that a couple of times. I have work to do. Terrific seeing you again," she said and started to stand. She needed to get away from this situation before she went crazy and said something she shouldn't. Gran would be hurt and she didn't want to do that to the only person on the planet who really cared about her. Charlie could go jump off a cliff for all she cared.

"No, no, sit back down. I made dessert and I have something I want to show you two. Stay put for just another couple of minutes, sweetie." Gran got up from the table and looked at Lark until she sat back down. "I'll be right back." She quickly turned and left the room.

She could hear Gran's footsteps on the stairs and then in the room above the kitchen. She and Charlie sat at the table. She felt uncomfortable and tried not to look at him, but noticed him stare at her - below the neck.

"Stop staring at the girls, Charlie," Lark said and crossed her arms over her chest.

Charlie took a gulp of air and looked up at her. "Sorry, you didn't have those when we were fifteen."

Lark stood, picked up bowls and plates from the table and took them to the sink. "Yeah, they've grown up since you've been gone. You need to get your hair cut." She walked to the coat hanger by the door and grabbed a sweater. She pulled it on and buttoned up the front. She went back to clearing the table and stopped. She looked at him. "What did I do wrong? Why did you cut us off?" she asked.

The silence in the room could be cut with a knife. Lark took her handful of dinnerware to the sink and put it down. She turned to head out of the kitchen, but met her grandmother in the

hallway.

"I can't talk to him, Gran. I'm going upstairs."

Her grandmother grabbed her arm and turned her back to the kitchen. "No you're not. Now sit down," she said and steered Lark to her chair. "I never told you about this, but while you were in college I needed a project. So, I put the pictures I'd taken of you two into an album. It's called 'scrapbooking' and I had a great time with a group of ladies. I put it together for you. This evening, I thought you might find it fun to look at and maybe find some good memories." She put the book at her place on the table. She looked at Lark and Charlie. "You two will have to scoot in so you can see." She sat down and looked at them again.

Lark felt horrified. The last thing she wanted this evening was a walk down memory lane with Charlie Stone. She stood up again. "Gran, I'm sorry, but I can't do this. I'll be in my office." She walked out of the kitchen and raced up the stairs to her office in the attic. She slammed the door behind her and leaned against it with her eyes closed. She wished the tears would go away, but they burned her eyes. Her throat felt tight and she wanted to sob uncontrollably, but wouldn't let herself break down over Charlie Stone.

She went to her desk and sat down. When she opened the bottom drawer and took a couple of things out, she saw the folder at the bottom. She took it out and the letter fell out onto the top of the desk. She hadn't looked at it for a few years. Charlie only wrote to her once the whole time he was in detention, but once was enough.

She picked up the envelope and gently took the letter out. Unfolding it she read:

"Dear Lark, I don't want you to come back here anymore. I hate you and we are not friends. Charlie."

A single tear slid down her cheek and dropped onto the page. Lark was heartbroken for weeks after that letter appeared in the mailbox. She'd never shown it to Gran.

After a month, she'd written him back and wanted to know what was wrong. She never got any reply from him. It took her a long time to get over the hurt feelings and now all that began to resurface.

She didn't want to know if he could explain it all away. She only wanted one question answered. *What had she done wrong?*

****

Charlie looked at Gran and smiled. "I guess we'll look at those pictures some other night."

"I'm sorry, Charlie. She went through a lot back when you were taken away. I never understood what happened between you two, but I thought she'd gotten over it. I guess not."

"It was my fault," he said. "I was pretty stupid back then." He looked at Gran who seemed confused. "It doesn't matter now. Will you tell her thank you for taking care of Fox all these years? I was going to tell her, but got sidetracked."

Gran put her hand over his. "You could tell her. She's up in her office. It's in the attic upstairs. You know where it is."

"No, she'd just feel trapped. I don't want to do that to her." He stood up from the table. "We'll do dessert another night. Thanks for a great dinner. It's terrific having home cooking for a change."

"Let me fix you a leftover bag." She jumped up and moved to a cupboard.

"That's okay. It gives me an excuse to come back for seconds. Breaker, come on, boy. Let's go." Charlie grabbed his coat from the hooks by the door and walked out into the dark, cold night.

He tried to figure out what he'd expected. He didn't think it would go so rough with Lark. He understood why she was upset, he'd hurt her deeply. When he first saw her in the kitchen doorway, he'd wanted to jump up and give her a hug. She'd grown into a beautiful woman and his body turned warm as it did when she'd entered the room. He could tell by the look on her face, though, that she didn't find him all that attractive. She'd never smiled once.

Breaker ran around the driveway in the snow and stopped a couple of times to sniff around the bushes and a tree.

"Breaker, to me," Charlie said and walked across the fresh snow to his house.

****

Aurora walked out of the kitchen and looked up the stairs. She knew her granddaughter held some sort of pain deep in her heart, but she was tired of it and wanted some answers. She went up the stairs and at the end of the hallway continued up the stairs to the attic. She knocked on the door and poked her head in. She saw Lark at her desk with a tissue in her hand.

"Hey Gran, come on in." Lark moved her chair around and faced her.

"Sweetheart, I don't know what happened to you back in June or thirteen years ago. I do wish you'd tell me, but I'll understand if you don't. I love you, and you'll always have my support, but this pity party you're having and taking it out on those around you doesn't make me happy."

"Gran, I know. I'm sorry I've been in a snit." She looked at her and a tear rolled down her cheek. "I don't know how you put up with me sometimes."

Aurora walked over and leaned on the desk. She reached her hand out and when she held Lark's, she squeezed it tight. "I wish you'd let me know what happened. In June, you just stopped talking to me and I've been worried sick. Now with Charlie's back..."

"It has nothing to do with Charlie. He just showed up at the wrong time and it brought up some bad memories." Lark stood up and wrapped her arm through Aurora's.

"That mail you received from the doctor's office...Lark, you're not sick or something?"

"No." Lark laughed. "Ironically, that was good news. I'm healthy as a horse with no bugs or anything."

"That's good." She held onto Lark's arm.

"Gran, I'll try not to fly off the handle anymore. I've got two really difficult decisions to make and once I get those figured out, I should calm down."

"It would be nice to see you smile again. I've missed that. Is Thomas still pushing for you to move to Denver?"

"Yeah." Lark sighed and wiped her eyes. "The last time I talked to him, he made noises about how I should sell out my half of the business. We had a pretty good argument." She pulled free of Aurora's arm and sat back in her chair. "He's being very obstinate about it."

"That doesn't surprise me. He does tend to act very snotty sometimes. I hope he'll make you happy, sweetheart." She saw Lark trying to look at her with a blank expression, but could read the pain and confusion in her eyes.

"Well, that's a good thought. I'm tired and going to bed, Gran." Lark stood again and kissed her cheek. "Love you."

Aurora saw the note on Lark's desk and turned it to look at it. "Sweetheart, what is this?"

Lark turned and she showed her the note. "It's nothing, Gran," she said and tried to pull it out of her hand. They locked eyes and she could tell Lark was sad. "Charlie sent me that when he was in Pueblo detention."

Aurora read the note. "Oh my Lord, no wonder you were so upset. Lark, why didn't you tell me about this note?"

"You always cared so much for him. I didn't want it to break your heart, too."

She could see Lark's eyes start to tear up again. She looked at the note and shook her head. "What was he thinking? Didn't he know that we wouldn't care where he was and no matter what he was a part of our family?"

"I don't know. Tonight I asked him what the problem was, but he didn't say a word. I still don't know what I did to make him write that note." Lark sniffed and wiped her eyes again.

"Let's get a good night's sleep. Things will be brighter tomorrow." Aurora said and set the note back onto the desk.

Chapter Five

The next morning, after Lark and Gran ate breakfast and drank a couple of cups of coffee, they got the decorations out of a storage closet and began to get the Christmas tree set up.

They spent a couple of hours at work on it to make it look just right. While Lark packed up the boxes, Gran went into the kitchen to prepare lunch.

Lark tried all morning to be as cheerful as possible. She thought the tree looked wonderful and for a moment forgot all her bad memories. She loved Christmas and putting the tree up with Gran was a tradition she didn't want to ever lose.

She turned into the kitchen and saw Gran stir a pan of soup on the stove. "I can't believe it's one o'clock."

Gran turned to her and smiled. "Didn't we say last year we were going to put the lights away a little more neatly, so they'd be easier to unwind onto the tree?"

"I think we've said that for the last twenty Christmases." Lark sat at the table and saw the photo album. She pushed it aside and did her best to ignore it.

There was a knock at the back door and when Lark looked up she saw Charlie. In an instant, she felt her anger return and didn't move from the table.

Gran looked at her and frowned. "I'm busy here. Would you please get the door?"

Lark looked at her and scowled. She shook her head, stood up and walked to the door. She opened it halfway and didn't greet Charlie, but just stared at him.

"Hi," he said. "I don't have a phone and I need to get someone to come and turn the heat on or at least figure out why it won't come on. The fireplace doesn't keep the house warm."

Lark wasn't going to open the door any further, but felt her grandmother's hand on her back.

"Open the door, sweetheart. Yes, Charlie, you can use our phone. Come on in. Would you like some soup to warm you up?"

Lark pulled the door open and let Charlie walk in. She felt like all her good Christmas cheer flew out the door. As she closed it and turned, she saw him take off his coat.

"That would be great. I have electricity, but I don't really have anything to cook with at this point. Thank you," he said to Gran.

"How convenient," Lark mumbled and went around him into the kitchen. She thought about going back up the stairs and let them have lunch without her, but decided she needed to keep Gran happy. She sat back down at the table.

Gran showed Charlie where the phone and phone books were and he spent a few minutes calling around to get emergency service.

She could see him in the living room. He looked at the tree and smiled. For some reason it pissed her off. As she watched Charlie talk on the phone and make notes, she felt something stir deep in her chest. She wasn't sure what it was, but spent a moment convincing herself that he wasn't attractive. Sure he was tall and fit, but that shoulder-length brown hair and five o'clock shadow looked stupid and sloppy. She was glad she'd told him last night that he needed a haircut.

Lark suddenly felt warm and realized he stared at her, while he spoke on the phone. He smiled a little and she couldn't tell if he was smiling at her or if the person on the phone said something humorous. She looked away, got up and poured herself a cup of coffee.

Gran latched onto her arm and whispered, "Just because you're angry doesn't mean we're bad hostesses. You need to offer him a cup of coffee, too."

Lark grabbed another cup, stepped into his line of vision and pointed at the cup. He smiled again and nodded. She poured it, took it into the living room and set it on the table by him.

She walked back into the kitchen. "He has coffee. Are you happy Gran?"

Her grandmother turned from the stove and huffed at her. "Don't act that way, young lady. Just be nice." Gran scowled at her and turned back around.

Lark sat at the table and heard Charlie hang up the phone. He carried his cup into the kitchen. "Well, that's one thing done." He sat across from Lark and took a sip of coffee.

"Will someone come out today?" Gran asked.

"Yeah, they said there would be a repairman out sometime between three and four o'clock. I hope they can get the furnace started."

Charlie and Gran chatted up a storm during lunch. Lark commented very little. The minute the soup and bread were finished, she excused herself and ran upstairs to her attic office. She claimed her work needed her attention. It did, but she found it difficult to concentrate. Her brain kept floating back to memories of her childhood and growing up with Charlie. She remembered the lanky kid who taught her to roller skate and ski. They rode their bikes all over Canon City and made their own adventures. They played cards and marbles and then Gran got her the first computer either one of them used and they'd discovered electronic games.

There were times, when Mr. Stone would be on one of his rampages, that Charlie climbed the cinderblock fence behind her house and showed up at her window. When they were young they had sleepovers and she always felt good about keeping him safe from his dad.

The one thing she'd always be grateful for was the way he defended her. For a while a couple of boys in their classes at school picked on her about being an orphan. No matter how they approached Lark, she'd always ended up in tears.

One Saturday, she'd gotten up and eaten breakfast really fast. She and Charlie planned to meet on the riverbank and come up with a new adventure. She raced out of the house and headed for the incline. She grabbed her stick, which she pretended was her light saber, and ran up the riverbank.

She found Charlie sweating up a storm and working on a new project. "Hey Ducky, what are you doing?" she asked and walked to where he did his work.

"I'm building a catapult." He smiled.

Lark swung her tree branch. "So, we're going to save the world from alien invaders in medieval times? Can I be a knight?"

"Lou, girls can't be knights. You'll have to be a princess," he said and shoved a big rock toward his construction.

"If I were like Princess Leia, I could use my light saber."

"No, you'll have a sword. They didn't have light sabers back then."

"What if the light sabers somehow got to medieval times by time travel, like when we watched the Time Machine?"

"Lou, now you're just being silly."

"Do you get to be a knight?"

"No, I'm the king." He stood up and grinned. "I need your help moving a big log."

Lark set her stick on the ground and followed him into the woods. He stopped and pointed at a medium-sized tree branch about twenty-five feet long.

"Ducky, that's really long. How are you going to get it to work?" She walked to the far end and figured out how to get it lifted into her arms.

"I've got an idea. It will be sort of like a teeter-totter."

They struggled to get the log out of the woods and brought it to the work site. Lark and Charlie worked side by side to get a pile of rocks stable enough to hold the log.

She stood with her hands on her hips and watched him shove a rock into place. She suddenly realized she was being pelted with a bunch of pebbles. She turned around and saw three boys walk toward them.

"Ducky, we've got trouble," she said.

Bobbie Reynolds and his two buddies, Dexter and Jamie, were walking down the incline. They'd picked on her since she first arrived in Canon City.

"Look guys, it's the Orphan Metcalfe. Where are your parents? Did they dump you off with your granny?" Bobbie whined.

Charlie stood up and walked in front of Lark. "You assholes need to think of something different. You've had the same shit spill from your mouths for so long, it doesn't bother us anymore."

"Look guys, it's the orphan's shitty boyfriend. Do you think she sucks his dick?" The three boys all started to laugh and Bobbie grabbed his crotch. "Here's a hot one for you, Orphan."

This was a new phrase to Lark and she didn't know what to say. She didn't have any idea what they were talking about. "Let's just leave, Ducky. They're not worth it," she whispered.

Lark saw Charlie close his hands into fists.

Bobbie walked up to him and stood inches from his nose.

"Hey asshole, I heard from your friends that your mamma and sisters suck you off all the time. Maybe they'd like something a little bigger than your puny cock," Charlie said in a really low voice.

Lark was surprised. She'd heard Charlie cuss before, but nothing like this. Bobbie swung at Charlie and hit him in the nose. It was just hard enough to start a trickle of blood. Charlie didn't move and laughed.

"That was a nice little love pat there, Bobbie. Maybe you're queer and want to suck me off, too." He tackled Bobbie around the stomach and landed on the ground on top of him. He grabbed the aggressor's shirt and pulled him up. "Apologize, asshole!" Charlie shouted in the kids face.

Bobbie looked up at Charlie and grinned. "Yeah, I'll apologize after I fuck her."

Lark saw one of the other boys, Jamie, move up on Charlie. She pulled her stick up and swung it hard. She hit him on the arm; he landed on his butt and grabbed the spot she'd hit.

"Hey, that hurt," he squawked.

She looked at Dexter and pointed her stick at him. "I gave him the flat end of the stick. If you move, I might give you the pointy end. No gang-ups." When she looked back at Charlie and Bobbie, who was crying, she smiled. Charlie apparently punched the kid a couple of times and was getting up.

He turned to Lark and held out his hand. "Come on, Lou. You're right, they're not worth it. Bobbie's a pussy and has no backbone."

They walked back to Lark's house in silence and she helped him get his face cleaned off.

He sat on the toilet with his head tipped back and she walked in with a bag of ice.

"Gran wants to talk to us when your nose stops bleeding." She pushed away his hand that held a tissue. "Let me see, Ducky." She dabbed at it and then put the ice bag on his face. "You're going to have a black eye."

"No biggie. I've had them before and at least this time it wasn't my dad. Is Gran mad at me?"

"I don't think so, but I think she's going to lecture us pretty good." Lark sat on the laundry basket and crossed her arms over her chest. "Ducky, my ears almost melted off of my head out there. I don't think I've ever heard you use such language and what does *sucking off* mean?" She grinned.

"Yeah, sorry about the bad stuff, but those jerks deserved it. The other thing I'll explain on a day when Gran isn't around. She probably doesn't like that kind of talk." He laughed.

"You'd better. I agree with you that Bobbie Reynolds is such an asshole."

"Don't let Gran hear you say that. She'll have a fit. I liked when you popped Jamie in the arm with your sword. I bet he gets a really good bruise."

"He acted like he was going to kick you. I couldn't let him do that."

"Thanks for watching my back, Lou."

"Anytime. You know, I don't think you should be king. I really think we need to knight you."

"Well, you're a princess. Can't you knight me?"

"I don't see why not." She stood up and grabbed her hairbrush and tapped his shoulders. "I dub thee a knight of the Canon City realm. You fought honorably today."

Charlie took her hand and kissed the back of it. "Thank you, m'lady."

She looked at him and for the first time felt a little uncomfortable. "Ducky, Bobbie called you my boyfriend. Is that what you are?"

He moved the ice bag down to his chest and reached for her hand. "I'd like to be your boyfriend someday. Would you want to be my girlfriend?"

Lark blushed and giggled. "Maybe, someday. Come on, Sir Ducky. We have to go get lectured." She took his hand and they walked down the stairs.

She smiled at the memory. That was one of their best days together. She really started to love him and couldn't even remember how old they were.

Lark started her computer and after a while got down to business. She checked the incoming orders and signed off on over one hundred new ones, so the floor staff could start getting them out in the mail on Monday.

Her cell phone rang at six-thirty and she looked at the caller ID. It was Thomas and she didn't really want to talk to him, but hit the answer button.

"Hey Thomas," she said.

"Hello, my dear. What are you up to today?" he asked.

"I'm just getting some orders ready for Monday."

"I understand you were in Denver last week. Why didn't you come to the condo?"

"Nancy and I were in meetings all week. Most nights we didn't get finished until late. I didn't want to disturb you if you were resting."

"It would have been nice to see you at least. I've missed you."

Lark didn't know what to say to him. The sentiment he spoke was nice, but she didn't believe he was sincere. In her opinion, the man didn't know the meaning of the words that spilled from his mouth. Since a very horrible night in June, she hadn't let him come near her and felt ill whenever she thought about being in the same room with him. The worst of it, though, was that he scared her and she was stuck on how to deal with him.

"I wouldn't have been any fun for you. It was pretty exhausting."

"Why don't you plan on coming up next weekend? We could have a quiet night and relax before the big Christmas rush starts."

"I'll see how things go this week. It will be pretty busy."

"Dear, are you all right? You don't sound like yourself."

"I'm fine, Thomas. I've just got a mountain of work to do. I'll call you later this week."

He said good night and hung up. Lark held the phone to her lips and wished she hadn't answered. She sat back in her chair and looked at the ceiling. *Is this my future? What am I thinking?*

She'd met Thomas five years earlier at a business meeting in Denver. She and Nancy were just getting the company off the ground and he gave her some good advice on advertising and marketing. He was an attractive man and impressed her with his knowledge of business and finances. They'd dated for two years and then bought a condo in Denver together. It was just after they'd moved into the dwelling that she'd become uncomfortable with some of his ideas of games to play. When he asked her to marry him two years ago, she'd agreed, but kept finding excuses to put off the wedding. He'd argued with her on several occasions and finally convinced her it would be in her best interests to give in and marry him.

Lark shook her head and wanted to stop thinking about Thomas. She tossed around the idea of getting some food, but decided she wasn't all that hungry. She walked down the stairs and found Gran at the kitchen table going through her recipe book.

"Gran, I'm going to head over to the rink. There's supposed to be a broom ball meet tonight. Do you want to go?"

"No, it's too cold outside and I'd rather not sit by the rink where it's just as cold. I'm getting my shopping list together for next week. I have pies to get ready for the festival." She pumped her fist.

Lark laughed. "Okay, I'll be back early."

Chapter Six

When Lark arrived at the rink, she saw Nancy sat on the bleachers with her three kids around her. She was putting a piece of duct tape on the bottom of her oldest son's tennis shoe. He'd need it to slide around on the ice during the game. She waved and started toward Nancy, but got sidetracked when she saw Jay Hager by the boards. His elbows were planted on the wood and he held a cup of coffee in his hands.

Like Charlie, Jay was tall. He stood six-foot-four inches and when he was still in high school, got drafted by a professional hockey team. He'd been sent to Portland to play on the pro-teams junior club and after his first year took a terrible hit during a game and broke his knee and leg. After five surgeries he'd given up the sport. That was the way he liked to put it. The team actually released him before a contract was signed. He'd been disappointed and depressed for a couple of months after, then went back to school and got his degree. He'd saved enough money to buy into the rink and turned the business around. He was doing really well. He and Charlie were friends in school and they often went on adventures with Jay as their third and some other friends.

"Hey, Mister." She smiled and stood next to him.

"Hey, Miss. Are you going to play tonight?" He straightened up to his full height and

gave her a half-hug.

"Maybe, if you need extra people for the adult game. I don't want to go out there with the kids. I nearly lost a knee-cap the last time I did that."

"We always need extra people," he said and watched the skaters move around the ice.

"I'll need to borrow some duct tape."

"No problem."

"Jay, I don't know if you're aware of this, but Charlie Stone is back. He bought the old house next door to Gran's." She saw Jay's head snap around to look at her and his eyebrows scrunched together.

"You're pulling my sore leg."

She shook her head and watched Jay turn back and put his elbows back on the boards. "Did he say where he's been all these years?" Jay asked.

"I haven't really talked to him much. Gran said he went into trucking after he got out of detention. He's been all over the United States. Now he's going to start veterinary school in the fall up in Fort Collin's."

"He always wanted to do that. Good for him. Is he staying at the old house?"

"Yes."

"Holy shit, he must have some bad memories of that place. I can't believe he went back there. Do you have any idea why?"

"Gran said it was cheap. I know it's a real fixer-upper. Who knows, maybe he's turned into a masochist." She shrugged and shook her head.

"Why haven't you talked to him? You two used to be thick as thieves." Jay looked at her with his brown eyes.

"I've tried, but he can't seem to communicate well with others. I ask a question and he stares at me. It's like he has post traumatic stress disorder or something."

"Lark, what happened between you two? You guys were always so close," Jay asked.

She looked at him and smirked. "Jay, why did you and Mandy Parker break up?"

He stood up straight again and looked annoyed at her. "You don't want to go there. Ever."

She raised her eyebrows and held her hands out with a silent question.

"Okay, point taken. There's nothing we need to discuss." He frowned and looked back at the ice.

Lark wished she knew what the problem with Charlie was, but she couldn't even begin to guess and really didn't feel the need to talk to him. "I'm going to go sit. If you need a player, let me know."

She went over to the bleachers and smiled at Nancy. Her four-year-old son, Jacob, waved at her. "Hi, Auntie Lark."

"Hi there, Jake. How's it going big boy?" She sat down and gave him a hug.

"It's okay, I don't get to play tonight because I'm too little. It sucks," he said and gave her a raspberry.

"Well, you can keep your mom and me company, all right?" She smiled as he nodded at her.

"The kids are playing first tonight, then the adults," Nancy said and cradled her nine- month-old in her arms.

"I doubt I'll play. I just needed to get out of the house for a bit." Lark put her elbows on her knees and watched the kids run around on the rink.

"Is everything all right on the home front?" Nancy nudged her shoulder.

"Yeah, all is good." Lark rubbed her eyes.

"Gee, the tone of your voice says different."

Lark looked at her and shook her head. "Do you remember   Charlie   Stone?"

"Should I?" Nancy asked.

Larked needed to remember Nancy was a couple years ahead of her in school and they didn't know each other until they were in college. "Charlie was my age and we grew up next door to each other. He accidently killed his father when he was fifteen and wound up in detention."

"Oh right." She nodded. "I do remember that. I didn't know he was your neighbor."

Lark decided she didn't want to go into the whole story tonight with Nancy. "It's not important."

"Liar." Nancy looked at her and rocked the baby.

"We'll talk about it later."

She stayed at the rink until after eight o'clock and then headed home before the adult game started. She pulled into the driveway and got out of her Bronco. As she looked up at the house, she decided to go for a walk. She was too wound up to talk to Gran and didn't want to sit in front of her computer.

****

As Charlie approached his front door, after he took Breaker for a walk, he heard a car door slam next door at Gran's. He turned and saw Lark walk through the snow toward the river.

She'd changed so much over the years, but in a way she'd stayed the same. He could still read the emotions that ran through her head, just by the look on her face. Her eyes were different though. He saw anger and fear when she'd looked at him and he realized the innocence she'd had as a young girl was gone. She was so beautiful, though. He found it difficult to think straight when she stood anywhere near him.

He saw she'd put on a jacket with a lamb's wool collar, a hat and her boots. She stomped across Gran's yard toward the incline.

Breaker woofed, focused his attention on her and took off toward the incline. "Hey, Breaker, get back here," Charlie called and followed the wolf. "Breaker, to me, now!" he shouted.

Charlie went down the incline toward the river bed and stepped carefully. There was a lot of snow and ice in the area. He looked to his right and saw Lark and Breaker in a stare down. She'd picked up a good-sized rock and didn't take her eyes off the wolf. He would have worried except Breaker's tail wagged.

"Charlie, get your stupid dog away from me. I can still hit what I throw a rock at," she threatened.

"Breaker sit," Charlie ordered and walked up next to the wolf. The animal sat and looked up at him. "He doesn't want to hurt you Lark, he just wants someone to play with."

She looked up at Charlie with a smirk on her face. "Right, we'll leave that to you. Why are you back?"

Charlie felt his heart drop an inch and twist with pain in his chest. He wondered if she had an alternate meaning tagged to what she'd just said. He didn't want to play games. "I'm starting vet's college next fall. Didn't Gran tell you?"

"So, you show up ten months early, buy a house and get in good with the neighbors. Why are you really back?" She leveled her eyes at him.

"That's why I'm really back. I'm starting school in the fall. What do you want me to say? I'm sorry I hurt you. Okay, I said it." He realized his feet moved, on their own accord, straight toward her. "Do you want me to say I was an idiot, and I was too stupid to realize I'd hurt the people I loved the most? Does that help ease your hurt? Does that make it better for you?"

He found himself standing in front of her and shouted in her face. He could feel her hot breath on his chin and suddenly wanted to wrap his arms around her and never let go. She closed her eyes and he could tell she was scared. "I screwed up Lark," he said, quieter. "I got help, but found out when I got released from detention that it was too late. Does that make it better?"

Lark looked up at him with tears pooled in her eyes and then took a step back from him. "Yeah, all better," she said in a sarcastic voice. She turned away and started down the riverbed. She then turned back to him. "I only have one question, Charlie. What did I do to you that made you send that letter? How did I screw up?"

He looked at her and found his tongue wouldn't budge. He watched her turn and start away again.

"Great, no answer." She stopped and faced him, again. "When you grow a pair and can speak again, let me know. That's all I want to know Charlie. How did I screw up our friendship?" She started down the river and passed the stump they'd once sat on. Breaker whined and woofed and stood back up. Charlie could tell the wolf wanted to follow her and so did he.

****

Lark followed the riverbed for two hours and then stopped in her tracks. The cold penetrated her thermal tights under her jeans and her gloves. She jammed her hands into her pockets and turned back. She didn't think it would be good to be found frozen on the river bank. It surprised her when she looked at her watch and it was after ten o'clock.

When she got back, Gran had already turned in for the night. She quietly made her way up to her room, put on her fleece pajama's and crawled under her warm comforter. She lay with her eyes open and remembered she needed to brush her teeth. She got up and noticed her cell phone blinked. She put in her code and listened to the message. It was from Thomas.

"Hi, babe. I just wanted to make sure you are okay. You didn't sound like yourself earlier and I just want to hear that you really are fine. I'll be out tonight, but I'll have my phone. Call me when you get the chance. Love you."

Lark hit the memory button with his number and listened to his answering message. When the buzz came she started, "Hey Thomas. I'm sorry I missed your call. I'm just in work mode too much, but all is well. I'll talk to you tomorrow." She cut it off and threw the phone onto her bed.

When she'd first started to go out with Thomas, he seemed like a nice man. He was five years older than she and when he gave her advice about starting a new business, he acted as though he cared for her. After six months, things changed. Thomas's weird tastes began to rear up. His bedroom games were sort of fun at first, but then he wanted to handcuff her to the bed or behind her back and strange sex toys began to appear. It interested her at first. She'd only slept with one other guy when she was in college, so she didn't have much experience.

One evening, he'd started talking about going out to sex clubs, and that was when she put her foot down. She didn't want to experience anything with a bunch of strangers standing around and watching. He'd let it go for a while, but the subject came up from time to time.

As the last year started, Lark felt more and more uncomfortable with his antics and started making excuses to not see him when she'd travel to Denver. When he'd proposed marriage, she was happy, but always felt a nagging pain in her head that said this wasn't a good idea. They'd been engaged for two years and finally agreed to have the wedding on New Year's Eve.

In June, she'd experienced the most horrible night of her life. It haunted her dreams and she'd withdrawn into herself around her grandmother and friends. She knew she couldn't marry that man, but now felt scared of him and how he might react.

After she brushed her teeth, she crawled back under the covers and tried to settle down. She thought about the evening's events. She felt, logically, that Charlie's apology should be accepted and she should let the past go. She should be able to let all the old feelings go and think about how she was going to deal with Thomas. She found she couldn't bring herself to move on, though and didn't know how to let go of the hurt she'd felt for so long. She just wanted her question answered. What had she done to make him write that hateful letter?

Lark was the type of person who wanted all the details from start to finish. Charlie didn't say what the problem was back then and that became a needle that stabbed her in the neck. She wanted him to explain what happened and make it clear to her, but she found it hard to consider being in the same room with him long enough for any explanations. When she looked at him all she wanted to do was cry over the lost time.

Around two in the morning, Lark woke up from a terrible nightmare. She found herself upright in her bed with tears rolling down her cheeks. She'd had these dreams off and on over the last six months, but not like this one. Charlie appeared in the dream and he laughed at her and said something, but she couldn't remember what came from his lips. It was impossible for him to be in these dreams, he wasn't here in June. She gave up the notion of getting any sleep and got up. She felt exhausted, but couldn't get her brain to shut off.

She went down to the kitchen and put the kettle on the stove to warm water for tea. She got a decaffeinated bag out of a cupboard and waited to catch the kettle before the whistle blew. Her stomach rumbled and she remembered she didn't eat dinner. She opened the refrigerator and pulled out the cheddar cheese. She put it on a plate and found some crackers in the cupboard.

She carried the plate and crackers to the kitchen table and saw the photo album that her Gran put together. After she put hot water in her cup, she carried it to the table and sat in front of the book.

She debated about looking at it and finally opened to the first pictures. She huffed and thought, *Where on earth did Gran get a baby picture of Charlie?* She looked at the page with her and Charlie's baby pictures side by side. Gran had pasted their names and birthdates under the pictures.

As Lark flipped through the pictures, and found Gran took more of them than she remembered. Some of the shots she could remember and others, she couldn't place. Gran marked the days on the pages to help remind her of the reason for the picture. She turned to the back of the album and the final pictures were taken on that great and terrible day.

Charlie was celebrating the fact he was finally taller than Lark. He'd had a growth spurt over the summer. It was a week before their freshman year in high school started and they were both fifteen years old.

They'd ridden their bikes out to Hirsh Ranch where Charlie's horse, Fox, was kept. Lark packed a picnic lunch and they were going to ride Fox into the foothills to their favorite pasture and have a fun day. They'd brought a small, travel-size checkerboard with them and a deck of cards.

Fox was a beautiful, big black horse that Charlie won as a prize when he was thirteen.

He'd worked very hard throughout the year to be the best newspaper delivery boy on the planet. His customers on his route felt he'd done an outstanding job and the newspaper gave him the prize of a young, black colt. Charlie found the Hirsh Ranch to stable his horse and in trade, did work for them, cleaning stalls, grooming horses and making sure the horses got enough food. It was then that he decided to be a large animal veterinarian.

They rode Fox into the mountains all the time, but this would be the last weekday they'd be able to do it until spring. Gran didn't like for them to ride during the winter. She was afraid they'd get lost in the mountains and freeze to death.

After eating lunch, they played a long game of War that seemed to go on and on. They laughed and threw cards at each other and then watched quietly as Fox made his way around the field finding grasses to munch on.

Charlie leaned on Lark. "You know, I'm worried about starting ninth grade."

"Why?" Lark asked as she pulled apart an Aspen Daisy.

"We're going to be in different classes. There will be new people at the school from around the county."

"That doesn't matter. We still have the same lunch hour and I'll need your help with algebra. And, we live next door to each other. It's not like you'll never see me." She threw the stem aside and looked down at him. "What's going on, Ducky?"

He brought his head up and looked her in the eye. "Lou, have you ever kissed a boy?"

"What? No. Why?" She frowned and moved away from him. She remembered seeing something in his eyes and for the first time since they'd been friends, she found him cute. "Ducky, do you want to kiss me?"

The color on his cheeks started to get rosy and he nodded. "I mean, if it's okay with you. I just thought...we've been friends for so long and...We did talk about being boyfriend-girlfriend once. It's just I think you're pretty and you've always been right there..." he went silent and continued to watch her.

"What kind of kiss do you mean?" she asked and saw a confused look on his face. "You know, like we see on TV? Do you want just a quick kiss, like you're the husband leaving for work or one of those open mouth things we saw in that movie when the man and woman on the beach started kissing?"

Charlie's brow folded. "I don't know. Which do you think would be best?"

Lark thought for a minute. "We could do like Gran says and 'play it by ear'."

"So, you wouldn't mind?"

She tilted her head and pursed her lips. "No, I think I'd like for you to be my first kiss ever. Have you ever kissed a girl?"

Charlie shook his head and turned to face her. He took her hands and looked her in the eye. He started to lean toward her and put his lips lightly to hers. After a few seconds, he sat up straight and they both opened their eyes.

"Huh," he said. "Maybe we should try the other way."

"Okay," she answered. "But, what do we do with our mouths open?"

"I don't know." He shrugged and leaned toward her with his lips parted.

She closed her eyes and felt his mouth close on hers. She let her lips open and his tongue moved around the front of her teeth. She started to grin and moved her tongue to meet his.

They'd continued kissing for a while and on the ride back to the Hirsh Ranch decided maybe they should consider being boyfriend and girlfriend. When they got back home, they'd spent a little time giggling in the driveway and made plans to go down to the river the next day to give kissing another go.

That night Lark saw red lights flash in her bedroom window. She jumped out of bed and looked out. She saw police cars at Charlie's house and an ambulance and a van with Coroner written on the side. She put on her tennis shoes and ran down the stairs. In the driveway, she found her Gran watching and went up to her. Gran wrapped her arms around Lark.

After a bit, the policemen came out with Charlie in handcuffs. They didn't find out until the next day what happened.

Lark slammed the photo album closed and stood up. "Damn, damn, damn," she mumbled and went up to her room. She crawled under the comforter to get warm and closed her eyes, but it took a long time for sleep to come to her.

Chapter Seven

The next week crawled by slowly for Charlie, and it was a mess. The furnace man came over the weekend and said the furnace couldn't be turned on until they got the air-ducts blown out. He had crawled around under the house and repaired some holes caused by varmints, but said Charlie had families of mice living in the ducts. If they didn't blow the pipes, he'd have baked mouse odor in the house and it would be a health hazard. Unfortunately, the furnace man couldn't make another appointment until the following week.

Then Charlie dealt with the plumber. He got the water running to the downstairs bathroom, but the pipes in the kitchen had frozen at some point and would have to be replaced. Charlie felt relieved to be able to shower and not have to run upstairs every time he needed to use the restroom, and it had become a pain in his backside to have to carry water downstairs just to make coffee. Now that water was downstairs again, even though it came from the sink in the bathroom, he wouldn't have to bring it from the upstairs anymore.

He also, wanted to get his truck over to Pueblo and get it sold. He needed something smaller just to go to the grocery store, but with all the workers coming in and going out, he didn't want to leave during the day, just yet.

****

Lark's week at work was busy. The Mile High email got inundated with orders for the holidays. It was good for the business, but hard work to get the orders packed and out to UPS for delivery. About half way through every day, she'd think they were getting caught up, when a whole new batch of orders would print off the web-site. There'd been a few hiccups with the folks that delivered their stock, but so far, everything was going smooth.

Lark left work at five or six o'clock in the evening, exhausted, and came home to a warm dinner and bath, and then she crawled under the sheets and sleep straight through the night.

On Friday afternoon, she decided to leave at four and headed home. When she walked into the house, she realized there were no heavenly smells coming from the kitchen.

"Gran, I'm home," she said and took off her coat. There was no response to her greeting. She frowned. Her grandmother's car was in the drive. "Gran?"

She hung up her coat and went into the kitchen. On the table she saw a note in her grandmother's handwriting. It said that she'd been invited out to dinner with some friends and there were lots of leftovers in the refrigerator.

Lark put the note down and tried to decide if she was hungry. She went to the door, took her boots off and put on her slippers. She started for the refrigerator when she heard a knock on the back door. She turned back and saw Charlie stood out on the steps. He smiled and waved through the glass.

"What?" she asked and opened the door part way.

"Is Gran around? I have a question for her," he said.

Lark saw he held a whisk in his hand. "She went out with some friends. What's your question?"

"I found this in the house." He held up the whisk. "What does it do and do I really need it?"

Lark looked at the device. "It's for scrambling things like eggs. It looks rusty, so unless you want lock jaw, I wouldn't use it." She started to shut the door.

Charlie put his gloved hand on the door frame to stop it. "Lark, could we talk for a minute?"

She looked at him and began to feel on edge. "I don't know that we have all that much to talk about, Charlie."

"I think we do. If we're going to be neighbors, I'd rather not be uncomfortable to just say *hi* to you."

She let him in the door and crossed her arms over her chest as he went past. "I asked you a question the other night and you didn't have the balls to answer. Now, all of a sudden, you're ready to talk?" She closed the door and turned into the kitchen. She moved to the counter and looked across the room at him. She didn't feel relaxed at the moment.

"God Lark, when did you become such a heartless bitch?" He looked at her and she saw anger in his eyes.

She stared at him and couldn't believe the words that just came out of his mouth. "I'm heartless? You were the one who cut me off all those years ago with no explanation. You're the one who let me devour myself with guilt for years. So if you're going to point fingers, you'd better go look in the mirror." She felt anger build in her neck and realized she was furious.

Charlie took a breath. "You did nothing wrong, Lark. I was young and immature. I never meant to hurt you."

She saw he tried not to shout at her and softened his voice, but it just made her more angry and she knew exactly where it came from. "You did hurt me and that was thirteen years ago. I'm glad you finally have the nerve to admit it, but it doesn't really make any difference."

She walked into the hallway and then turned around again. "You need to remember something. You were the one who wrote to me one time only. It was the most hurtful thing anyone has ever said to me and I can quote it verbatim. *Dear Lark, I don't want you to come back here anymore. I hate you and we are not friends.* You must remember stabbing me in the heart with that letter. You obviously didn't give a crap about me. You never explained what I'd done to cause such a response. What was I supposed to think?"

Charlie moved closer to her and looked down at her. Lark saw his cheeks were red and his teeth clenched. He slammed his hand against the hallway wall next to her.

Every fear she'd felt over the last couple of months bubbled to the surface and she couldn't look at him. She closed her eyes. The fear she'd kept tightly sealed away spilled into her gut and she found it hard to breathe. She could hear those men laughing at her.

"Enough, Lark! I know I fucked up. You'd laugh if you knew how many times I've kicked myself over the years," he said through his clenched teeth.

****

Charlie's anger started to build, and it was something he'd fought for many years. It reminded him too much of his father. He suddenly hit a brick wall when he looked at her and realized she was hyperventilating. "God, Lark, what..." He started to bring his hand up to her, but saw her flinch back flat against the wall.

Her hand came up to his chest and she tried to push him away. "Don't," she hissed and sucked in air.

She continued to push against his chest and shook her head.

He put his hand on her arm and was at a loss for how to help her. "Lark, what can I do?" He watched her as she tried to catch her breath and suddenly thought about sandwich bags.

"Just don't." She tried to pull away from his hand, but he wouldn't release her arm.

He moved to her side. "Lark, bend over and try to relax," he said and put his hand on the back of her neck.

****

Lark felt his hand on the back of her head. He tried to make her bend over and she heard his words, but everything from six months ago slammed into her. She could still hear the laughter and the voices from that night.

She found as much strength as she could muster and swung her hand up. She slapped his cheek with force. "Don't touch me," she hissed between breaths and ran toward the back door. She flung it open and went out to the driveway. She grabbed the front of her sweater and tried to get her breathing under control. Her chest burned and she wanted to claw a hole in her neck if it would help just to breathe. She moved to her Bronco and put her hands on the cold hood. The ice and snow on the SUV and around helped her cool off. She grabbed a handful of snow and put it up to her cheeks. The voices started to fade and then she heard footsteps behind her. Looking over her shoulder, she saw Charlie stop half way to her. He held her coat in his hands.

Lark turned around and leaned against her SUV. She continued to suck in air and still couldn't talk. Charlie held the coat out to her and she grabbed it. She held it against her chest and wouldn't take her eyes off him. As her throat tightened and tears welled in her eyes, she thought about the boy she used to know and care about. Was this him? Was it really her Charlie?

"Lark, I didn't mean to scare..." he started.

"Don't," she said and waved her hand. She looked into his eyes and tried to find her voice. "We will never be friends, again, Charlie, if that's even what we were. You said that in your letter. Just stay away from me and everything will be fine." She moved quickly past him and went into the house. She locked the door and slid down to the floor and then buried her face in the coat and cried.

Chapter Eight

Charlie looked at the back door and wanted to go make sure Lark was okay. She'd said some very intense things to him that he was going to have to think about. All those months ago, when he'd decided to come back to Canon City, he knew he'd need to deal with hurt feelings, but he never expected anything like this.

He felt bad that she was so angry with him and hoped they could get past it, but he also felt that there was something else brewing just under the surface. Why was she so frightened? He knew from his own past experiences it could be hard for her to talk about. He stared at the back door for a long time and then decided to leave it alone for now.

Charlie turned up the drive to head back to his house, and shook his head. He didn't know how to help ease her upset.

****

Lark cried her way up to her room then lay down on her bed. Her chest was on fire from her anxiety attack. She put her hands up on her head and wanted to scream. She'd just done something to Charlie that he wouldn't understand.

After she accused him of withholding information about what she'd done to make him cut her off, she'd let what happened back in June effect her and she'd done the same to him. She rolled over onto her side and began to think it was unfair of her to do that to him, no matter how angry she let the past make her feel. Charlie had no way of knowing what her problems were and he would probably try to find out from Gran.

Lark couldn't have that. Gran could not be told anything about that night. She felt so stupid back in June. The blame fell on her for that night. She'd wanted to trust Thomas, but couldn't after she found out about his lies and indiscretions. Gran would never understand any of it and Lark didn't want any of it to get out.

She got up off the bed and changed her work pants to a pair of flannel-lined jeans. She put on a heavier sweater and socks, too. Looking at herself in the bathroom mirror, she saw the puffy rings under her eyes and tried to cover them up a little. On her way out of her room, she stopped in the attic and grabbed Charlie's letter.

At the back door, she put on her coat and boots. Once outside, she realized it was freezing cold, but at least the snow stopped. The sun set and she could see stars shine bright. She stomped through snow and found herself at Charlie's front door. Raising her glove, she didn't have the first clue what she would say to him, but she needed answers and knocked on the door.

Lark put her hands in her pockets and heard the dog woof. Then footfalls came to the door and the lock clicked. Charlie opened the door with his pants half way undone and a bare chest. They stared at each other for a moment.

"I need some answers," she said and pushed past him into the front hall. The house was as she remembered. It was dark and looked sad and empty. "First of all, I want to apologize for freaking out on you."

"Okay." He closed the door and hit a switch on the wall that turned on the light. "I planned to take a shower, but I suppose it can wait."

She looked at him again and her breath caught in her throat. She turned away and looked at the kitchen. "I came at a bad time. I can come back later," she said.

He shook his head and frowned. "No, it's okay." He pointed toward the living room.

Embers glowed in the fireplace and she went over to it to get some warmth. On the mantel she saw what looked like a bunch of letters bound together with a rubber band. She turned back to him and saw Charlie bent over to pick a thermal shirt up from the floor. He pulled it over his head and buttoned his pants.

"Do you want a cup of coffee? I bought a microwave oven and can warm it up in no time." He put his hands together and waited.

"No. No coffee." She moved forward and felt something under her feet. She stood in the middle of his sleeping bag. His wolf, Breaker, sat by it looking up at her. "Charlie, please, tell me the truth. What happened? Why didn't you get in touch with me?"

"You said it doesn't make any difference anymore." He scratched his jaw. "So it's not important. You've moved on and I'm going to start college next fall. That's all that matters now." He reached for a wooden chair, the only piece of furniture in the room and set it by the fireplace. "Have a seat." He sat down on the hearth and Breaker sat next to his feet.

Lark walked to the chair and sat. She'd said those words to him in the midst of her panic. She needed to calm down. "It is important. I was having an anxiety attack and blabbed the first things I thought. Charlie, I've carried a load of guilt on my shoulders for thirteen years and now I can get the answers. What happened?" She took off her gloves and looked at him. Charlie stared at his hands and seemed to be deep in thought.

He laughed. "When I was first put into detention, I got into a lot of fights. There were other boys there who got their jollies by picking fights. The new kid always got tested." He looked at her and arched his eyebrow. "You know how I was back then. I didn't take crap from anyone."

"You were fearless," she said.

"The second year I was in there a new therapist started working with those of us with anger issues. I got counseled the rest of the time I was in juvie. The last two years I met three times a week with this lady therapist and got a lot of my own guilt and fears worked out. My number one fear was that I'd turn into my dad. I didn't mean to scare you earlier, Lark. I still have moments when I worry about being my dad."

"I don't think you need to worry about that. My reaction came from something else and wasn't your fault."

He nodded. "The crap that went on with my mom and dad wasn't my fault, either, but for a long time I'd thought it was and since they were gone, I blamed you for everything that went wrong while I was in detention. I was pretty mixed up."

"Blamed me for what? I don't understand."

He looked at her. "Did you go to the prom?" he asked.

"Yeah, I went. What of it?" Lark couldn't figure out where this conversation was headed.

"With Zack Strom?"

"Yeah. What does that have to do with anything? It was twelve years ago."

He shook his head. "Unbelievable. You go to the prom with the one dick I could never stand. He was an arrogant bully then and I suppose he still is now."

Lark couldn't stand the look in his eyes. It seemed to go from anger to confusion back to anger in less than a heartbeat. "So, I wasn't supposed to go to the prom?"

Charlie stood up so fast from his seat he almost stumbled on the hearth. He went to the other side of the room and crossed his arms. "You were supposed to wait for me. You promised to wait," he shouted at her.

Lark stood up with her fists clenched. "How long was I supposed to wait, Charlie? Five years, ten? Christ, was I supposed to become Miss Havisham and wear my wedding dress until I died? How long, Charlie? I was only fifteen. When we were eighteen years old and you didn't come back, what was I supposed to do?" She saw a new expression on his face. "Let me guess, you never read Great Expectations? Figures. I thought we'd be able to once and for all put the past away, but even though you were counseled it would seem you're still angry. I'm still angry. I guess it would be better to wait until tomorrow." She turned and started out of the living room.

Charlie followed behind her and in the hallway, grabbed her arm. She looked up at him, shocked. He spun her around and pushed her against the front door. They were both breathing hard and Lark could feel tears start to burn her eyes. She kept telling herself this was not June and Charlie wasn't one of those men.

"Answer my question, Charlie. Why did you cut me off?" she whispered. "Gran and I tried to see you every month, but you refused to see us. Why?" She looked up as his brows creased.

"I was so pissed off at you," he choked. "You were supposed to wait and now you're engaged. I just can't win. I came back here when I was released from juvie and Gran told me you were up in Boulder going to the university. I spent two weeks watching you on the campus and it was obvious you fit right in there. It was best for me to leave."

She felt him press his pelvis against hers. A warm tingle began to work its way down her legs into her feet and thaw the ice that surrounded her heart. He still held her arms. "You didn't answer my question, Charlie. Why did you cut me off?" She felt the grip lessen on her arms, as his bottom lip lightly trembled. She was able to bend her elbow and brought her hand up to his face. She lightly touched his lip and looked into his eyes.

"I was so fucking jealous of you, but you were my friend and I needed you," he whispered.

Lark didn't say anything. She felt there was more to spill and didn't want to interrupt his train of thought. She moved her hand along his jawline and around his neck.

"The week you sent me the letter about going to the prom with Zack, my mom came to visit." He let her arms go and backed to the other side of the hall. He leaned against the wall, but didn't look at her. He laughed. "It's so funny. I was in detention for saving her from my dad." He glanced at Lark. "I never had the love you got from Gran. I always wished she was my Gran, too, but then that would have meant you and me were related. I had a terrible crush on you back then." He ran his hand through his long hair and coughed. "Anyway, when Mom came to see me, she said she was very disappointed with me. She asked what was I thinking when I killed my father. I told her that I was trying to save her ass." He shook his head and his voice began to fade. "She frowned at me and said *your father never would have hurt me.* Christ, he beat her all the time, why on earth would I think he was trying to kill her? He was drunk as shit and had a death grip around her neck." He went silent and squeezed his eyes shut. "Then came the real kicker. She said, *you know, I never wanted a baby. Your father was Catholic so I couldn't have an abortion.*"

Lark's heart was being ripped apart in her chest. A tear rolled down her cheek and she was unable to move or say anything. It was all she could do just to breathe. She couldn't believe the hell Charlie lived through.

"She stayed about ten minutes and when she left she said she didn't expect to see me ever again. Great family, right? Gran told me she died a few years ago. So much for mending that fence." He brought his eyes up to Lark's and stared at her. "You are so beautiful and

I see it. Crazy me, back then I thought we had a tight connection, but I got that letter the same day she visited. You were out here living life to the fullest and there I was unable to move anywhere without being watched. I did hate you and knew if I saw you I'd be a dick about what the cards dealt. I would have said something mean and would have hurt you worse. I cared for you too much to do that."

It was all she could do to keep from crying her eyes out. She moved up to him and put her hands up on his shoulders and then pulled him into a tight hug. She put her head on his chest and didn't say anything. She felt his hands move around her waist and he tightened his hold.

After a moment, she looked up at him again and touched his face. She pushed up on her toes bringing her lips to his and brushed them gently. "I'm sorry. I never knew, Charlie. I never meant to hurt you," she whispered.

He picked her up and lowered his head. She felt his lips and tongue graze against her mouth and she pulled to him tight. It was the kiss she remembered from so long ago and it warmed her, but the guilt in her heart stabbed at her. Tears continued to roll down her cheeks as they gently kissed.

He brushed his hand through her hair. "Don't cry Lark. It's in the past. I know it." He let her back down, but left his hand in her hair and massaged her neck.

"You have nothing to be sorry for. I was too young and it was easier to run away." He sniffed and chuckled. "You know what's funny?" She shook her head. "At least we know what to do with our tongues now."

She wiped her eyes on the sleeve of her sweater and laughed. She looked back up at him. "If it's any consolation, prom sucked. Zack got stoned with his buddies and I rode home with Jay Hager and his date." She backed away and sniffed. "Talk about being a third wheel. I think it was all they could do to keep their hands off one another. I think they talked about getting married, but broke up after graduation. Zack works for his dad at the savings and loan and, yes, he's still a jerk." She leaned against the opposite wall and smiled at him. "We still have a lot of past to go through, Ducky. We both have a lot to forgive."

"And you're supposed to be getting married New Year's Eve, Lou."

Lark had an *Oh right* moment, but felt so elated they'd both used the nicknames from their childhood. "Feel like having an all night talk session? I'll bring the tissues and vodka or maybe Gran's hot chocolate."

"I don't drink and I better get some more wood for the fire. It's chilly in here," Charlie said, grinning. "Aren't you tired? You've had an upsetting evening so far."

"I think I'm getting a second wind. I'll go get the chocolate, you get the fire roaring. I'll be right back."

As she walked back to her home, she thought about that kiss. It surprised her how warm and tingly it made her feel. She thought about Thomas, and how he hadn't made her feel that way for a very long time.

She ran the rest of the way home and found the special chocolate powder her grandmother mixed. She left it on the counter and ran up the stairs to her room. She pulled open her closet door and hunted around for a particular box. Finding the one she wanted, she took it out of the closet and set it on the corner of her bed. She rummaged through it and found exactly what she wanted. She stuffed it in her pocket with the letter and went back down the stairs. She remembered her Gran was still out with her friends. She stopped at the table and turned the note over. She wanted Gran to know where she was and not worry. She grabbed the can of powder and a jug of milk from the refrigerator and then turned off the light and went back out the door.

Chapter Nine

Charlie got the fire blazing and heard his microwave turn on. He must have been outside when Lark came back. He stood up and went into the kitchen. She was at the counter putting spoonfuls of powder into his two cups. She'd taken her coat off and wore a fuzzy, soft looking sweater and tight straight-legged jeans. Her blonde hair caught the light from the stove top and seemed to glow. He liked the view and felt his blood start to warm. She looked over her shoulder at him and smiled.

"Lou, I don't know if this sounds crude, but you have a great ass," he said and smiled.

"Thanks for the compliment." She left a spoon in one of the cups and walked over to her coat, which hung on the back door knob. She pulled something out of a pocket and flipped it to him.

He caught the yellow, rubber duck and was surprised. "Hey, where did this come from?"

"I was on a walk to somewhere one day when your mom still lived here. It was garbage day and her cans were on the curb, loaded with a ton of stuff. I saw

Mr. Ducky on one of the piles and had to grab it." She turned back to the microwave as the ringer went off.

"You've turned into a garbage picker?" He grinned and looked at one of the few things, besides Lark, his horse and his bike that ever meant anything to him. It was given to him as a birthday present when he turned five.

"Yeah, it's like those guys on the History Channel say. You never know when you'll find gold." She turned and carried two steaming cups.

His brows creased. "You're not really picking garbage cans?"

She handed him a cup. "No, that was my one and only time." She smiled.

"It's warmer in the living room. Let's go out there. I should have heat and water in the kitchen on Monday. I have field mice living in the air-ducts and once they're cleaned out I'll be able to turn on the furnace. Until then, it's like camping in here. I don't want mice poop flying through the air. The furnace guy started to ramble about twenty-six letter diseases I could get. It gave me the willies."

"I guess, it's probably a good idea not to turn it on then," she said.

They walked back to the living room and she moved the chair to face the fire and sat. She took off her boots and put her socked feet up on the hearth. Breaker was stretched out on the sleeping bag.

"So, tell me about your pup. Where did you find him?" she asked and took a sip from her cup.

Charlie sat back down on the hearth and stretched out his long legs. "He sort of found me. I was at a rest area in Montana, just taking a break. I heard something whine outside the truck and when I looked there was this little scrawny puppy dancing around. I thought he might have rabies, but now I know he was just trying to get my attention." He looked down at Breaker, whose tail started to wag. "I named him Breaker, because I was on a break. It wasn't until I took him to a vet for shots and to get him neutered, that I found out he's a gray wolf. We've been partners ever since."

"He's beautiful and seems very attached to you."

"Yeah, I'll have to put Mr. Ducky up, so he can't get it. Breaker would tear the thing to pieces." He looked at the rubber duck again and squeezed it. He stood up and put it on the mantel next to the stack of letters.

"I noticed the letters before..." Lark started and he saw her blue eyes look up at him. "I brought your letter over. Maybe we could have a sacrificial burning."

He put his hands on them and smiled at her. "I don't have much and the things I do have are precious to me. There is no way I will ever throw them in the trash or burn them." He sat down on the end of the hearth and stretched his legs out, again.

"I saved your letter. It was the only one I ever received. I tried to read between the lines to figure out what I'd done wrong, but I couldn't ever figure it out." Lark arched her eyebrow and looked at her cup.

He sipped his cocoa and smiled. "You know, I searched high and low over the years for a cup of hot chocolate that could match Gran's. I never found it. I travelled in all parts of the country and never found anything as good as this." He sipped again. "It's missing the little marshmallows though."

"Gran mixes the powder in her secret kitchen and it's packaged down at my warehouse. I've been selling it online for a couple of years. It's one of our best sells. Sorry about the marshmallows. I forgot them."

"I tasted a really strange mix once down in New Mexico. It had one of those hot peppers mixed into it and was spicy, but just not what I remembered. Do you know what the secret ingredient is?"

"No. Gran says its love, but since I'm not eight years old anymore, I'm pretty sure it's one of her favorite spices."

They sipped the cocoa and he watched Lark look at the flames jump in the fireplace. "You know, I have some anger demons that I work really hard to keep buttoned up. They rear their ugly faces every now and then, but I learned some techniques to help quash them. They started to surface earlier and I am really sorry if I scared you."

"It wasn't you, Ducky. You have no reason to be sorry. Do you remember the time we built the catapult on the beach and that jerk, Bobbie Reynolds and his pals showed up and mouthed off?" Lark asked. He nodded. "Was that one of the times the anger demons appeared?"

"Yep, they've been with me a long time. My dad really kicked my butt when Bobbie's dad came over and tried to get my dad to pay for the medical bills." He grimaced and looked at Lark. "I guess I broke Bobbie's nose. You know, I hate to admit this, but there are times when the anger is a good thing to have around. Like everywhere else in the world, there are some pretty mean drivers out on the roads and there were times I felt thankful for those demons."

"Yeah, well Bobbie deserved worse and I felt proud that you were able to pull away from him without going overboard. He's still here in Canon City and is a jerk. There's a rumor about him dealing drugs, but I think he started it to pump up his weird ego. I heard Jamie moved down to Texas and became a cop or something like it. Dexter owns a bar up on I-25." She gazed back at the flames. "Sorry, I shouldn't waste time giving you their histories."

"Lou, I'm sorry about that letter. Once I got my head straightened out with the therapist, I realized it was one of the dumbest things I'd ever done. I started millions of letters to you the last six months in juvie to try and apologize, but just couldn't get the right words down." He looked at her and wanted to touch her face and kiss her lips. "Every now and then over the years, I'd pull your letters out and re-read them. I still kick myself for being such an idiot. It's my fault we lost all those years."

"We were always able to talk about things, Charlie. I wish we'd been able to just talk then." She set her cup on the hearth and folded her hands in her lap. "I never meant for my letters to torment you. I thought it would help keep you connected to us if you knew what was going on here and that we were thinking about you. It wasn't supposed to hurt you."

"I know. Since I can't go back in time and change my reaction, hopefully, now we can at least become friends again. I missed that the most." He put his hand on her foot and gave it a squeeze. He wanted so much more from her, but would have to accept friendship. "So, tell me about this loser you're planning to marry. Is he good to you?"

"Thomas isn't a loser, and, yes, he's good to me," she said and had a pinched look on her face. For some reason Charlie felt she was lying to him, but let it go and thought she didn't want to discuss her relationship.

"How long have you been together?"

"About five years. He asked me to marry him two years ago on New Year's Eve. That's why we decided to have the ceremony this New Year's Eve. It's just a few weeks from now. I don't know why I thought it would be a good idea. We've been pretty busy at work. He'll be here in a couple of weeks for the dance."

"What dance? Please, not another prom?"

"No. It's the Methodist Church Christmas festival. A few years ago they moved it from the basement of the church to the community center. Now, the whole town gets involved. Gran, Mrs. Bickens and Mrs. Hager, Jay's mom, have baking wars every year. It can be fun."

They went silent for a few minutes and Charlie began to feel a little uncomfortable. "Why did you wait so long to finally decide on a date for the wedding?"

"The time was never right." She laughed. "One thing after another kept getting in the way - his work, my work. I'm determined this year will go smoothly."

Charlie saw her look down at her hands and frown. "Lou, you don't sound very excited about it. You sound like you're trying to convince yourself it's going to go smooth." He moved his hand up to her ankle.

"We still have one issue to work out. He wants me to move to Denver, but..." She looked up at him with her beautiful blue eyes.

"But?"

"I don't want to be so far away from Gran and I can't move the warehouse up there. I have fifteen employees who need the jobs. They have got children in school and homes. They count on me and Nancy, and wouldn't be able to follow if I moved everything north."

"That sounds like two very good reasons not to move to Denver." He couldn't stop staring at her. "I'm sure you'll get it worked out."

Lark nodded and looked at the fire. The reflection from the flames bounced on her face and hair. Charlie's heart began to pound. "I only wish one thing." He saw her eyebrows go up and she tilted her head. "We never got to have our date the day after the picnic. We were going to walk down the river bank and watch the rafters take off."

She smiled. "I remember and we were going to work on our kissing technique."

"Do you remember the card game that went on and on, until I won?"

"Yeah, and excuse me, you didn't win, I did. I was the War champ. Lord, I thought we'd be out in that field all night trying to get that game finished." She shook her head. "Do you want some more cocoa?"

Charlie heard what she asked, but couldn't answer. He put his cup aside and slid from the hearth down onto his knees. He moved toward her and wedged himself between her legs. He pulled her slightly forward and hugged her, putting his head on her shoulder. He felt her hands move to his back and touch his hair.

"God, I've missed talking to you so much," he mumbled. "Last week, before I saw you, I was so scared. I'd never admit that to anyone but you. After that first dinner, I went from being scared to really sad. I didn't think you'd ever forgive me and wondered why I'd bothered coming back to Canon City. I could have easily gotten an apartment in Fort Collins." He moved back, rested on his feet and left his hands on her thighs. "Lark, I...we..."

She put her finger over his lips. "Ducky, don't hyperventilate." She looked at him and leaned toward him putting her lips on his.

Charlie moved one of his hands up to her face and put the other around her back. Her tongue tenderly caressed his lips and it made him want her more than he ever thought he would, but she broke the kiss and moved her head back. He opened his eyes and saw the confused look on her face. She didn't take her hands off of his shoulders. They were both breathing hard.

"Ducky, I have a few things to work out here. The one thing I do have to say though is that our kisses have gotten a lot better than our first one, so many years ago. Although, that first kiss did stick with me for a long time. Have you been practicing?"

He rested back on his heels again and moved his hands down to her waist. "I've been with a few women in the last thirteen years and they were all one-night stands. No one could ever be you."

She smiled and put her hand on his cheek. "I better get out of here. We both need to get some sleep. Thank you for your honesty."

Charlie pushed himself up and helped her stand. "Do you want me to walk you home?"

"No, I think I can find my way." She stopped mid-way through the living room and looked up at him. "I'll leave the cocoa powder I brought. Just put two scoops in the cup with milk. It only takes about two and a half minutes to warm it up."

Chapter Ten

Although Lark felt exhausted when she got home, she found it hard to get to sleep that night. She lay in her warm bed and stared up at the ceiling. Charlie turned into a really good kisser and she found it difficult to think about anything else.

As the sun started to come up, she felt herself start to drift off. The next time she was alert, she looked at her clock and it was just before noon.

She put on her sweats and slippers and made her way down to the kitchen. Gran sat at the table with a pile of papers and her checkbook.

"I was wondering when you'd get up. I heard you stomp in here pretty late last night. What was going on?"

"I wanted to get the air cleared with Charlie or I was never going to sleep right again." Lark poured a cup of coffee and sat at the table.

"Did you two get things worked out?"

"Yep, I think we did." Lark brought her leg up and rested her chin on her knee. "We talked about some old hurts."

"Good, I didn't like the way you acted at dinner the other night. Poor Charlie seemed so uncomfortable, but tried to make the best of it," Gran said and looked over the top of her glasses at Lark and then went back to her bills. "Did he explain what happened and why he turned us away?"

Lark adjusted herself in her seat and wondered how much she should tell Gran about the last thirteen years. "I wrote letters to him when he was in detention. I'd tell him all about what I was doing at school and the creative stuff you and I would work on. I wrote to him about going to prom with Zack Strom and he received it on a really bad day. He never said that it bugged him"- she didn't want to give Gran a bad impression of Charlie - "but I guess he got jealous that I was living and he wasn't. His mother visited him and said some very hurtful things to him the same day the prom letter arrived. I never realized that his mom treated him so bad. I always thought it was just his dad. Anyway, one thing led to another, and when he got out he didn't feel like he could come back and fit in." She shook her head.

"Charlie's mom was the classic abused woman. I saw her once with a black eye and asked what happened. She gave the usual *I bumped into something* response. When I'd talk to her about Charlie it was obvious she didn't care one way or another about what happened to him. It broke my heart for him. Charlie has

99

such a big heart and he deserved so much better. It's a miracle he turned out to be a decent man. You know, I thought about reporting his parents to children's services, but he begged me not to say anything."

"Yeah, he told me about that. He was afraid he'd never see us again." Lark sipped her coffee and silently agreed with her grandmother. "What are you working on?"

"I'm just paying some bills. Do you want lunch?"

"No. I'm going to drink too much coffee and then head over to the warehouse."

"It's Saturday, Lark. I think you need a day off," Gran said.

"Thank you. I'll get time off after Christmas. We're too busy right now."

"When are you going to go for your dress fitting?"

Lark nearly choked on her coffee. "Oh Lord, I completely forgot about that. I haven't had time to even think about getting back up to Denver this year. I don't know what I'm going to do about that."

Gran put her pen down and moved her hand to Lark's arm. "Sweetheart, the wedding is in three weeks. Are you sure Thomas is the one?"

Lark froze for a moment and remembered the kiss with Charlie last night. She shook her head. "Yes, Gran, I'm sure. I'll talk to Nancy. I'm sure she'll have a suggestion or know someone who could alter the dress.

I'll arrange to have it sent down from that shop in Denver."

****

Charlie woke up and felt better than he had in a very long time. He strolled out to the kitchen and saw the can of hot chocolate powder. He grinned and thought it felt good to smile for a change. He followed Lark's instructions to mix the cocoa and while it warmed in the microwave, he fed Breaker.

It was a slightly overcast day, but there wasn't any breeze to chill the air. The trees stood stock still. He decided it would be a good day to try and get some work done outside. He wanted to get under the house and see if there were any animals living or dead down there. The furnace man hadn't seen anything but the holes in the air ducts. He also wanted to see if the shed behind the house was still standing or if it rotted away to nothing.

He and Lark spent a lot of weekends weaving tales in that shed. They even imagined pirates invading Canon City once. It was also his injured animal hospital. When his dad found out what the kids were using the shed for, he'd whipped Charlie with his belt. Charlie still heard the snap and some nights could feel the stings.

Charlie put on his gloves and opened the back door stepping into the breezeway between the house and garage. He hadn't gotten the chance to look at what condition it was in and figured there would be varmints living out there and probably mountains of spider webs. He put his shoulder to the garage door and pushed to get it open. When he entered, he hoped to find a broom, but was surprised. Whoever lived in the house last, left behind furniture, a barbeque, hoses and a large number of boxes stacked around the room. The garage was loaded wall to wall.

"Holy crap," he mumbled. He walked towards the double doors and slid them up to get some light. He wondered why the real-estate agent hadn't mentioned any of this stuff. Laughing at himself, he thought, *Why didn't I check out here when I bought the place?* He would have to call the garbage collectors and find out if they'd pick some of it up if he left it on the road. He stopped and thought, *I need to get a phone.*

He pulled things around and went through some of the boxes. There was a couch that was home to several families of field mice and a couple of leisure chairs with more families living in the cushions. He did find a small square dining room table and four chairs he could use, a glass fronted bookshelf unit and two boxes with plates and bowls. Now all he needed was silverware and he'd be set.

He cleaned off the table and chairs and carried them into the kitchen. He took the shelving unit into the living room. He planned to put the plates up in the cupboards, but decided to wait until the water was hooked up in the kitchen. He should probably clean them up before he used them. He stacked the boxes along the wall. He went through more of the boxes and found some pots and pans. He started to laugh and looked at Breaker.

"I guess I'll have to learn how to cook," he said to the wolf and ruffled his neck.

Breaker woofed at him and followed him back and forth into the house. He was about to stop and fix himself a peanut butter sandwich, when a Jeep pulled into the driveway.

Charlie walked to the front of the garage and watched Jay Hager unfold himself from the Jeep. Charlie couldn't believe his eyes and started to laugh. "Where the hell did you come from?"

"Me? Where the hell have you been?" Jay walked up to him and grabbed Charlie's hand. "It's been too long, man."

They shook hands and Jay slapped him on the shoulder. Charlie shook his head. "I can't believe I'm actually looking you in the eye. You were always way taller than me."

"It looks like you took your grow vitamins like a good boy." Jay laughed and patted him on the head. "I saw Lark at the rink last weekend and she said you were back. I was in the neighborhood and thought I'd drop in for a little visit."

"Rink?"

"Yeah, I own the rink now."

"That decrepit old place? I thought you were going to be a big NHL star?" Charlie took off his gloves and leaned against the garage door rail.

"Yeah, that was the plan. I got hit really bad in the juniors and busted my knee and leg to pieces. I couldn't pass the physical after that and put my energies elsewhere. The rink is no longer that decrepit old building. We've remodeled and business is pretty good. Do you have any kids that need skating lessons?"

"No, no kids."

"Well, every Saturday night we have a broom ball match. The kids play first and then the adults get out there and tear up the ice. I expect to see you there." Jay arched his eyebrow and stared at Charlie.

"That sounds like fun. I'll mark my calendar as soon as I get this place up to snuff."

"I was a little surprised that you bought this house. Are you trying to make yourself nuts?"

Charlie looked at his old friend and laughed. He explained to Jay about his reasons for coming back and they spent about an hour getting caught up. Jay filled him in on all the local gossip about the jerks from their school days and Charlie told about his journeys across America. They agreed to get together soon for dinner and then Jay took off.

Charlie turned around and looked into the garage. One side was cleared and swept. He did find a broom.

The other side had pieces of furniture that would have to go to the dump. Since he spent most of the morning in the garage and it was after two o'clock, he put off going under the house. The furnace people would blow out the air ducts on Monday and he could wait until spring to go below.

He walked up to the shed and pulled the door open. The building shook a little and he could tell there was a lot of mold.

"Charlie, are you around her somewhere?" he heard Gran's voice call from the breezeway.

"I'm here, Gran." He turned and moved to the back of the house.

Breaker ran to the end of the walkway and wagged his tail with wild abandon. Gran appeared and bent over the wolf, scratching his neck and back. The pup was in heaven and seemed to be smiling. He rubbed up against Gran's legs making a strange squeaking noise.

"I saw you out front working your butt off. I didn't realize the garage was such a mess. Was that Jay Hager I saw pull up in the Jeep?" she asked and walked up to him.

"Can't get anything past you, can I, Gran? Yeah, I guess Lark told him I as back. It was good to get caught up with him." He smiled. "Hey, I have a question. How many years has it been since someone lived here?" he asked.

"I guess that family left about four or five years ago. He worked over at the prison, but got laid off at some point. They stayed as long as they could, but eventually just packed up and left."

"They left a ton of stuff behind. It's really crazy. I have almost a complete kitchen set up. I just need to get a toaster and some glasses and silverware. Although, I haven't gone through all the boxes, I may still find those things." He laughed. "It's sad to think they just left it all behind. I don't get it."

"Well, they had three kids. Sometimes it's too expensive to move furniture and everything else. I remember they had a U-haul trailer. It was probably just the beds and personal stuff." She looked around the back yard and then at the shed. "Is there more in there?" She pointed.

"I don't know. I was just going in, when you called. Want to see if there are any more families of field mice in there?" He grinned at her.

"You bet," she answered.

They went to the door and looked. It was dark in the shed, but Charlie had his flashlight in his pocket. He turned it on and pointed it in. It was full of gardening equipment, more hoses, a lawn mower and outdoor furniture.

"You know, when I bought this place, I thought I'd have to spend a lot of money on this kind of equipment." He shook his head. "I think all I'll need is bedroom furniture and a couch."

"I saw a couch in the garage. Can't you use it?" Gran asked and backed away from the door.

"Ah, no. There a couple of families of critters living in it and I'd have to evict them. If you pull up the cushions there's not a much underneath except springs." He looked at Gran and grimaced. "It smells pretty nasty, too."

"Well, why don't you get finished and clean up. Then bring Mr. Breaker and yourself over for dinner. I'm making meatloaf and mashed potatoes. It will be a ready in about two hours. Lark should be back from the warehouse by then."

"Gran, you're going to spoil me rotten. I'll agree if you and Lark will let me take you out for dinner tomorrow?"

"I don't see any problem with that, but I'll have to check with Lark."

Chapter Eleven

When Lark reached the warehouse, the packing crew was hard at work getting orders ready for mail-out on Monday. She walked up the stairs toward the offices and found her partner, Nancy Frye, sitting in her office.

"Hey, Nan. I was just down on the floor and Mac mentioned about not getting the delivery of tins for the hot chocolate mix. What's up?" Lark asked and stood in the doorway.

"I'm not sure. I've been trying to reach Frank all morning, but I only get his message machine. Hopefully, he'll call back. I checked the orders and it looks like we're going to need two trips to the UPS on Monday. There are over 150 orders just for the hot chocolate. We need to get the tin problem sorted out today, or tomorrow at the latest." Nancy stood up from her desk.

"I have Frank's personal number. I'll try that and if it doesn't work, I'll call Sheila. She always answers her phone. I thought you were going to take the weekend off?"

Nancy smiled at her. "I have a son that will want to go to college in a few years. I need the money."

"Right. I'll go make a call." Lark turned and continued down the hall to her office.

Once she'd settled in, she looked through her Rolodex for the cell phone number she wanted and dialed it. The line rang a couple of times and a female voice answered.

"Hey, Sheila. How are you doing? This is Lark," she said.

"Hi there. We're getting ready for the holidays. Frank's mom and dad are coming down from Montana for Christmas and then my brother and his wife and kids will be here over New Years. They're hoping to get some skiing in and I guess there's a storm front moving in for next weekend, so there should be plenty of snow. How are you and your grandmother?"

"We're fine. Same as you, we're just getting ready for holidays, but without all the company. Is Frank there by any chance?"

"Yeah, I'll get him."

She heard the phone put down and Sheila's voice at the end of the line started to shout for her husband. Lark laughed. Frank must have forgotten she was one of Sheila's bridesmaids at their wedding and they were friends since high school.

The phone picked up. "Hi, Lark."

"Hey Frank. I won't keep you on the phone long, but what's up with the tins? Can we expect them to arrive soon? We've got a lot of cocoa orders," she asked.

Lark heard a brief silence on the line and Frank cleared his throat.

"I'm not sure. Listen, I was over at the BPO lodge the other night having a beer and there's a rumor going around that Mile High is either getting bought out or closed down," he said. "I wasn't sure what to think. I called Frank Sebastian up in Denver and he said he'd heard the same thing. He said he was holding back stock for now."

"Who did you hear the rumor from?"

"A couple of different people were talking about it. One of them works at the savings and loan. What's going on, Lark?"

"As far as I know, Frank, we're not going anywhere. There's nothing in the pipes except getting orders out and believe me, there are a lot for the hot chocolate. Can you please deliver the tins either today or tomorrow? If we don't get the orders filled by the end of the week, they won't arrive in time for Christmas and my customers will be very unhappy."

"Sure, I'll get them over there tomorrow afternoon. Lark, please, don't keep us in the dark. If I'm going to lose your business, it will hurt," he said.

"I assure you Frank, there is no problem and if something comes up, my suppliers will be the first to know. Thanks for the information. I'll talk to you soon." Lark hung up her phone and stood.

She walked down the hall to Nancy's office. Her partner looked up at her and Lark explained what she'd just heard.

"I guess that explains why the suppliers up in Denver were holding back. I wonder where that rumor got started. We're doing great for the year and are totally in the black," Nancy said and leaned back in her chair.

"Frank will have the tins here tomorrow. I'll call Mike Strom at the bank on Monday and see if he's heard anything. This is really weird though. I can't figure it out."

Lark did some work in her office for a couple of hours and then went down onto the floor to help box orders. She spent a few more hours down there and then called it a day and headed home.

When she walked into the house, she smelled Gran's meatloaf cooking in the oven. It was one of her favorite meals and her mouth started to water.

"Hey, Gran, I'm home," she said and took her boots off at the door. She found her grandmother in the living room watching the weather report. "What's Mr. Weatherman reporting?"

"There's a storm front that's going to be moving in during the week. The worst of it should hit on Saturday or Sunday. They're calling for eight to ten inches of snow and it's supposed to get really windy. They're saying possible blizzard conditions. I hope it holds off until Sunday. I'm supposed to make a lot of pies for the dance on Saturday and already have most of what I need." She looked up at Lark. "If it hits on Saturday, we could be eating pies until Valentine's Day."

Lark smiled at her. "I could handle that. Your pies every day until February, sounds like heaven to me." She looked at the Christmas tree and saw her grandmother was busy with the scissors and tape. "Oh, damn, Gran, you've been wrapping. I haven't even had a chance to think about Christmas shopping," she whined and went to the tree. "We are going to put up our stockings for Santa this year, right." She turned and looked at Gran with a goofy grin on her face.

"Lark, you're silly," Gran said and stood up. "Charlie's coming over for dinner again tonight and he wants to take us out tomorrow night. You're not doing anything, are you?"

She could see by the way her grandmother looked at her that they *were* going out for dinner tomorrow night. When Gran wanted something, it didn't take much to get Lark to agree and Gran did like to get out of the kitchen every now and then. "I think that sounds just fine, Gran."

Chapter Twelve

Lark was in bed reading. She felt tired, but her brain was going in fifteen different directions. She tried to piece together this rumor business and couldn't make heads or tails of it. She couldn't figure out who would have started the rumor and why. She thought about Charlie and his wonderful, warm lips and then tried to not think about him, but it was difficult. She thought about Thomas and found she really didn't want to think about him. She realized she'd read the same page for an hour and put the book on her night stand and turned off the lamp.

She scrunched down into the covers and looked up at the ceiling. Gran's dinner tonight tasted so good. She thought about going downstairs and having another slice of meatloaf, but decided she felt too comfortable in her bed. Gran was the best cook and always prepared something tasty. She could even make Brussels sprouts taste good.

Charlie was very charming during dinner and scored all kinds of points with Gran. Lark smiled to herself. He'd volunteered to help wash the dishes after they ate and looked great with a kitchen towel tucked into the top of his pants. After he'd gone home, she'd heard Gran rearrange the plates and silverware in the dishwasher. Lark asked her what she was doing.

"Okay, so I'm a control freak about my dishwasher. If it's organized properly, the dishes wash better, and if you put the spoons with spoons and forks with forks in the silverware tray it's quicker to get them put away." Gran smiled at her and laughed. "So I'm overly-efficient with my dishes. Does that make me weird?" Lark laughed about that one and told Gran *no she wasn't weird.*

She thought about Charlie again and smiled. He'd asked her if she could run him out to Bicken's ranch tomorrow. He wanted to get reacquainted with his horse, Fox. He said he'd pay her back for the years she'd paid to have the horse boarded, but she wouldn't accept anything monetarily from him. Fox became one of her friends over the years and she went out to the ranch as often as she could to ride him up into the mountains. He was sure-footed and a very smooth ride. Lark always felt that horse possessed a gentle soul and she loved him more than anything.

Charlie also asked if it would be possible to go into town to the furniture store. He wanted to find a couch and some bedroom furniture. Gran mentioned that Lark's old set was stored in the garage and he was welcome to it.

Charlie frowned. "Do you mean all that white furniture and the bed with the pink canopy?"

Gran smirked at him and rolled her eyes. "You don't have to use the posts. You'd have a double bed frame and all you'd need to get is a mattress and box spring. And as far as the white night stand and chest of drawers goes, you could refinish those and I wouldn't be unhappy. They've been sitting in the garage for years. Would you mind if he repainted them Lark?"

No, she wouldn't mind if he refinished it. After she'd graduated from college she'd bought a new bedroom set in blonde wood and never wanted a pink canopy again. If Lark took him into town, it would be a good time to start her Christmas shopping.

There was a light tap coming from somewhere in the room and it took her a second to realize the sound came from her window. She sat up and looked. Charlie was on the outside tapping and waving. He wore a huge grin on his face.

Lark got out of bed and went to the window. She unlocked it and slid the window up. When they were kids, Charlie spent millions of nights with her. They'd have sleep overs all the time and it kept him safe from his father's rage. When they'd turned fourteen or fifteen, Gran got a little weird about him staying in Lark's room. She put the foldout couch together for him and insisted he sleep in the living room. Gran never explained why and Lark couldn't figure it out until now when she was older. She didn't want them to get physical at such an early age and Lark appreciated the sentiment now.

"Charlie, what are you doing? Are you crazy?" she whispered.

He climbed in through the window, peeled off his coat and boots and crawled into her bed.

"What are you doing?" she asked and closed the window.

"I'm free..zing." He shook under the comforter. "The fire went out dur..ing dinner and the wood I..I..I brought in is wet and won't light. The house is a freezer," he said and his teeth chattered. "We...we used to do this all the time when we were kids. I couldn't think of anyplace warmer."

"You could have broken your neck out on the roof."

"Naw, it was like riding a bike." He shook again and pulled the over tighter around his neck. "The cinder block wall is still goo...good, but there was a little ice on the roof. I slipped a couple of times, but made it okay." He looked at her. "Please, get in here and warm me up."

She walked to the other side of the bed and started to get under the comforter. "Where's Break....oh, my Lord, you're an ice cube tray. I can feel your feet through your socks and mine." She snuggled close to him and let him wrap himself around her. "Why didn't you get in your truck?"

"I thought about that, but by the time the thing warmed up, the neighbors would have complained to the police about the noise. To keep it warm, I'd have to leave the engine running. I didn't want to wake everyone up."

"Where's Breaker?"

"I left him outside. He does well in cold weather with his fur coat." He shivered. "God, you feel good."

His face was pressed up against her chest and her arms held onto his back. "This really brings back memories."

"Yeah, all those times I slept over here...you saved me, you know?"

"Charlie, come on."

"No, you did." He propped himself up on his elbow and took her hand. "Those nights when my dad was drunk, it really helped to know there was a safe place I could go. You and Gran never turned me away. I have so much to thank you for; I don't know how to get started." He kissed her hand and scrunched back down under the comforter.

"Well, you saved me, too. Back in our school days, when that bitch Sally Hoskins and her buds made fun of my name and called me Meadow Lark, you kept me grounded. I was never much of a fighter, but I really wanted to beat her up." She put her hand in his hair and snuggled closer.

"I knew it made you sad, because your mom gave you that name. I brought you chocolate, flowers and that movie newly released on VHS...what was it?"

"The Truman Show. I loved that movie."

"Right, and we made popcorn and Gran fell asleep in her rocker," he said.

"When the movie ended, you went out the back door, like you were going home and then you climbed up the wall and we had a sleepover." She looked down at him and felt the tingle start in the lower half of her body. "You know, Gran was aware of your being up here. When we were a little older, she tried once to discuss exactly what we were up to when we had sleep overs." She laughed and it must have been contagious because Charlie laughed, too.

There was a light knock on her bedroom door. They both stopped laughing. "Come in," Lark said.

The door opened and a large wolf landed on the middle of the bed, stepping on both Charlie and Lark.

"Breaker was scratching at the back door and seemed lonely. He came right up the stairs and stood at your door. I wondered why for a second, but then I remembered. He'll make sure you two behave. Good night kids," Gran said and closed the door.

Breaker rubbed up against Lark and pushed Charlie to the other side of the bed. He parked himself right between them and got comfortable.

"I should have left you at the house, you dork," Charlie said to the wolf.

Lark scratched behind his ears. "No, you shouldn't have done that. He'll be fine."

The bedroom door reopened and Gran leaned in, again. "Speaking of which, Charlie, there is a really nice sleeper sofa downstairs. I'm just saying," Gran said and left the room.

Lark turned on the bedside lamp and looked at Charlie. The both laughed.

"I think Gran just gave us a hint," Charlie said and lay back on the pillows.

"She has nothing but our best interests at heart," she replied and continued to pet Breaker. "Are you warmed up yet?"

"Yeah, my teeth aren't chattering anymore."

"Come on, boys. I'll help you get the sleeper set up." She climbed out of bed and held her hand out to Charlie.

He pushed Breaker off the bed and took her hand. They stopped at the hallway closet and she loaded his arms with sheets, blankets and pillows.

They pulled the cushions off, which Breaker found very comfortable. Lark spread the fitted sheet over the mattress and crawled up on her knees to reach the other side. She heard Charlie quietly whistle behind her and felt his cold hand through her flannel pajama bottoms. Her heart pounded in her chest and fear crept into her stomach. She could hear the men laugh. After she closed her eyes and remembered June was in the past and it was only Charlie who touched her rear-end, she calmed down.

Lark looked over her shoulder. "Ducky, that is a place I would rather you didn't feel." She tried to stop her voice from sounding tense. It was just Charlie who touched her. He wouldn't hurt her.

He looked at her and didn't smile. "This may be rude, but I told you before. You do have a great ass, totally gorgeous. Sorry."

Lark smiled and felt his hand move down her leg. "Damn," she whispered and turned around on her knees to face him. She crawled toward him and felt his hands move around her waist. "You are too tempting." She put her finger on his lips and moved her hands around his neck.

He leaned his lips down to hers and his tongue swirled in her mouth. She nibbled his lips and let her own tongue trace over his teeth. His arms tightened around her and she did likewise wanting to touch every inch of his body with hers. The room grew warm and she felt sure he wouldn't be frozen anymore.

He pulled her up and wrapped her legs around his waist. He gently laid her out on the mattress and pressed down on top of her. Their kiss didn't separate and Lark felt as though she'd never been truly kissed before. Every nerve in her body tingled and she didn't want to let him go.

That was until she felt a wet, slurpy lick on the side of her face. Charlie got it, too, and put his hand up to the wolf.

"Breaker, get down." She watched the animal obey. "Good boy, now lie down, go on, lie down." The wolf's head disappeared below the sleeper.

Charlie looked down at her and kissed her lightly. "Where were we?"

She ran her hands through his hair and caught her breath. His hand was moving up under her fleece nightshirt. "Ducky, what is your hand doing?"

He wiggled his eyebrows and grinned. "It's feeling your nice, firm breast. It's so soft, but firm." He pinched her nipple and she sucked in air. "Do you like that, Lou?" he whispered and lightly bit her chin.

She opened her eyes. "Gran is right upstairs and the zipper on your jeans is rubbing me the wrong way and killing the mood."

"Would you like for me to take them off?"

Lark smiled. "You wish." She pushed him off of her and rolled onto her side. "I think we can safely say there are some old emotions resurfacing between us."

"Lou, we only ever shared one kiss and we were kids. I had no idea what any of our parts were for until I read Playboy magazine. We were friends and now I think the relationship is finally getting the chance to grow up."

"I'm engaged to another man, and getting married in three weeks. I'm glad you came home and we've had a chance to forgive one another, but..."

"But what?" He moved his hand up to her face and touched her hair. "You can't tell me you're not feeling something. That last kiss was extremely hot and I know I want to keep touching you. Lou, I want more. I want us," he said.

"I know you do. I have a whole new ball of guilt forming in my heart, because I don't want to lead you on. Your kisses are wonderful, but that's as far as it goes, Ducky." She moved off the sleeper and started to pick up a flat sheet.

He sat up. "I can finish making the bed. Thanks for warming me up, Lou."

He stared at her and she couldn't read his look. It seemed the emotions he wanted to release boiled below the surface and it was hard to tell what he was thinking.

"We'll talk more tomorrow. Goodnight, Ducky." She turned and went back up to her room.

She pulled the covers over her head and couldn't figure out what just happened. They'd been all over each other and she did want him to make love to her, but was stuck. She wanted to be faithful to Thomas and didn't want to sleep around the way she knew Thomas did. She needed that honesty. She didn't want to play games and said it earlier. Charlie was too tempting and he'd woken something up in her that she'd feared was dead. She hadn't felt any kind of sexual hunger for months and wondered if she were to go farther with Charlie would she be able to put the horrible past behind her.

Chapter Thirteen

On Sunday morning, Lark drove Charlie into Canon City to search for a couch and bed. He'd left Breaker with Gran, who seemed to have become very attached to the wolf.

They didn't discuss what occurred the night before or how little sleep they'd both gotten. Charlie didn't know if he was coming or going when he looked at Lark. She was everything he remembered and everything he wanted in his life. Yet, he understood he put her in a difficult situation and cared for her too much to pull at her emotions.

After he'd found mattresses and a couch, and arranged to have them delivered, they stopped at a thrift shop where he found some mis-matched pieces of silverware for a nickel a piece and a couple of drinking glasses for fifty cents. He also found a desk and chair for a reasonable price. When Lark questioned the purchase, he said he'd need somewhere to do his school work in the fall and it was in good enough condition. After unscrewing the legs off the desk, they were able to get it loaded into the back of her Bronco.

Charlie realized he didn't have bedding and when they looked at the remnants of sheets and comforters at the thrift store they were all musty and stained. Lark wouldn't let him buy any of them and they ended up in Sears where he found what he needed. He also got some towels and a flannel shirt at half price. While he looked at sheets, Lark wandered over to table cloths and he saw her look through the shelves. She came back over and showed him the one she'd picked. The cloth was a lacy royal blue and he thought Gran would like. Lark smiled and said she felt good about getting her first gift for Christmas bought.

They dropped Charlie's purchases off at his house and headed out to the Gorge. Lark drove the Bronco carefully to the Bicken's Ranch. The road was not on a main thoroughfare and hadn't been plowed.

They were quiet. Charlie didn't want to bother her and get them stuck in the snow, even though she handled the road beautifully. As they neared the gate to the ranch, the road smoothed out and Lark seemed to relax.

"Lou, I want to apologize for my behavior last night. You said it about me and I feel the same about you being too tempting, but I need to keep my hands off you." He saw her brow crease and she glanced at him with a frown. "Not that I want to keep them off, but I understand your heart is elsewhere. I have to respect that."

"Thank you, but you don't need to apologize. We're both adults and I think all three of our kisses have been started by me. I could have walked around the sleeper and put the fitted sheet on standing up, but, no, I was lazy and, since you seem to be a butt man, I guess I tempted you." She pulled the Bronco into the driveway, passed a huge two story house and followed the road down to the stables. She drove the SUV to an area with a couple of other cars parked and turned off the engine. She reached between the seats and grabbed a paper sack from the back seat.

"On good days, Mr. Bickens releases the horses out into the pasture so they can run and prance." She looked up at him. "They need the exercise." They got out of the Bronco and she steered him toward a fence that circled around a huge field. She set the paper sack down and pulled out a plastic bag that held apple slices.

He watched as she stepped up on the bottom rail of the fence. She pinched her lips together and let out an ear piercing whistle. He looked out at the field and could hear a horse reply.

"That's a good whistle, Lou. Where'd you learn how to do that?" he asked.

"My dad taught me when I was seven or eight. I used to do it all the time when we were kids. You don't remember?" She looked down at him.

"Vaguely. I don't remember it being so loud."

"Thanks for the compliment. Fox should appear any second." She took her gloves off and pulled out a couple of slices.

Charlie felt a grin curl his lips when he saw the beautiful black horse step down the hillside. He'd named the horse after one of his favorite TV characters. When Fox reached the field he galloped toward them. "Damn, he's incredible."

The horse shook its head and slowed down as it approached the fence and headed straight for Lark. He put his head over the top rail and whinnied, nudging Lark's arm.

"Hi there, beautiful boy," she said and held out her hand with the apple slices. The horse gobbled them down in no time and let Lark rub his neck and ears. "I've got a surprise for you Foxy boy."

Charlie saw her smile. "He won't remember me."

"Yes, he will. Come here, Ducky." The horse watched Charlie approach and blew steam out his nose. "Hold your hand up to him."

Charlie did as he was told. Fox whinnied again and moved to sniff his hand. The animal nodded his large head and let Charlie move closer.

"Hey there, buddy. God, I've missed you," Charlie said and rubbed his muzzle. The horse moved as close as he could get to the fence and put his head on Charlie's shoulder, who put his hands on either side of the horse's neck and gave Fox a hug. "I should have known you'd remember. I learned something and I haven't started veterinarian school, yet."

When Charlie pulled back he realized tears pooled in his eyes. He cleared his throat and saw a sympathetic look on Lark's face. "He looks so good, Lark. I'll never be able to thank you enough for seeing that he was well cared for and happy." He cleared his throat again. "I will repay you for the boarding fees."

"Yeah, we can argue about that later. Let's see if Mr. B. is around. We'll get his saddle and you can go for a ride," she said and handed him the bag of apple slices. "Hold your hand flat when you feed him those. He loves apples. I'll be right back."

"You'll ride with us, right?" he said to her back as she walked away.

"Not today. You need to get reacquainted."

Charlie watched her walk toward the barn and saw an older man come out. He was tall with gray hair and a mustache. Charlie remembered him from his days as a newspaper delivery boy.

****

"Hey there, Mr. B. How's it going?" Lark asked and smiled.

"I can't complain, Miss Metcalfe." He took his glove off and shook her hand. "Are you going for a ride today?"

They both turned and walked toward Charlie. "No, not me. Mr. B. I don't know if you remember

Charlie Stone? He is the real owner of Fox. I've just been keeping an eye on things while he's been away."

She saw Mr. Bicken's squint his eyes at Charlie and thought he probably knew the story. In a town the size of Canon City it was hard to keep secrets.

"Well, I'll be a bear's bud." The old man smiled and shook hands with Charlie. "Didn't you used to be our paperboy?"

"Yes, sir. I was."

"We haven't had a decent one since. It's never on time and I don't think the kid we have now has ever heard of rubber bands." Mr. Bickens reached up and rubbed Fox's nose. "So you want to take this boy out?"

"Yes, I would," Charlie said.

"No problem. Are you sure you don't want to ride today, Miss Metcalfe? It's a good day for it."

"Not today. It's too cold and I want to see what Mrs. Bickens is mixing up in the kitchen."

"Yeah, she's barricaded herself in the kitchen baking up a storm. She won't let me near, because she knows I'll eat the batter before she can get it in the oven." He chuckled. "I'll go get a saddle. There's a gate down there if you'll bring him out."

Lark helped Charlie get the big horse out of the pasture and Mr. Bickens brought a saddle. He got it set right and Charlie pulled himself up on the horse's back. The stirrups needed to be adjusted for his long legs.

Lark worked the buckle on one side and noticed Charlie looked down at her with something in his eyes. There was a warmth and intensity that almost caused her to hold her breath.

"Lou, are you sure you don't want to ride? You could sit behind me," he said and smiled.

"No. As I said, you need to get reacquainted." She backed away and put her hands in her pockets to keep him from seeing them shake. "Take your time. We're in no hurry." She waved at him and headed toward the house.

****

"There's a trail head on the other side of the field over there." Mr. Bickens pointed. "It's up hill for about half a mile and levels off some. Fox knows the trails pretty well. You shouldn't have any problems."

Charlie turned the horse and said, "Let's go, boy." He nudged the animal's ribs and headed to the path. He took it slow and easy with Fox. He hadn't been on a horse for a long time and felt it was like riding a bike - he just needed to get his bearings.

As they slowly made their way up the hill, Charlie thought about Lark. He wished she'd come with him, but understood she wanted to give him time alone with Fox. They needed to solidify their relationship and he wasn't sure if he was thinking of her or the horse.

Lark was still one of the nicest people he remembered from his childhood. There were times when she treated him like a little brother and other times they were equals. He reminded her more than a thousand times that he was older than she by three months. It didn't matter. She and Gran would always open the door for him and treat him well.

He felt like he was out of her league when it came to dating and having a closer relationship. She was a respected business woman in Canon City. Today, when they'd shopped for his furniture there were a number of people, young and old, who'd come up to her just to say hello and he was astounded.

She was also engaged to another man and he knew it was wrong to touch her, but it was all he could do to keep his hands to himself. Only two nights ago, she'd been so pissed off at him and he was scared stiff she'd hate him forever, but he still wanted her. He wanted to wake up with her every morning and lay with her every night. He wanted to put his hand under her shirt and feel her warm, soft skin. Her lips were so tempting and he fantasized about covering her mouth with his and feeling her tongue twist and lunge with his. He wanted to taste every single inch of her and hear her moan his name. He loved watching her walk. Her bottom and long legs were built perfectly and he didn't think he'd ever get enough of that view.

Charlie realized he hadn't been watching the trail. He adjusted his pelvis in the saddle and sucked in his breath when he discovered his penis was hard as a steel rod and he'd wedged it against the saddle horn. He slid back in the seat and squeezed his eyes shut.

"Oh crap!" he grimaced.

Fox's head twisted around and looked at Charlie. He then shook his head and whinnied. Charlie opened his eyes and saw the horse's big brown eyes look at him.

"Sorry, boy. That's what I get for thinking about a really gorgeous woman." He leaned forward and scuffed the horse's neck.

They came around a corner and Charlie heard something clink below him. "Whoa boy." He pulled back on the reins and looked down at the ground. Standing up in the snow was an iron shoe. Charlie could see patches of rock underneath the horse.

He got down from Fox and picked up the shoe. "Does this belong to you?" he asked. The horse nodded and butted his head gently against Charlie's shoulder. He bent over and ran his hand down Fox's leg and picked up the hoof.

Sure enough the horse had thrown a shoe and from what Charlie could see he might have stepped on a rock. The pad, sometimes called the frog, was a little red. He slowly let the hoof down and looked at his watch. He wished he'd noted the time when they'd left the ranch.

"Okay, boy, it looks like I'm on foot. We'd better head back." He turned and held the reins. They followed their footprints back toward the Bickens. He wasn't sure how far they'd come, but it couldn't have been more than an hour. Charlie felt glad he'd worn his snow boots.

****

Lark sat in the Bickens kitchen talking to Bernice and sampling baked goods as they came out of the oven. She thought she'd better stop. Charlie was taking her and Gran out for dinner tonight and she didn't want to ruin her appetite.

She looked at her watch and realized she'd been sitting with Mrs. Bickens for almost three hours. Her brows came together.

"Bernice, I'm sorry. I've bent your ear for too long. I'd better go see what happened to Charlie." She stood and grabbed her coat from the back of the chair.

"I've enjoyed having the company, sweetie. Tell your Gran she'll have lots of competition at the dance this year. Mrs. Hager is making her rum-apple cakes. Those always sell out fast." Mrs. Bickens came toward Lark and gave her a hug. She then put a small paper bag in her hand. "These are for Charlie. He'll probably be hungry when he gets in."

"Thank you. We'll see you on Saturday." Lark left the kitchen and walked toward the barn. She looked across the field and saw Charlie exit the tree line. He was on foot with Fox walking next to him at the same pace. She stopped and watched him walk with the horse. It looked like he was talking to the animal.

Lark felt her lips curl at the ends and a tingling in her pelvis. As he came around the end of the fence, she felt her heart flutter in her chest. He was very handsome in his faded jeans and jacket. He needed a haircut, but his blue eyes looked so clear. She watched him put his arm under Fox's neck and hug the horse, rubbing his face against the hair. Her breasts started to hurt and she noticed warmth spread into the lower half of her body. She wished for a moment that was her and he was rubbing against her chest. She blinked and realized she was holding her breath. She let it out and could hear crunching behind her.

Mr. Bickens came out of the barn. They both walked toward Charlie.

"What happened? Did Fox toss you on your butt?" Lark asked.

Charlie and Fox stopped and he dug in his pocket and pulled out a shoe. "He threw a shoe. The frog looked a little red and I didn't want to risk making it worse by riding him." Charlie handed the piece of iron to Mr. Bickens.

The old man leaned over and pulled up Fox's leg. He looked at the hoof. "I see what you mean. He probably stepped on a rock." He set the hoof down, straightened up and patted Fox on the chest. "We'll get him a new shoe and he'll be right as rain."

Charlie rubbed the horse's neck and leaned into him. "I'll see you soon Foxy boy." The horse's head nodded and moved against Charlie's shoulder.

"See, I knew he'd remember you," Lark said and smiled.

Mr. Bickens took the reins and led Fox to the barn. Charlie watched them go. "Thank you, Mr. B. I should have a phone next week. I'll call and see how he's doing."

"That will be fine. It's good to see you again Charlie."

"You can always use Gran's phone." Lark nudged his arm. She took her keys out of her pocket.

Charlie watched the horse disappear into the barn. "I didn't even think about that." He looked down at her. "I'm sorry. I didn't expect to be so long."

"No problem." She handed the bag of cookies to him. "Those are from Mrs. B."

"What's this?"

They got into her Bronco and she started the engine. She watched him open the bag.

"Oh man, I am in heaven. I can use about ten of these right now. Do you want one?" He asked and pointed the open bag at her.

"No, I've already eaten four." She steered the car down the drive. She gripped the steering wheel tightly, but it wasn't because of the snowy road. It was all she could do not to stop and throw off all her clothes. She heard Charlie say something and tried to pay attention, but her body was definitely on fire.

"That was great. Fox does seem to remember me. I can't thank you enough, Lou. Why did you move him from the Hirsh's ranch?"

Lark looked in the review mirror and couldn't see the Bickens house anymore. She braked and pulled the Bronco to the side of the road. She turned off the engine and reached under her seat to grab a lever and move it back. She unzipped her coat and threw it to the seat behind her.

When she looked at Charlie, the burning became worse. She wanted his hands on her. He'd stopped chewing and looked at her like she'd lost her mind.

"What?" he said with a mouthful of cookie.

"Finish your double chocolate chip." She slid her snow boots off and saw him swallow. She took the bag out of his hand and put it on the back seat next to her coat. She started to move to him and when he seemed to realize what she was doing, he helped her onto his lap. She put her knees on both sides of his legs and straddled his pelvis.

"Oh," Charlie said.

She reached down to the side of the seat and pulled another lever. Charlie's seat back flattened fast. She looked down at him and felt his hands on her hips. "I'm sorry. I'm being aggressive again." She leaned over and lightly touched his lips with hers. She licked at them and when his mouth opened she teased with her tongue and nibbled his lips. "You taste like cookie. I'm probably being a slut, but it's been a while since I felt this way."

His hands moved to her bottom and pulled her closer. "No way are you a slut. To be honest," he pushed his fingers through her hair. "I gave myself a hard-on when I was riding. All I did was think about you."

"I watched you walk back in with Fox and it...you walk really nice. I'd never noticed it before." She kissed him again and smiled. "You do know it's all I can do not to tear all my clothes off and let you devour me. It's too cold..." She moved her legs a little and adjusted her pelvis. She looked down at him. "Oh dear, what are we to do?"

Charlie laughed. "Oh dear is right. Try walking down an incline with an erection. It's definitely a learning experience." He smiled and moved his hands up under her sweater. "I'm getting one of my wishes right now."

"What is your wish, me sitting on you?"

"That is one of my wishes, too, but I love the feel of your skin. It's so soft." He moved his hand up her back and unlatched her bra.

She sat up and looked down at him. "Your hands are being very naughty."

"Yeah, they have a mind of their own. I hope it isn't a problem?" His hands moved up the front of her sweater and cupped both breasts under her bra. He put his bottom lip out. "Can I see, please?" he whispered.

Lark pulled her arms out of the sleeves and took her bra off. She then put her arms back in and let him lift the front. She took the bottom of the sweater and held it up. She watched him gaze at her chest. His hands moved up her stomach and his fingers lightly tickled her overly excited buds.

"Lou, you are the most beautiful woman. Always have been, always will be," he said and leaned his head to her right breast. His mouth covered the tender, hard tip and his tongue and teeth teased her nipple.

She sighed and closed her eyes, letting Charlie perform magic. Her body flamed inside and out. She'd felt excited in the past, but nothing like this. She wanted him, all of him.

"Oh Ducky," she moaned.

She felt one of his hands move down to the hot V between her legs and pressed on the right spot causing Lark to moan, again.

"Sweetheart, does the back seat flatten out? If I don't get inside you soon I'm going to bust."

She looked down at him, not paying attention to his words. His hands were making her crazy. She glanced out the back window of her Bronco and saw a truck coming towards them. That seemed to register.

She leaned back and pulled her sweater down. "We can't do this here. There's too much traffic."

"What?" He saw where she pointed and looked. She saw him glance at the truck and take in a deep breath. "Let's go back to my place." He turned back to her.

Lark put her hand up to his face and ran her thumb along his brow. "You don't have any furniture, Ducky."

He kissed the palm of her hand and grinned. "According to Playboy magazine there are other ways of making love around the house. I've always wanted to try some of the moves."

"Charlie Stone, you're going to make me have a stroke." She kissed him and moved back to her seat. She started the engine.

"Lou, are you going to put your boots back on?" he asked and put his hand on her thigh.

She grinned at him. "Maybe I'll put them back on, but right now I'm hot..."

"Scorching hot, baby." He leaned over, put his hand around her neck and brushed her lips with his.

She pressed toward him, let him take her mouth with passion and felt amazed at what a great kisser he'd become and how he woke up her raging hormones. "Ducky," she said and kept her eyes closed.

"Yes."

"I don't know if I can drive with your hand on my crotch." She opened her eyes and saw him look down.

"Tit-for-tat, baby." He grinned.

Lark didn't even realize her hand was cupped on his jeans over his penis. She felt him twitch through the fabric. "Hmmm, can I get us home in under thirty minutes? I wonder." She straightened in her seat and shifted the Bronco into Drive. "Buckle up, sweetie." She arched her eyebrows and grinned.

Chapter Fourteen

They made it back to the neighborhood in twenty-six minutes. Lark drove carefully and did her best to not spin out. She kept her Bronco steady on the road and didn't put them into a ditch.

"Maybe we should leave Breaker with Gran. He might think we're playing and want to join in the fun," Charlie said.

Lark grinned. "I'm only interested in human animals, Ducky."

He grinned back at her. "Quack."

They both laughed and she turned the Bronco onto Pine Ridge Road. As they approached Gran's driveway, Lark could see a black Lexus parked down by the front of the house. Her stomach instantly tied in knots and she stopped laughing.

"Whose car is that?" Charlie asked, as she slowed down.

"Crap, reality never seems to give it up. My fiancés." She pulled the Bronco behind the Lexus.

"That's a mood breaker. Lark..." He looked at her.

After she put the SUV into Park and turned off the engine, she leaned over to put on her boots. "Don't

Charlie. We were having too much fun and I shouldn't have led you on."

He sat back in his seat. "Definitely a mood breaker," he mumbled. "I guess dinner's off."

She stamped her foot down to get her boot all the way on and looked at him. "No it's not. Gran is really excited to go out with us tonight. We're still on." She looked back at the car in front of hers. "I don't know why he's here. My phone was on all day and I don't have any messages."

"I better come in and round up Breaker."

She watched Charlie get out of the Bronco. She grabbed her coat and the bag of cookies off the back seat and got out. As she approached the back door, Charlie stopped and waited for her to go into the kitchen ahead of him.

Lark handed him the cookies as she walked past and looked up at him. She wanted to say something, but couldn't find the words. The flame that built inside of her earlier at Bickens Ranch had waned to a small ember and she suddenly felt very cold.

She opened the door and saw her Gran come in from the living room. "There you are. I didn't think you'd be gone riding so long," Gran said with a question on her face.

"Fox threw a shoe, so it took longer to get back in. It's my fault," Charlie said.

Lark took off her coat. "Where's Thomas?" she whispered.

"In the living room," Gran answered.

"Where's Breaker?" Charlie held out his hands in question.

"Oh, I had to put him up in the bedroom. He made Thomas uncomfortable."

Lark saw Thomas stroll into the kitchen, his blond hair combed perfectly and an annoyed look on his face. He wore a pair of dark grey flannel pants, a blue turtle neck and grey jacket. He was a handsome man, but she realized she didn't really have any feelings for him. What was she thinking about when she accepted his proposal?

"Thomas," Lark said and went to stand by him. "Why didn't you let me know you were coming down?"

"I left several messages, darling." He leaned over and kissed her quickly. He turned to Charlie. "You must be Mr. Stone. Aurora explained your relationship with the family. I'm pleased to meet you."

Lark looked up at Thomas and knew he'd just lied to her. There were no messages on her cell phone. She looked back down and thought he put on a good act, but she could hear the ice in his voice.

Charlie nodded. "Yeah." He looked at Gran. "I'll go up and take Breaker home. Is half an hour enough time for you ladies to get ready for dinner?" Both Lark and her Gran nodded. He walked past them and disappeared up the stairs. In less than a minute he came back down with Breaker keeping pace beside him.

When they entered the kitchen, Lark saw the wolf's fur stand on end and heard a low growl in his chest.

"Let's go Breaker. I'll be back," Charlie said and shut the door behind him.

Lark stared at the door and wanted to follow him. She looked up at Thomas and smiled. "I'm going to change." She turned and headed to the stairs and he followed her to the bedroom.

He closed the door and leaned against it. "So, you have assisted the needy, I see." He smiled.

Lark stood at her closet and looked over her shoulder. "Charlie isn't needy. He's a bit scruffy around the edges, but he's a college graduate and knows his way around." She almost sucked in her breath when she realized she had taken off her bra and it was still out in the Bronco. She walked to her dresser and pulled out a pink one. She took her sweater off and put it on with her back to Thomas.

"Is that so? Your grandmother said he was going to veterinary college. How exciting for him," Thomas smirked.

Lark thought Thomas might be feeling a bit of jealousy and wanted to smooth things over. She didn't want him here right now, but would have to make do until she could figure out the best way to discuss their relationship. "Will you come with us for dinner?"

"I came down here to spend time with you, not your grandmother and the next door neighbor. Why don't we have dinner somewhere without them?"

Lark zipped up a pair of red pants and slipped a red sweater over her head. "We can't do that tonight. Charlie doesn't have a car yet and I've volunteered to drive."

Thomas crossed his arms over his chest. "You know it's interesting that you're wearing red. It matches your face."

She'd bent over to pull on her boots and straightened up. "What's that supposed to mean?"

He walked up to her and put his hand under her chin. "They match your swollen red lips and cheeks. It makes me wonder."

She moved her chin away from his fingers and took a step back. "Thomas, it's cold outside. My ears are probably red, too."

"Be very careful, my dear."

"Okay, I give. What's that supposed to mean?"

"If I find out there's another explanation than just the cold, we'll have to discuss it very seriously."

Lark wanted to scream at him to mind his own business, but knew he would only get very angry with her. If she challenged his position he could turn mean. "Thomas, there is nothing happening here. It's cold outside and that is all." She bent over, again and pulled her other boot on. "Look, you can join us or wait here. It's your choice."

He landed a heavy hand on her shoulder and wound his fingers into the sweater. "Why is this so important, Lark?"

She put her hand on his arm and looked up at him. She'd had a knot in her stomach since she parked the SUV and it just kept getting worse. "It's not that important, but I committed to it and, as you know, I hold to my commitments."

"I'd rather spend the evening alone with you, my dear," he said in a quiet tone. He put his hand up into her hair and grabbed a handful.

"I know, but in three weeks, after we're married, we will probably spend so much time together that you'll get tired of me." She tried to get him to release her sweater and her hair.

He moved his hand out of her hair, put it around her waist and leaned in for a kiss. Lark thought it was interesting that when Thomas kissed her, there never was any fire, anymore. The more she thought about it she realized she'd never felt much for him physically and became confused.

Thomas always approached kissing and making love like he felt angry at the world. He'd jam his tongue in her mouth and never acted very tender. She remembered Charlie's lips on her breast and almost smiled, but stopped those thoughts and focused on Thomas.

She pulled back. "Please, come out to dinner with us."

"Where are we going?" he asked.

"I'm not certain. Gran got to pick the restaurant and its likely going to be Black Angus. She loves that place."

"You know I don't care for places like that."

"I know, but they have a big menu and I'm sure you can find something acceptable." She felt his fingers begin to loosen on her sweater. "I'll ride with you and Charlie can drive Gran in the Bronco."

Thomas arched his eyebrows and slightly smirked. "That would be acceptable."

"Good, good." She latched onto his arm and moved towards the door.

When they got downstairs, Gran was waiting with Charlie, who'd changed into a tan pair of jeans and the flannel shirt he'd bought earlier in the day. He still wore his jean jacket. She found it difficult not to look at him.

"So, Thomas is coming with us." She glanced at Charlie. "Would you drive Gran in my SUV?"

"Sure."

"Great, let me get the keys." She headed to the coat hanger and pulled her jacket off the hook. She took the keys out of her pocket and handed them to him.

"Where are we going?" she asked and slipped on her coat.

****

Charlie watched Lark and could tell something bothered her. She wasn't her usual easy- going, mischievous self. She looked stiff and kept her hands folded in front of her.

Gran hooked her hand around Charlie's arm and they walked to the Bronco. After Gran was settled and buckled into her seat, he walked around to the driver's side. He slid in, moved the seat back and started the engine.

He backed the SUV out to the road and pulled forward slowly until he saw the Lexus headlights in the rearview mirror. Charlie noticed Gran fumble with something around her feet. "Is everything okay over there?" he asked.

She looked over at him and smiled. "Yeah, I'm fine." She sighed and sat back in her seat. "I don't like that Thomas very much. It seems like whenever he's here from Denver, Lark is on edge." She looked out the front window. "I never understood why she accepted that man. He seems so arrogant and stuffy. I wish I'd chosen Burger King for dinner instead of Black Angus. That would have turned him on." She laughed.

"I think I only said five words to him and got the arrogant attitude completely. He seems like a jerk. You know Gran, Burger King works for me."

"No, let's do Black Angus. I love their Fire-grilled Artichoke. It's so good. I don't know, maybe he's the way he is because we're small town folks and he's big city," Gran said.

"If that's the case, I'll stick with the small town folks. We're much warmer and friendly."

He stopped at a red light and lost sight of the Lexus. He figured Thomas, not being familiar with the roads, might be driving slowly. He thought about waiting for them to catch up, but the light turned green and he decided to go.

They got to the restaurant parking lot and Charlie wedged the SUV into a spot as close to the front door as he could.

He helped Gran out and they walked carefully to the entrance. Charlie arranged for a table and since it was Sunday night, the place wasn't that busy. They would only have to wait a few minutes.

Just as the hostess pulled out the menus, the door opened and Lark and Thomas entered. Thomas held on to her upper arm and steered her into the entrance. Charlie could see what looked like blood on the corner of her mouth.

Gran moved quickly to Lark. "Sweetheart, what happened?" She pulled a small package of tissues from her purse.

Lark pursed her lips together and looked down. "Dorky me, I slipped on a patch of ice getting out of the car and bit my lip." She looked up at Charlie and he instantly knew it was a lie. She shook her head slightly at him.

Gran took her arm. "Let's go get it cleaned up." She led Lark toward the ladies room and they disappeared.

The hostess led the men to a table. They sat across from each other and Charlie stared at Thomas. He felt he knew exactly what happened to Lark and the hairs on the back of his neck stood on end. He watched Thomas reach for the wine list and glance at it.

Thomas looked up from the list at Charlie and smiled. "Fine dining," he smirked.

Charlie wanted to fly over the table and beat this asshole into a pulp. He'd seen this kind of behavior too often with his mother not to recognize it.

The ladies returned and both men stood up to assist them. Lark sat next to Thomas.

Charlie didn't look at her, but continued to stare at Thomas across from him. The waitress came and took their drink orders. Thomas ordered a glass of red wine, Charlie and Gran had coffee and Lark, a cup of tea.

Charlie watched as Lark started to take her coat off. Thomas turned to help her and she flinched ever so slightly. It verified his suspicions. He felt the anger build and continued to watch Thomas.

The waitress brought their drinks and pulled out a pad to take down their food orders. When she turned to Charlie, he held the menu up to her. "New York strip, medium well with a baked potato, no sides."

Thomas laughed. "You didn't even look at the menu."

"I have it memorized." Charlie frowned at him.

"Have you worked here?" Thomas asked.

"No," Charlie answered and that was all he said.

****

Dinner seemed to drag on forever, although they only sat at the table for about an hour and a half. Charlie paid the waitress in cash and looked at Gran. "Are you ready to go home?"

"Yes, thank you for a great dinner. How did you like the artichoke?" she asked as she stood.

Charlie helped her with her coat. "It was fine. The pesto sauce was really good."

"Yes, it was very good. Thank you, Mr. Stone. You really didn't have to pay for all of it, but it was an interesting meal," Thomas said. He stood next to Lark who struggled into her coat and turned to leave.

Charlie felt worried about her and wanted desperately to talk to her. She'd barely said two words since she sat down. He really hadn't said much himself and when Gran asked him a question he'd asked her to repeat it more than once. He felt guilty for not paying better attention, but it was all he could to keep his eyes off Lark. He wanted to go over and wrap his arms around her and to protect her from the dick sitting across from him. At one point he thought he saw tears in her eyes.

As they walked out, he heard Thomas tell Lark he was going back to Denver and she would have to ride home with her grandmother. He said he'd see her on Saturday for the dance.

Charlie got Gran into the Bronco and looked toward the Lexus. Lark and Thomas stood by the trunk. Thomas reached for her, but she stepped back and started toward the SUV.

Charlie felt fed up. He shut Gran's door and started toward the Lexus. He walked past Lark and went straight toward the asshole. Thomas looked surprised. Charlie put his hand on the man's shoulder and grabbed the collar of his coat. He pulled him close and moved him to the driver's door.

"Let me explain something to you, fuckhead. If you ever so much as think of hurting Lark again, there will be consequences to pay." Charlie shoved him against the car.

"Get your hands off me," Thomas said and struggled against Charlie's hold.

"I just want to make sure you understand what I'm saying clearly. If you ever touch her again, you will pay for it."

"She is my fiancée, Mr. Stone. I can do what I like."

"See, you've got that all wrong," Charlie said between clenched teeth. "If you do whatever you want, then I will become angrier than I am now. I have experience with making people stop breathing. So if you want that, just try me. I'd be more than happy to attend your funeral."

He let go of the coat and saw the look on Thomas's face. He felt he'd gotten through to the bastard maybe just a little. "Drive carefully, asshole. I have friends in big rigs out there who would love to take you out head-on," he said and turned.

"Is that a threat, Mr. Stone?"

Charlie heard that and laughed. He turned back to Thomas. "If that's the way you want to take it, then fine, but remember what city you're in. I have friends here, too." He walked back and saw Lark still stood in the same place. "I just wanted Thomas to know how nice it was to meet him." He smiled at her and held out his arm.

Chapter Fifteen

When they got back to Gran's, Charlie saw the ladies into the house and then said goodnight. He told them he needed to take Breaker out for a walk, and left.

Lark and Gran took off their coats and moved into the kitchen.

"That was a nice dinner. Would you like a cup of tea, sweetheart?" Gran asked and started to fill the kettle.

Lark sat at the table. "Yeah, no, I'd rather have some cocoa. I want to sleep tonight." She moved the sleeve on her arm a little and looked at her wrist. She saw a bruise forming and when Gran approached, she moved it back down. Her grandmother sat next to her and crossed her hands. "Gran, why did my mom call me the stupid name of Larkspur?"

"It isn't stupid. It's a beautiful, wild mountain flower. Your mom loved wild flowers so much. She said when she first saw you that you were so beautiful that Larkspur was the only name she could think of. I'm just glad she didn't call you Bistort or Tansy Astor. Those would have been really strange names."

The kettle started to whistle and Gran got back up and poured. She brought the cups over and set one in front of Lark.

"Thanks, Gran." She picked up the cup and blew on it, taking a sip.

"Lark, what happened on your way to dinner? Did you and Thomas have an argument?"

Lark looked at her and wondered how much to tell. "Yeah, we had an argument. Gran, he hit me." Her eyes welled up. "It was my fault. I smarted off to him and..."

"Lark, no." Gran stood and wrapped her arms around her granddaughter. "Oh sweetheart, I'm so sorry."

She didn't think she would cry, but she did and having Gran's arms around her made her feel safe. She leaned forward and got a napkin out of the holder. "It's not your fault either. There's no reason for you to be sorry, Gran." She sniffed and tried to get the waterworks stopped.

Gran sat back down and held onto Lark's hand. She wished she hadn't said anything, her grandmother looked so worried.

"Has he done that to you before?"

"Yes, a couple of times." Lark hated telling this secret to her grandmother, but she didn't want to lie to her either. She needed to be honest now that Thomas had done this on several occasions. "Gran," she looked up, "I don't think there's going to be a wedding at the end of the month." She blew her nose and wiped her cheeks again. "There's been something brewing for a while now and I have to finally be honest with myself, I don't love Thomas. I should never have accepted his proposal."

"I'm glad, sweetheart. I have to be honest, too. I have never really cared for him all that much. He always seems fake and at times he's treated me like I didn't know which side the butter went on the toast."

"Yeah, he did that to me, too."

"Why did he hit you tonight?"

Lark took in a deep breath and felt warmth start in her cheeks and spread down her neck.

"Why are you blushing, sweetheart?"

Lark looked up and thought *Okay, she's an adult, just tell her.* "On the trip back from the Gorge today, Charlie and I had a moment." She didn't want to go into too many details.

"A moment?" Gran's eyebrows came together and then rose as her eyes opened wide. "Oh...a moment. Did you two make love?"

"No, we didn't go that far, but we enjoyed an extremely hot moment and if Thomas hadn't been here when we got home, we would have."

Gran stood up and walked to her coat. She pulled Lark's bra out of the pocket. "This got tangled under my boots when we left for dinner." She handed it to Lark. "You may want to throw it into the wash."

"Thanks. I wondered where it went. Thomas could tell I wasn't wearing it and asked me why. Silly me, I wanted to be honest and he asked me some other questions that aren't appropriate for normal people and I made a smart aleck remark." She squeezed her grandmother's hand. "Please, don't tell Charlie. He went through so much with his parents and I don't want him thinking about all that."

"Sweetheart, I may be way out in left field, but I believe Charlie already knows."

"What?" Lark sat up straight.

"He didn't say as much, but during dinner he looked mad enough to eat bolts. I tried to talk to him and he said that he didn't have anything to add to the conversation. I think he probably knew when you walked in the door with blood on your lip."

"Yeah, and that's more than likely why he walked Thomas to his car door." She put her head into her hands and shook. Her eyes were closed and she thought she might have a mental break down. "Damn. Poor Charlie. What have I gotten him involved with?"

"Lark, you know I love you very much, but there are times when you're a little dense."

She opened her eyes and looked up at Gran.

"Charlie has been nuts about you for years. Anything you asked of him, he'd do his utmost to accomplish. I also think he wants to protect both of us. He acted that way when he was a kid and it's part of his nature, I think."

Lark sat back in her chair. "I've got to get some sleep. Hopefully things will be clearer in the morning." She stood up and kissed her grandmother's head. "Night, Gran."

"If you want to talk some more, I'll be up for a while."

She went up the stairs and started to take off her clothes. She looked at her breast. When Thomas stopped the car on their way to the restaurant she'd felt very scared. After he hit her in the face, he'd hit her chest, grabbed her breast and squeezed hard. It hurt so very badly and when she'd started hitting at him to release it, he'd grabbed her wrist and nearly pulled her arm off. The bruise on her wrist ran up her forearm and was almost to her elbow. The bruise on her chest seemed to have gotten bigger.

She shook her head and put on her fleece top. She crawled under the covers and clutched at one of her pillows. "Please, God, let me get a decent night's sleep."

Chapter Sixteen

Charlie walked up to Gran's back door with Breaker at his side and knocked. When the door opened part way, Gran stood with a dish towel in her hand. He and Breaker just stood there and looked at her. He wasn't sure what to say and cleared his throat.

"I want to apologize to you, Gran. I think I was a little rude at dinner and you didn't deserve that. I'll have to make it up to you and Lark."

"Charlie, no apology is necessary. Why don't you two come in out of the cold?" She opened the door all the way and the wolf strolled in.

"I still can't get the fire started. Can we do one more night on your very warm and comfortable couch?" He said and closed the door behind him.

"Of course you can. I wouldn't be happy if you caught pneumonia."

Charlie took his coat off and hung it up. He looked at Breaker who danced around Gran's legs.

"Hello, there Mr. Breaker. Would you like a treat?" Gran rubbed behind his ears and the wolf sat down on her foot. "I got on the Internet and found a recipe for doggy treats. I made a batch this afternoon."

"Gran, I think you've made a friend for life." Charlie smiled at her.

She walked back to the sink. "Breaker was a good wolf earlier, weren't you? He protected me from that nasty mean man." She looked up at Charlie. "Why don't you go up and talk to Lark? She went up about ten minutes ago. I don't think she's asleep yet."

"I don't want to bug her, Gran. I'm sure she has a lot to think about."

"Charlie." She walked up to him and turned him toward the hallway. "Go on. I can tell by the look on your face, you want to check on her."

"Am I that transparent?"

She laughed. "You're a man in love, honey. It's written all over your actions."

He leaned over and kissed her cheek. "Thank you. Breaker, stay. Protect this fine lady," he said to the wolf. Breaker woofed at him and sat next to Gran.

Charlie headed up the stairs and stopped in front of Lark's door. He lightly knocked and heard her say, "What?" He opened the door and stepped into the dark room.

"Lou, if you want me to leave, I will," he said. She was quiet for a moment and then he heard her move and turn on the bedside lamp. He watched her look up at the ceiling and shake her head.

He could tell she'd been crying and it made him want to put his arms around her and give her some comfort, but he didn't know if that was what she needed.

"Are you okay?" he asked.

"I will be. What did you say to Thomas?"

Charlie nodded and sat on the foot of her bed. "The basics of it were that I enjoy attending funerals."

Lark frowned at him. "You threatened him."

"I made him a promise. I knew what happened the minute I saw you at the restaurant.

Sorry, Lou, but it's not acceptable for people I care about to be treated so bad."

"I appreciate that." She pulled down the sheets on the other side of the bed and patted it. "Shoes off, Ducky. You're too far away from me."

Charlie took off his boots and flannel shirt. He wore a long-sleeved thermal undershirt.

"If you're wearing long john's you can take off your jeans, too."

He stopped by the side of the bed and smiled. "Sorry, babe. I'm au natural. No drawers or anything. And" - he flopped onto the bed - "Gran would kill me." He hoped she'd laugh, but he could tell she was being serious. He propped up on his elbow and crossed his legs under the sheet and comforter. "Do you feel like talking about it?"

She shrugged. "He hit me. I was honest that you and I had a hot moment this afternoon, but that nothing really happened. He asked me if I'd let you fuck me and

I smirked at him and said no, but that I'd wanted you to. I told him it was the first time I'd felt anything for a man for a while. I should have kept my mouth shut." She swallowed. "He's done this a couple of times before and always found a reason it was my fault. I feel stupid enough that I let him manipulate me, in the past. This time it was a wake-up, though." Their eyes locked. "I'm going to break off the engagement."

Charlie took her hand and was going to kiss it, but could see darkness on her wrist. He sat up and moved the sleeve of her night shirt up her arm. "Oh, babe..."

"Charlie, look at me."

He lifted his head and gazed into her beautiful blue eyes.

"It's only a bruise. It will fade. The whole memory will fade to nothing, but it'll take some time. I've still got a bunch of crap to unload." She laughed. "It's weird. A few days ago, I felt so angry with you and now I can't lose you again. Not ever. Please be patient with me."

"You just try to get rid of me, Lou," he whispered. He put her hand on his cheek and kissed her bruised wrist.

"It's not going to happen, ever." She leaned back, smiled at him and reached up to run her fingers through his long hair. "After our first kiss thirteen years ago, I day-dreamed about you. I'd sit by the river and make up all these scenarios about you coming home. I'd sit on our stump and you'd walk up the river bed toward me. When I got older, the scenes stayed the same, but became much hotter and, no, I'm not giving you any details. I...well, I want to say something to you, but I'm afraid to, Ducky."

He leaned forward and kissed her lightly. "Lou, don't ever be afraid of me. I'll never hurt you again; I swear it on my life. I'm yours no matter what happens." He watched her lick her lips and look down at her hands.

"Charlie, I love you. I've always loved you, but now it's more than friendship."

He put his fingers under her chin and moved her head so she looked at him. "Say it again."

"I love you."

Charlie felt his throat tighten and knew his eyes were filling up. "This is without a doubt the happiest day of my life, Lou," he whispered. "I never thought I'd hear those words and the fact that they're coming from your lips makes me want to act really goofy." He laughed and cleared his throat. "Would you like to know something really stupid?" She nodded. He felt a tear roll down his cheek. He brushed it off and cleared his throat. "When I was little, I got to meet my grandmother. We spent the summer on her farm in Iowa. She was the only other person on the planet who ever said that to me."

"Charlie, that's not stupid." She put her good hand up to his face and cupped his cheek. "I love you, Gran loves you and even Breaker loves you."

"I love you, too. I was in love with you when we were kids and it's never changed. You've always been my light at the end of the tunnel." He looked at her sore wrist again and pulled the sleeve down. "Did the asshole hurt you anywhere else?"

Lark laughed. "Yeah. I'll have another bruise on my chest and maybe one on my chin."

"Babe, if I ever see him again, I'll more than likely have to beat the shit out of him."

She smiled at him and shook her head. "No, my daring knight. I appreciate your bravery, but Thomas would want revenge and there's no way I'll risk you either getting hurt or winding up in jail for assault." She started to lean to kiss him, but stopped. "I also refuse for either one of us to lower ourselves to his level. You and I are much better than that."

He felt her lips softly touch his. Her tongue worked its way into his mouth and moved along his gum line and teeth. He wrapped his arms around her and pulled in close. She nibbled at his bottom lip and chin.

Charlie sighed. "You know I want you more than I want to breathe right now, but..."

"Gran is downstairs watching TV and it would be embarrassing if I started to shout your name real loud and we banged the bed against the floor," she finished his thought.

"Yep, that says it all." He smiled at her.

"It's okay. I'm kind of pooped." She hugged him and kissed his neck.

"I will have a bed on Wednesday." He moved her down and put the comforter around her.

"Hey that's right. I think we have a date." She smiled at him.

"It will be the three longest days in the history of the world." He leaned over and kissed her lips. "Are you cold?"

"No, I'm quite warm just at the moment." She reached up and turned off the bedside lamp.

Charlie scrunched down under the covers and lay on his side. "I don't want to hurt you. If I put my arm over you like this is it all right?" He put his arm across her stomach and touched her other hand.

"Yes, it feels just right."

"So since we are lying here together, you won't mind if I maybe spoon you with my arms around you and protect you while you sleep?"

"Oh Ducky, that's sounds wonderful and I would like to accept the offer." She rolled onto her right side and he wiggled in close to her.

"You smell so good," he said. She pulled his arm up under hers and kissed his fingers. "Goodnight, Lou."

"I love you, Ducky. I think I'm going to like saying that to you."

"I know I'll love hearing it. I love you, too."

Chapter Seventeen

The next morning, when Lark woke up with Charlie wrapped around her body, she'd wanted to stay in bed the whole day, but knew she needed to go into the warehouse. It was two weeks until Christmas and they needed to get as many orders out as possible.

She got out of bed without waking Charlie and showered. After she put on her makeup and dried her hair, she got dressed and heard her door creak open. Breaker poked his nose into the room.

"Hi boy, come here," she whispered and squatted down. She rubbed his ears and back. Lark looked up and saw Gran at the door with a smile. She winked at Lark and closed the door. "Why don't you go wake up your papa?" she said to the wolf.

Breaker's ears popped up and he seemed to grin. He turned, jumped up on the bed and started to lick his daddy's chin. Charlie began to make a funny grumbling noise. He turned on his side and sat up. Lark smiled and watched Charlie stare at his pup.

"I love you, too, Breaker, but you aren't the warm and fuzzy I was dreaming of this morning. Get off the bed you brute." Charlie looked at Lark and arched an eyebrow. "Good morning, my love."

Lark's heart almost burst out of her chest. She crawled up onto the bed and straddled his hips, then leaned over and brushed his lips. "Good morning to you."

His mouth opened and she felt his hands move up her thighs. He swung her around and the next thing she knew she was on her back with him between her legs. He kissed her with the passion she wanted desperately.

"Lou," he whispered. "We're being watched."

They both turned their heads and found Breaker with his fore paws on the edge of the bed. He woofed at them and wagged his tail.

"He wants some attention." Charlie kissed her jaw.

"I'm not supposed to kiss him, too?" Lark whispered in Charlie's ear.

"No one kisses these precious lips but me." His hand moved to her ribs and started tickling her.

"Stop, stop. You're starting a bad tradition," she laughed.

"Come back to bed," he said and kissed her again. He moved closer to her and stopped tickling her.

"I have to go to work, but I should be able to cut out at three or four o'clock." She smiled at him.

"Hmmm...if I could get Gran to babysit a certain pup, we could continue where we left off yesterday and forget that awful dinner."

"I like that idea very much, Ducky. I might even find a way to be here by one or two."

Charlie propped his head on his hand and looked down at her. "My dear, I have work to do today, too. The furnace people are coming and so is the plumber. Now I'm going to have a hard on all day until you get home." He kissed her nose and rolled off her. "Think on that."

"Oh yum, I should be good and wet when I get home. Thinking about your hard on will make packing boxes not as dull as it usually is." She put her hand under the covers and moved it down his chest. She traced it over the front of his pants and grinned when Charlie got a surprised look on his face. She curled her fingers over his penis and gave it a light squeeze.

"Larkspur Metcalfe, I am completely shocked by your behavior." She squeezed again and grinned when he sucked in air. "Oh woman, if this is the way I'll wake up every day, I'll worship you until my dying breath." His eyes crossed and his hips moved.

"As much as I would like to continue tormenting you, I can't." She kissed him again.

"How are you feeling this morning?"

"My chest is a little sore and my wrist." She held it up and wiggled it. "It feels like it's bruised, which it is. All in all, I'm all right. I took an ibuprofen."

He kissed the inside of her wrist. "I hear kisses make it all better."

She shook her head and smiled. "I'll see you later." She got up off the bed and walked back to her closet.

"Not if I see you first," he said and swung his legs over the side of the bed and sat up.

"Ducky, that's a really old saying." She grabbed a sweater and started to the door. "Later alligator." She laughed and he threw a pillow at her, which Breaker leapt on and claimed.

She went down the stairs and filled a travel mug with coffee. She put her boots on and grabbed her coat. "I'll be home early, Gran," she said as she opened the back door.

"Hey, don't you want some breakfast?" Gran asked and walked into the kitchen.

"No, I've got to get moving. Charlie will be down in a few minutes. He'll need a good breakfast." She zipped her coat.

"So, you were good kids last night? Yes?"

"I'll never divulge our secrets, Gran." Lark laughed her way out the door.

"I'll get answers from Charlie. He's weak when it comes to bacon," Gran said from the back door.

Lark laughed all the way to her SUV and said to herself, "Maybe we were good kids last night, but definitely going to be bad this afternoon."

When she arrived at the warehouse, she actually felt light on her feet. She grinned, and thought she was a dork for the bounce in her step, but didn't care. She and Charlie were back together and she couldn't be more thankful.

She met Nancy in the hallway. "We've got a problem," Nancy said and looked none too happy. She followed Lark into the office.

"Hold that thought one second." Lark walked to her desk. "Alicia, come in here a second." She took off her coat and put her purse in a drawer.

Her secretary followed Nancy into the office and carried a notepad and pen.

Lark grinned at her. "Sweetie, I know you are incredibly efficient and still have the email addresses and snail mail addresses for the guests for the wedding."

"Yeah, I have a folder in a file," her secretary said.

"Great. This morning I need for you to send a general group email and snail mail out. The note should say the wedding at the end of the month is cancelled and there should be no *I'm sorry to announce* because I'm not sorry. Okay?" Lark said and leaned on her desk.

"Got it. Do you want to check the note before I send it?"

"Nope, I trust you." Lark smiled and Alicia left the room. She looked at Nancy. "What problem do we have to deal with?"

"Wait a minute, what the hell is going on?" Nancy asked.

"The long and short of it is I had a big wake-up call this weekend. Thomas hit me and I realized I've never loved him and never will. I suppose when Alicia sends the email one of his friends will call him and he will call me wanting to know what my problem is." She shook her head. "Believe me; I haven't a problem in the world. Charlie Stone is home and I'm happy for the first time in years."

"Charlie Stone? You mean the guy that lived next door to you and...The guy you were talking about at the rink the other night?" Nancy stopped.

"The very one and we'll go over that later. What's up?"

Nancy shook her head. "Oh right, we've got an accountant here who wants to go through the books. He won't say who he represents. I called Ryan Barton, who's doing some checking. He will call us back with whatever information he finds. In the meantime, Mr. Accountant is in the break room, drinking our coffee."

Lark let this run through her head. "What on earth? We don't usually see accountants until the first quarter."

"I know. Call me paranoid, but with the rumor about our selling the company last week and now this, don't you think we should be worried?"

"I'm not sure." Lark started out of her office and Nancy followed.

She went down the stairs to the employee break room and saw a middle-aged, bald man sitting at a table with his electronic tablet. "Hi, I'm Lark Metcalfe. May I ask who you represent?" He grinned and Lark thought he resembled the Cheshire Cat.

"I'm sorry, Miss Metcalfe, but I'm not at liberty to say."

"Could I see some ID please?" She held out her hand.

The man continued to grin and reached into his pants pocket. He pulled out his driver's license and handed it to her.

"Thank you, Mr. Dumphy." She almost started to laugh at his name. She looked at the picture on the card and noted the birth date. She also glanced at his wallet, which he held open in his hand. She handed the license back and turned to leave the break room.

She and Nancy walked side by side out to the warehouse floor and started up the stairs.

"Nance, do you have a pen?"

Nancy watched Lark write some numbers on the palm of her hand as they continued up the stairs. "What are you doing?"

Lark held her palm up. "Mr. Jason Dumphy's driver's license number and birth date." She continued up the stairs and went into her office. She sat at her desk and hit the speed dial button for the lawyer's office.

"When did you become such a smart woman?" Nancy said and sat across from her.

"It's in the Levi's, ha, ha. That's a Gran saying." When the phone was answered she picked up the handset. "This is Lark Metcalfe for Ryan Barton, please." While she waited for her lawyer to answer the phone, she looked at Nancy. "How are the orders going?"

"We have everything from last week out, but got almost another one hundred over the weekend."

"I think we should post a cutoff date on the website. We can guarantee before Christmas delivery if ordered by...what do you think?...The twentieth?"

"The twentieth is a Friday, it would work. Then after that, we guarantee before New Year's Eve delivery. I like it."

"That would be good." Lark held up her hand and the lawyer got on the line. She gave him the information and he asked her to hold on again. They waited in silence for a few minutes, and she listened to hold music. When he came back on, Lark put the call on speaker so Nancy could hear.

"It looks like Mr. Dumphy is from National Savings and Loan in Denver. He's an accountant in acquisitions. I've got a call into Canon City Savings. I'm wondering if they're trying to sell your loan. That could be a problem," Ryan's voice said on the speaker phone.

"Mike Strom is on vacation until after the first of the year. He'd be the one to talk to," Nancy said.

"I've got another contact over there. I'll let you know what I hear. Let Mr. Dumphy see the sales only accounts. If he presses for the purchasing numbers tell him to come back tomorrow. Give him some noise about the computers being overloaded right now arranging orders. We'll find out what's going on."

"So in other words, stall him?" Lark said.

"You got it. I'll be in touch." The phone when dead.

Lark hit the cut off button and looked at Nancy.

"Want to Roshambo who goes to set Mr. Humpty-Dumphy at a computer?" Nancy asked.

Lark laughed. "No, I'm going down anyway. What would you say is the noisiest, most unfriendly computer location in the building?"

"That's easy. Nick's office, next door to the compressor is the worst. He's been asking to move to the other side of the building. It's really hot in there, too. Nick's gone until Thursday." Nancy stood and smiled.

Lark laughed harder. "Lordy me, I do love us. We can be so evil sometimes."

They high fived each other and then went their separate ways. Lark set up their packaging manager's office. She got the computer warmed up and made sure the desk was locked. Then she steered Mr. Dumphy into the office and left to go help package orders.

Lark worked until the afternoon on the floor. She got a sandwich from the auto-cantina.

After she ate half the sandwich and drank her cold coffee, Lark called her Gran.

"Hi, I just wanted to let you know I'm going to be a little late. We're really busy today. Could you do me a favor, Gran?"

"Of course, sweetheart," Gran answered.

"Would you run over to Charlie's and let him know I'm going to be late?"

"You two have certainly become close rather quickly. I'm glad for you both."

Lark smiled. "I'm really happy about it, too. I have another question, Gran. On the church phone directory, is there a home number for Mike Strom?" She could hear her grandmother open a drawer.

"Let's see. There is a cell phone number."

"Great." Lark wrote the number down and said goodbye. She dialed the number and after four rings got a message and a bing to leave a recording. "Hi Mike. This is Lark Metcalfe over at Mile High Bread. I know you're on vacation, but Nancy or I really need to talk to you. We've had an accountant here all day going through the books. He's from National Savings and Loan in Denver. I talked to Ryan Barton and his theory is that National might be trying to buy our loan from Canon City S and L. Could you give me a call any time? Thanks."

She hung up and her cell phone instantly rang. She looked at the caller ID and saw it was Gran. "Hey Gran, what's up?"

"Hey, this is Charlie. I borrowed Gran's phone. I know with the holidays and all you're crazy busy. Come over when you get home, no matter how late. I have heat now and the plumber says I should have water in the kitchen by the time he leaves today. I also have a surprise for you," he said, out of breath.

Lark smiled and laughed. "Do you want me to pick up a pizza or something else? We'll have to share with Gran."

"That would be great. I'll let her know not to cook dinner. I can't wait to see you."

"Same here. I shouldn't be too long." She hung up and glanced at her cell phone. The message light flashed and she hit the Receive button. It was from

Thomas. She pushed the Erase button and didn't listen to the message.

There was a knock on her door. She looked up to see her secretary waiting patiently in the doorway.

"Should I start looking for another job?" Alicia asked.

"No, not ever. I'll give you advanced warning if things go south, but don't worry yet." "Okay." Alicia walked into the office and stood at Lark's desk. "The email went out and I'm already receiving condolences. You'd think someone died. Do you want me to forward them to you?"

"Nope, just erase them." Lark smiled.

Alicia put a letter on the desk in front of her. "This is the letter. I need your signature."

"How many do you have to mail?" Lark grabbed a pen and signed her name.

"About thirty. I just have to stuff the envelopes and Ed will be here in about an hour to pick up the mail."

"Great." Lark looked up at her. "Alicia, please don't worry. We're in the black for the year. One way or another everything will be fine."

"No, it isn't that. I know we're doing okay with sales. I can see the bruise on your chin. Are you all right?"

Lark looked down and pulled her sweater down. She could see the bruise on her chest spread up. She smiled. "I am going to be fine, too. My ex-fiancé stepped over a line yesterday. I'm afraid I'm the kind of girl who only allows one strike and I've let him have more than his share of first strikes. He's out of here."

"Good," Alicia said and smiled. "I'll get this out." She turned and left.

Lark sat back in her chair and heard her cell phone ring. She looked at it and saw it was Thomas calling again. She turned the phone off and set it on the desk.

At five o'clock, she stood up and stretched. She walked into the front office and saw Nancy's light still on.

As she passed Alicia's desk, she stopped. "Why don't you cut out early tonight? We'll just have more to do tomorrow."

"Thank you," Alicia said. "Have a good evening."

"You, too." Lark leaned into Nancy's office. "I've left three messages for Mike Strom. Hopefully he'll stop skiing for a few minutes and check his messages."

"We've got the website updated. I made an executive decision and changed the date to the nineteenth which is Thursday. That will give us four mailing days and I feel we won't be as late with deliveries."

Lark leaned against the door jam. "Ack, late is late, but the nineteenth is fine. I'm heading home." She started to turn, but stopped. "Have you heard anything from Ryan?"

"No and, knowing him, I'll bet he's on his way home, too."

"Okay, see you tomorrow."

Chapter Eighteen

Lark stopped and picked up a pizza. She, Charlie and Gran enjoyed a nice dinner together. They laughed and reminisced about the past. Breaker was in wolf heaven and enjoyed leftover pieces of crust.

Charlie helped Gran wash the dishes, again, and then they took Breaker for a walk along the river. It was a cold clear night and they held hands for the first time ever as a new couple. They'd held hands when they were kids, but Charlie knew this was different. His heart thumped in his chest and he didn't think he'd ever been so nervous.

"I hope you're not too disappointed about this afternoon, Ducky." She looked up at him and bumped his shoulder.

He let go of her hand and put his arm around her waist. "No, ma'am. No disappointment on this front."

Her hand moved around his waist and she latched a finger in a belt loop. "Do you remember when we protected Canon City from the alien invasion?"

"Lord, yes. We carried our faithful saber sticks and our canteens were full of Androvian power juice. You were a great second in command."

"Thank you, major general. You were very good at strategy and always fought heroically." She smiled.

"Yes and we are protected even more since we've recruited master sergeant Breaker. He will protect us from evil vermin and birds. He has an ever-watchful eye."

"Ever-watchful?" Lark laughed.

"Yes, he's very devious that way." Charlie pulled her into his arms and swung her around.

When they stopped, Lark looked up at him and touched his lips. "Ducky, remember yesterday we talked about your house not having furniture?"

"I have a vague memory of that, yes. Didn't someone mention Playboy?" He moved his hand down and put his fingers into the back pocket of her jeans. He felt her jump and shake. "What's the matter?"

"Nothing. It's just chilly out here." Her eyebrow arched. "Do you think Breaker's been out long enough?"

Charlie stood still and then fought against Lark's pocket as he tried to get his hand free. "Breaker, to me, boy." He got his hand out and looked for the wolf. "Did I mention to you earlier on the phone that I have a surprise for you?"

"I think you did, yes," she said. "I do need to ask one question, Charlie." She took his hand and pulled him around to her. He made sure he paid attention. "You do have real protection, right?" He felt his brows came together. "I'm on the Pill, and it's not that I don't trust you, but..."

Charlie looked at her and got what she spoke about. He smiled. "Oh, you mean protection. Yes, at least I used to. At one point in my travels I thought I wanted to be a lover. After those one-nighters, I decided it wasn't worth it. I should have the leftover's in my truck." He took her hand. "Breaker, come on boy. Where is that wolf?"

Breaker bounded through the bushes onto the river bed and ran to them. He danced around them and loved the attention.

They walked quietly back to Charlie's house. He unlocked the door and they walked in. The house was warm and it felt good after the cold night air. He saw Lark look down the hall into the living room and a smile spread across her lips when she saw his couch.

"Hey, your couch arrived." She walked into the living room and leaned over the couch to look at it. He loved the view he got when he stood in the doorway.

"Yeah, the store delivered it early. I found the coffee table in the garage. It isn't really my taste, but it will work for now." He stood next to her and tilted his head.

She turned to him and unzipped her coat. "If the couch arrived, does that mean the bed is also here?"

He looked down at her and smiled. "Yes, it does and I need for you to wait here one second. I'll be right back." Charlie turned and ran out the front door.

****

She heard his truck door open and after a few seconds, it slammed. He ran back into the house and slid into the living room. "One more second, babe. Stay right there." He turned and pounded up the stairs. She heard his footfalls on the ceiling and had to laugh.

Lark took her coat off and removed her boots. She knew that this evening would end up in his bed and felt warmth slide down her limbs into her pelvis. She was relieved she felt something that eluded her for the last several months. She heard him start down the stairs and she turned around. He'd taken off his coat and boots, too.

****

Charlie turned into the living room and stopped in the doorway. Lark stood by the couch and in the darkened room he could see her only in shadow. It made him admire her more than he ever thought possible. She looked so beautiful.

She leaned against the back of the couch. "Ducky, do you think if we make love it will ruin our friendship?"

He crossed his arms and leaned against the door jamb. "No, I wouldn't think so. We know each other's history and we're comfortable together." He saw a look on her face that he couldn't identify. "We're still growing and we're just taking another step."

"What do you like?" she asked.

He heard the question, but felt a bit confused. "What do I like about what?" he asked and wondered where she was going with this conversation. The expression on her face told him it was serious.

"I've only ever been with two men. One of them was in college and he didn't have any idea about foreplay. He just wanted to get it on and fall asleep." She took a breath. "Thomas, on the other hand..." She crossed her arms and brought her hand up to her face. "He always wanted me to face away from him. The excuse being that he could play with my breasts easier, but I always felt he thought it gave him more dominance over me. He was into toys and he loved being sucked off. I'm just wondering if you have any favorite positions and such?"

"No, no, no." Charlie walked to her and took her hands. He held them to his chest. "Babe, I've read about the weird games that people play and I'm not all that interested in dominating anyone. I'm not into playing games either. I've always liked the idea of sharing the moment." He kissed her hand. "Besides, I don't think that I'd like you in black leather and I'm so not ready to be spanked." She smiled and he felt glad and relieved. "Lou, you'll always be my best friend. I'll never do anything to hurt you, ever again. I swear it."

"The hurt was all a long time ago. Don't you think it's time we let it go?"

He looked at the letters on the mantel. "Maybe we should have a sacrificial burning of the letters."

Lark turned and reached for her coat. "I've been carrying this around since Saturday morning." She pulled his letter out of the pocket. "It's a good idea to get rid of them."

He took the letter out of her hand and looked at it. He threw it on the couch, Breaker jumped up on the cushions and then lay on top of it.

"Let's do that later. Breaker stay," he told the wolf. He put his arm out for her to take. "I want to show you the surprise. Come with me."

They walked up the stairs, but when Lark started to turn left to go to his old bedroom, he pulled her to the right.

"I'm the master of the house now. I get the big bedroom," he said in a low tone and laughed. They turned into the room and he let her walk ahead of him. "What do you think?" He put his hands on her shoulders and stood behind her.

"Oh Charlie, it's wonderful," she whispered.

Charlie had set up the bed in the middle of the long wall so he could look out the windows when he lay down. Lark's old nightstand sat next to it and her dresser was against the wall by the closet. He'd made the bed and even turned it down. Around the room he'd set up and lit several candles which gave the room a warm glow.

"I found the candles in a box in the garage. I think I'm going to need some lamps. The ceiling fixtures don't put out much light," he said into her ear.

"Ducky, you've become an old romantic." She turned and wrapped her arms around his waist. "It's so nice." She put her head on his chest.

"Lou." He ran his fingers through her hair and kissed her neck. "Are you feeling all right about all of this?"

"I'm having a shy moment." She looked up at him. "It just occurred to me that you might want me to take my clothes off. You've never seen me naked."

"Oh Lord, you're right. I didn't think about that." Charlie swallowed.

"We are adults and I'm sure we'll both probably act like kids and giggle our heads off."

Charlie became more nervous, but when he looked into her eyes he felt warm and calm. He put his hand on the side of her face and leaned over to move his lips along her chin and jaw. "Should we bite the bullet and undress each other or turn our backs and meet under the covers?"

"What if you stand on one side of the bed and I'll be on the other? We'll each take off one piece of clothing at a time." She opened her eyes.

"Yeah, we could do that. It would be sort of like strip - not poker, since we're not playing cards - strip something. I'm sure at some point I won't be nervous and will want to strip you myself, but let's try your idea for now."

They parted at the foot of the bed and stood on either side. "Wait a minute; you have on more clothes than me. You're wearing a bra." He grinned.

"No we're equal, you have on a long sleeved under shirt. Oh wait, are you still au natural?" He nodded his head. "I do have more on. I'm wearing panties."

"If you leave them on, do I get to take them off?"

"Sure, but what if I take the panties off and leave on my socks?" She teased.

"I hadn't thought of that. Would it bug you if I took them off and kissed your toes?" He looked across the bed at her.

"I've never had my toes sucked. I'll have to think about that. Are you ready?"

"Ladies first."

"What a gentleman," she said. She put her finger on her chin and looked up at the ceiling, as though faking thought. She reached down and pulled her sweater over her head. She held it out to her side, let it drop and showed off her white lacy bra.

Charlie thought he might fly over the bed, but contained himself. "Nice bra." He unbuttoned his flannel shirt and pulled it out of his pants. He copied her and let it drop to the floor. He showed off his undershirt and acted like a body builder.

"Nice," she laughed. She bent over and took off one of her socks.

"I see, you're going to tease me. I, my darling, am a bit bolder." He touched the top of his pants and acted like he was going to unzip them. He then pulled at the bottom of his under-shirt and took it off.

He saw her nod her head. "What's the scar on your stomach?"

"Appendicitis. I had to get it removed in Baltimore. You're stalling."

Lark put her thumbs in the top of her pants and undid the button. He watched as she slowly let the zipper down and turned to the side. She slid her pants down and arched her back which made her bottom curve out. She wore white lace bikini panties that matched her bra. She sat on the edge of the bed to get them all the way off and then bounced up on her feet.

Charlie felt his mouth go dry. She was beautiful and he wanted desperately to get his pants off. He'd put up with a semi-hard on all day, but now it pushed against his zipper. He leaned over and took off a sock.

She did the same and took off her last sock. She arched her eye brow. "One sock and one pair of jeans. Hmmm...what will it be?"

He couldn't take it anymore and opened his pants. He slid them down and copied her turning to the side. He pushed his bottom out and looked at her as sexy as he could manage. He puckered his lips and sent her an air kiss.

Lark whistled and looked at his bottom. As he straightened, he noticed her eyes looked at his penis. He was definitely ready to go. He got his pants off and turned to face her.

"Hmmm...what will it be? Panties or bra?" He smiled.

She reached around her back and loosened her bra. "When you said you'd take my panties off it gave me chills up my back and made my pelvis very warm." She pulled the straps down and slid it off her arms. She held it out to the side and dropped it on top of her sweater. "You better take your other sock off," she said.

He looked up at her eyes and then walked around the bed and put his hands on either side of her face. He gazed into her warm blue eyes. He leaned in and barely touched his lips to hers and felt her warm breath surround him. "You are so beautiful," he whispered and pressed his mouth to hers.

He straightened briefly and looked down at her chest. He could see the bruise spread up to her collar bone and neck. He lightly ran his fingers over it. The color was pinkish purple and he could see what looked like finger prints on her breast. "Does this hurt?"

"It's a little tender."

"You'll let me know if I'm hurting you, right?"

"I will, but I don't think you'll make it uncomfortable. What was it you said? *Kiss it and make it better.*"

Charlie felt all the blood rush to his shaft and thought he might pass out from too much happiness. He turned her and whispered, "Lie down and let me get those panties taken care of." While she flattened out on the comforter, he leaned over and took off his other sock. When he looked back he sucked in his breath and held it. He looked down at her. Lark put her sore wrist over her head and her other arm was at her side.

Charlie let his breath out. "Sweetheart, I have to say something now, before I get hypnotized and don't make any sense. I love you more than anything else on this planet." He looked at her body and then up at her eyes. "I've always loved you." He leaned his knees against the bed and ran his hand up her leg. He wrapped it around her thigh. "The first time we kissed kept me going for a very long time, but when we kissed in the hallway the other night..." He suddenly couldn't find the words he wanted to say.

She reached her hand out to him. "I know, darling man."

"No, see...I've read a lot, but I've never really done much and..."

"Charlie, we have all the time in the world. We'll teach each other."

He felt calm and very warm. He leaned over and kissed her above her V. The skin on her stomach was so soft. He licked around her belly button and felt her legs part. Her feet hooked around his waist and pulled him towards her. He kissed his way up to her breasts and lightly sucked a nipple. His mind raced, but he felt so calm. With his tongue he traced over to the bruised breast and kissed it. He heard her moan and looked up.

"Did that hurt?"

"God, no. It feels great," she whispered and arched her back pushing her breast up to him.

He explored her chest and took note of what made her moan and what didn't. He finally slid the rest of the way up to her and felt his shaft rub against her wet, warm folds. He kissed her neck and chin and found her mouth open and waiting for him. Their tongues danced and pushed against each other and he nibbled on her lips. His hand moved down her side and felt her hip. He moved up and his shaft slid up and down along her core. He hummed low in his chest at the warm slick feel that came from her and felt an electrical charge run through his system. His penis twitched and he wanted to be inside her desperately.

"Oh Ducky, who's teasing now?" she sighed and moved her pelvis to continue the rubbing.

He lifted his hips and moved his hand into the curls around her folds. She was so warm and he wanted to take her now, but didn't want to rush anything. His middle finger slid into her channel and she sighed and moaned at the same time.

"I thought you said you didn't know much? This is incredible, babe." She arched her back again and he moved his finger around in circles. He found her spot with his thumb and tickled it lightly. She continued to move her pelvis and he watched her face. Her eyes were mostly closed but would suddenly open and she would let out a groan. Her head turned to one side and then the other and her hands grabbed onto his shoulders. When her face came back around, she took his hand and pulled it up to her mouth. She bit and licked his fingers, sucking on each one in turn.

Charlie felt the blood pump in his penis, but knew he couldn't take her yet. He wanted to give her the pleasure he'd read about in all those magazines and only experienced a few times. He wanted her to know it was him giving her a gift. He pressed his thumb harder on her spot and picked up the speed of the circles. It amazed him to watch her; the expressions that passed over her face were gorgeous. Her head snapped back onto the bed and she started to pant. She held his hand against the side of her face and moved her hips against his hand.

"Oh God, Charlie, yes, don't stop, please don't stop." She panted harder and her back arched and held. His thumb continued to circle and his finger slid in and out of her.

When her breathing started to slow down, he slid his finger out, took hold of his penis, and put it to the opening of her channel. He adjusted his arms on either side of her head and pushed his shaft all the way in. When she raised her legs and wrapped them around his waist it made him enter her further. She felt so warm and her muscles tightened around his penis, which caused him to groan and give her a pump.

She opened her eyes and looked up at him. "No fair, I wasn't ready." She continued to breathe hard.

"Do you want me to stop?" he asked and pulled his pulsing shaft out and pushed back in slowly.

"God no, you feel great." She put her hand on the back of his neck and lifted up to kiss him.

He held the position and kissed her chin and licked her neck. He pushed up on his arms and looked down at her.

"What? What's wrong?" she asked.

"The protection. I forgot to get it out," he whispered.

She looked up at him. "I am on the Pill and I trust that you don't have any diseases, right?"

"As far as I know."

"If you pull out of me now Charlie Stone, I'll be very unhappy with you. I want you right where you are and that's all I have to say." He felt her hand move down his side to his butt cheek and pinch. "Except, I do have to say that you feel so good. I can feel you twitch inside me and if you don't take me now, I'll...oh...I don't know. Just don't leave," she said and tightened her ankles around his waist.

"Lark, I love you," he said and started a slow pumping.

"I love you, too. Yes..."

Charlie lost all track of time and didn't think he'd be able to go so long, but when she pulled him down on top of her it was the final straw. He let out a moan that followed the increased movement of his hips and he came with a blast of lights behind his eyes. Electricity ran up his body into his head and back down into his legs. He put his forehead on the pillow she was on and felt her below him.

****

Lark loved the way it felt to have Charlie on top. It was wonderful to be able to kiss him and watch the expressions on his face change while he made love to her. Thomas had only done it once or twice in the first year of their relationship. He then claimed it was too hard on his back and he couldn't tease her nipples.

She felt like she'd gone to heaven and didn't want to move. Charlie pushed up on his arms and moved off of her. Lying on his side, propped up on his elbow he looked down at her and his warm hand rested on her stomach.

"Lou, do you remember the catapult we built?" he asked and ran his hand up to her chest and moved his fingers over nipple.

She signed and smiled. "Of course, I do. That was the day you made Bobbie cry and Gran lectured us for over an hour and then gave us chocolate chip cookies."

"I was walking Breaker the other day and I noticed the rocks are still stacked in a pile there by the river."

"Do you want to try and finish it? We never got back to get it done." She put her hand over his on her breast.

"No, I just think it's funny that those rocks never got moved. I wonder what happened to that long-branch we lugged out of the forest."

Lark rolled onto her side to face him and snuggled close. "Ducky, do you want to know a secret?" She said, quietly between breathes and kissed his chin.

He kissed her forehead and held her around the waist. "Yes, ma'am."

She looked up at him. "That was my first." She saw his brows come together. "That was my first orgasm with a man and I loved that it was you that helped me experience it." She kissed his lips lightly.

He pushed himself up on his hand and looked down at her. She felt his hand move up along her side, gently touching her hip, waist and ribs. A finger traced the side of her breast and along her neck. He tucked a couple of stray hairs behind her ear. "Thomas never did that for you?"

"No, he was too busy worrying about his own pleasure. He wasn't into sharing."

"Lou, the more you tell me about this guy the less I like him. You mentioned at dinner that you'd cancelled the wedding, do you think he'll find out?" Charlie kept moving his hand over her body.

"I think he already knows. He left several messages on my voice mail that I erased. I don't want to hear him right now. He'll probably be up on Saturday for the dance and I'll talk to him then or maybe he won't come up. Who knows and I don't really care." She ran her hand up Charlie's arm.

"I don't want you to be alone with him. It worries me that he'll try to hurt you again."

"We'll be at the dance together and there will be lots of people around. You can keep an eye on me."

Charlie frowned. "Why don't you just call him and get it over with?"

"I don't want to talk to him now. I want to focus on us this week. I don't want to waste one single minute on him. Besides going to work, you've got my attention completely and after this Thursday, work will settle down and I may not let you get out of bed until after the New Year." She smiled and kissed his chin.

"What about oral sex?"

"What about it?"

"You said this was your first. Didn't Thomas ever do the oral thing to give you an orgasm?"

"He liked it when I sucked him off, but he didn't...he wouldn't even lick...never mind. It's too embarrassing." She looked away from Charlie and wanted to kick herself. She started to choke up and didn't want to cry. Not tonight. She felt too happy and relaxed. "I put up with a lot from him. I was pretty stupid."

"No, don't say that, Lou."

"When I started going out with Thomas I thought I might as well stay with him. It seemed like I'd never see you again and there wasn't any chance that we'd ever be together. I don't want to talk about him anymore. I don't want to think about him." Lark felt like such an idiot and tears welled in her eyes. She looked up at him and a single tear ran out of her eye into her hair. "I'm so glad you came home, Ducky. I can't wait to start experiencing life with you."

Charlie put his lips on hers and licked along the inside of her mouth. She met his tongue and sucked on his bottom lip. He lifted his head and moved his fingers through her hair.

"About oral sex, I've read about it, but I don't know. It just seems rude to stick my cock in your mouth when it would rather be somewhere else."

Lark started to laugh and wiped her eyes. "I appreciate your sentiment, more than you'll ever know. It's not all that bad, as long as you don't grab my hair and pump your penis really hard." She saw his questioning look. "Do you want me to show you?"

"What? Now?" he said and started to sit up.

She pushed herself up and put her hand on his chest. "Just lay back down flat and relax. I've never done this the gentle way and I've always wished to try it with someone I really cared about." When he'd flattened out, she pulled the sheet off his legs and straddled his thighs. "Now just close your eyes and remember to breathe."

"That's easier said than done," he mumbled and looked up at the ceiling. He then looked back at her and didn't take his eyes off her.

Lark looked down at him and smiled. His penis twitched slightly and she thought he might be ready to play again. She leaned over his stomach and kissed around his belly button. She licked his salty skin and nibbled down until she felt his curly hairs brush her chin. She put her hand around his penis and felt it harden in her grip. He moaned and sucked in a breath as she smoothed her hand up and down his pulsing shaft.

She licked her lips and lowered to kiss the tip of his member.

She glanced up and saw he still stared down at her. There was a little curl to his lips which signaled that he enjoyed her movements. She rubbed her breasts on his thigh and went back to kissing around his hips and pelvic area. She backed up just a little and moved his penis around her chin and brushed the head with her lips.

"Oh, Lark...Fuck, this is crazy incredible," he whispered and his arms reached over his head. He put his palms flat against the wall.

She smiled and let her tongue wonder down to the base of his hard member. She worked her way back to the top, and then took the head into her mouth and tongued it in circles. She saw him watch her again and let the shaft slid into the back of her throat and swallowed. She slowly came back to the head and continued the up and down movement for several minutes. Charlie groaned. She saw his eyes were closed and he pushed against the wall.

She brought her hand between his legs and cupped his testicles, massaging them gently. Charlie arched his back and began to move his hips in a rhythm with her. They moved together slowly for several minutes and Lark thought, *This is the way to do it so it feels good. I could really get used to doing this.*

"Lark, babe..." he shouted. "I don't want to come in your mouth. Not tonight, but you're killing me."

She licked up his penis one more time and then got up. She scooted forward and put her opening over the head. She slowly moved down and let the shaft push up into her channel. When he was all the way in, she looked down at him and smiled. "Is this where you want to be?"

"Oh God, yes, I'm in heaven," he hissed and started to move.

She moved her hips and he reached up and put his hands on her breasts. He pinched her nipples and she arched her back as she moved. She felt him shake and realized he was coming. He exploded into her and she held her position long enough for him to expel every last drop.

When she looked down at him, there was sweat on his chest and forehead. He stared at her with a huge grin on his face. She leaned over and kissed his chest. He put his hands on her shoulders and pulled her body up so her mouth was closer to his.

He touched her face and hair. "That was amazing. I'm going to want more of that. Oh my Lord, woman you are so hot. I knew I'd missed out on a lot over the years, but, wow! I am so glad I waited for you."

She lightly kissed his lips. "And you know what?" His eyebrows rose as he continued to breathe hard. "I've never done it that way. I never got to be on top with he-who-shall-not-be-named anymore. That was another first for me, too."

He wrapped his arms around her and sat up. He kissed her shoulder and neck. "I love you so much Lark. Don't ever leave. Please, be mine forever."

She hugged him back. "I'm yours, babe. Always and forever."

Chapter Nineteen

Lark played with the mouse on her desk. She was supposed to be reviewing orders, but found it easier to let her mind wander. Every time she pictured Charlie in her mind, she felt warmth flow into her pelvis and legs. It was only eleven in the morning, but she wanted to go home, find Charlie and undress him. Quickly.

When they woke up this morning, they got out of bed and Charlie pulled her into his shower with him. It was something she'd never done before and loved every minute of it. They splashed hot water at each other and when she kissed him, it was supposed to be a quick smooch. The hot water apparently started his engine and he kissed her back, tongue plunging into her mouth and sucking her lips with abandon. His hand worked its way between her thighs and he slid a finger in and out of her channel while his thumb lightly teased her nub.

The next thing she knew, he'd wrapped her legs around his waist, pushed her against the wall under the shower head and slammed his hard, pulsing shaft inside her tender walls. The hot water flowing down on them increased the heat between them and they'd orgasmed at the same time; Charlie groaned loudly and she huffed out breath after breath and tried to keep from screaming.

He let her down gently and grabbed a bar of soap off the holder. She thought he was going to clean himself, but he instead started to move the soap around her breasts and pelvis. His hands were so tender. He then opened a bottle of shampoo and lathered her hair. He kissed her neck and chest, lightly flicking her nipples with his tongue as bubbles ran down her chest. His fingers then went back to her channel and he tormented her for several minutes. It thrilled her, and he made her come again and it was all she could do to continue to stand upright.

She then did the same to him, lathering his hair and soaping up his body. Her mouth moved over his penis causing it to harden again. Using her lips, tongue and hand she tormented him in the same way he'd done to her. When he braced his arms against the side of the shower she squatted in front of him and let his penis slide into the back of her throat. She grabbed onto his buns and held him in as long as she could and then slid down, tonguing the tender part of his pulsing shaft. When she let him push in again, he roared and warm jets of semen poured into her throat and she swallowed, taking him all the way into her body. She almost started to cry when she realized this was the first time she wanted Charlie or anyone to be a part of her inside and out. Now she knew what he tasted like and how he smelled and she thought she would have to hurt someone if this turned out to be a dream.

When she looked up at him, Charlie breathed hard, but managed a smile. It was then they both realized the water had turned lukewarm and headed for cold. They rinsed the soap off and laughed.

Lark borrowed a towel to wrap her hair. She'd have to dry it at home since Charlie didn't have a dryer. They dressed and then walked hand in hand through the back door of her house and saw Gran at the kitchen table.

"Good morning, kids. Did you have a good evening?" She smiled. "Let me guess, you talked until late and fell asleep?"

For a second they both looked like they'd been caught stealing cookies. Lark looked up at Charlie and grinned. "Gran, we're a couple now." She walked to her grandmother and kissed her cheek. "I've got to dry my hair and change for work. I'll be right back."

She raced up the stairs to her room, changed her clothes and got her hair dry. She put on make-up and smiled at herself in the mirror. She felt a little bad deserting him, but knew he could handle Gran.

Lark sat at her desk in her office and smiled. She moved her tender nether region on the seat of her chair and sighed. She knew if she kept thinking about this morning she'd never get any work done. She was so happy that Gran felt tickled that they'd found each other again.

She looked at her computer screen, tried to focus and continued to play with the mouse. More orders were coming in and she wanted to be able to keep up with them.

****

Charlie felt slightly uncomfortable for a minute when Lark went upstairs, but when Gran came over and gave him a hug, he started to relax.

"Do you want some coffee?" she asked.

"Yes, please."

"You go ahead and sit. When Lark comes back down, I'll fix you both some breakfast." She poured a cup for him and put it at a place at the table. "Charlie, I only want to say one thing."

He felt a knot form quickly in his stomach and became nervous. "Okay."

Gran smiled. "Welcome back to the family. I'm so glad you came home. It's good to see Lark smile again."

He let out a breath and smiled. He felt his throat tighten and almost started to cry. "Gran, would you hate it very much if I became your grandson-in-law?"

She turned around from the stove and took a step forward. "Did you...?"

"No, no. Not yet, but I'm thinking about it. I've got to get over to Pueblo and sell that truck. I don't want to break into my college savings, but I want Lark to have the most beautiful engagement ring I can find. I've got to do it this week."

"Why this week?"

"I can't keep asking you and Lark to drive me around everywhere and I want to ask her to marry me before Christmas. It just seems important."

****

When Lark came back downstairs, she found Gran hugging Charlie and she was sniffling.

"Oh God, what happened?" she asked from the doorway. Gran looked up and patted Charlie on the back. He smiled at Lark and she could see tears in his eyes. "What?"

"Oh nothing, sweetheart. I'll get breakfast started," Gran said, and moved back to the stove. She poured eggs into the pan and started to scramble them.

Lark saw Gran turn to look at Charlie and gave him a wink. She shook her head and went to the cupboard to get a cup. After pouring some coffee, she went to the table and sat next to him.

She saw Gran continue to look over her shoulder at them and Lark became a little uncomfortable.

"What is going on?" she finally asked.

"I'm really glad you two found your way back to each other. You know, I think it was meant to be. I read a book once about this couple and they were destined to be together. I think that's you two completely." Gran sniffed again and continued to scramble the eggs.

Lark felt her own throat tighten and stood. She walked over to her grandmother and they gave each other a hug.

Charlie put his chin in his hand. "My two favorite ladies hugging. How hot is that?"

"Charlie Stone, are you saying you'd be interested in a threesome?" Gran asked and laughed. He sat up straight in his chair.

"Grandmother!" Lark stepped back, truly shocked. She looked at Charlie, whose eyes were huge and his mouth hung open.

"I'm not as square as you think, Larkspur. I've read some really racy stuff in my time and remember, I was in my twenties during the 1960s. I know all about free love, peace, granola and all that." She patted Lark's hand and went back to her cooking.

"But you're my grandmother," Lark said.

"How on earth do you think your dad got here and you for that matter?"

"Gran, we don't want to go there. Not ever. That would be too much information and I don't know if I have a nervous system that would understand." Lark went back to the table and sat down.

"Larkspur, my darling girl, you've got a lot to learn and over time you'll learn it. Now stop being such a prude," Gran said and spooned the eggs onto their plates. She carried them to the table and got toast out of the oven.

"Gran, I am not a prude. It's just too early in the morning for this type of conversation."

After breakfast, Charlie walked her to the Bronco and gave her the sweetest kiss she'd ever experienced. She asked where he'd learned how to kiss so great. He smiled at her and said it was on a late summer day thirteen years ago, on a picnic, with the most beautiful girl he'd ever met. She gave him a kiss back, called him an old romantic again, and left for the warehouse.

Her serene moment at her desk was interrupted by a knock on the door. When she looked up Alicia stood in the doorway.

"Ah, are you here, Lark?" Alicia continued to look at her. "I buzzed you. Thomas is on line three and he's insisted he'll hold until you're ready to talk to him," she said and backed out of the office.

Lark stared at the blinking phone line. The last thing she wanted to do was talk to him. It was a good mood wrecker. *Just get it over with Lark*, she thought. She hit the button and lifted the receiver.

"Yes, Thomas."

"Why the hell haven't you returned my calls?" his voice snarled at her.

"Well, number one, I've been busy with work. You know, 'tis the season and all. Number two, I have nothing to say to you except that our wedding isn't going to happen and you can fuck off."

"Yeah, I've been very embarrassed getting calls from my friends, who want to know what happened. I felt like an idiot."

"Too bad for you. What do you want?" She tried to sound as uninterested as possible.

"I want to discuss your rash decision."

"There is nothing to talk about, Thomas. You hit me, again, and I've learned to respect myself enough not to put up with your crap anymore. I tried to be honest with you about events earlier in the day and that was that." She wound the telephone cord around her finger and wanted to pull it out of the wall.

"Oh Lord, you are over-reacting, as usual. I didn't hit you that hard." He sounded incredulous.

"I have bruises on my wrist, face and chest that prove it wasn't a love tap. Speaking of..." There was a knock on the door and Nancy looked in.

"Ryan's here," Nancy said, quietly.

"Look, there's nothing to discuss, Thomas..."

He cut her off. "I'm still coming on Saturday and we *will* talk. We'll have to miss the dance, but I think you owe it to me to tell me to my face what your problem is," he ordered.

"Whatever," she said and hung up. She looked up at Nancy and shook her head.

Lark followed her partner to another office. She felt very angry at Thomas and didn't want to see him again ever. They stopped outside the door.

"Are you okay?" Nancy asked.

"I'm not one hundred percent, but I will be."

They walked into the office where their lawyer Ryan Barton sat with a cup of coffee in one hand. He stood up and shook hands and they all sat down at a conference table.

"So, to get down to brass tacks, it would seem that Canon City Savings and Loan, for some unknown reason, has decided to sell off a bunch of business loans. They've spoken to National up in Denver. My connection here said it looks like someone is trying to buy out the loan."

"Someone other than National?" Lark asked.

Ryan nodded. "Yeah, and I haven't found out who the buyer is, yet."

Nancy sat back in her chair. "Why would someone want to buy the loan? That doesn't make sense."

"Can either of you think of a competitor who would be interested in buying you out or closing the doors?" Ryan looked at them.

Lark and Nancy exchanged looks. "There was that group back in New York that made an offer two years ago, but nothing serious," Nancy said.

"They were pushy, but gave up when we wouldn't budge on our counteroffer. Three billion wasn't in their ballpark." Lark laughed.

"I have a meeting this afternoon with Zack Strom over at the savings and loan. There's a clause in the contract that says they need to give warning sixty days in advance before they start selling off loans. It's to give business owners the opportunity to pay off the loan. Since they haven't done that, we could take them to court to stop the process completely," Ryan said.

"I've left several messages on Mike Strom's personal phone. He's on vacation until after the first. I know he's retiring, but I don't think he'd want this. He said to me once he wants to keep local businesses alive and functioning. I think maybe he's not aware of what his son is trying to pull."

"How'd you get his personal phone number?" Ryan asked.

"He's listed in the Methodist Church directory. I have big connections," Lark said.

They all laughed, talked over some other matters and then Ryan left. He said he'd call them after he spoke to Zack Strom.

Nancy frowned. "How come I feel like there's something else going on here?"

Lark looked at her friend. "Paranoid?"

"I don't know, maybe. Ever since we were in Denver last week something's been nagging at me, but I can't quite figure it out."

"We'll be okay. See, I'm staying positive." Lark smiled.

Nancy looked at her closely. "You're too cheerful. Did you have good sex last night?"

Lark stood up and smiled. "No comment." She walked to the door, but before she opened it, she looked at Nancy over her shoulder and grinned. "It wasn't just good; it was great, cha, cha, cha."

Nancy laughed. "It's good to know someone is getting great sex. You know I'll want details eventually." She walked up to Lark and hooked her arm. "You never acted this way with Thomas. I'm glad you're not going to marry him."

"Me, too."

Chapter Twenty

Ryan called later in the day and said Zack Strom cancelled the meeting at the last minute. They rescheduled for the next week and Ryan was pissed. He asked if they heard anything from Mike Strom to let him know.

Lark and Nancy both worked the floor in the afternoon and were almost caught up when the woman who handled most of the orders showed up with another one hundred and two. Lark's secretary was right behind her and handed Lark a stack of envelopes.

It was going on four o'clock and she was tired. Charlie wore her out the night before and this morning. She did look forward to the speech she was about to give, though. Christmas was her favorite time of the year.

She and Nancy called a meeting with all their employees down on the main floor. It was a pep rally of sorts. When everyone quieted, Lark stepped forward.

"You guys have kicked ass the last couple of weeks and I know the hours you've worked have satisfied a lot of customers, but probably worn you guys out. Nancy and I appreciate your hard work. We've made the cutoff date the nineteenth, which is only two days away. So, we decided to close up shop early tonight. Everyone gets to go on home, or, like me, do last minute Christmas shopping. We'll start up tomorrow and in the next two days get as many orders filled and out as possible. Before you all leave, stop here." She held up the envelopes. "Its bonus time," she said in a sing-song voice.

The employees clapped and cheered and lined up for their checks. Lark handed them out with a grin and wished them all a Merry Christmas. Once they'd cleared out, Lark went up to her office, put on her coat and shut off the light. She met Nancy in the hallway and they walked out to the parking lot together.

"I really like bonus time of the year." Nancy switched off the lights for the main floor and moved to the exit. "I think they like us for a few days after we hand out those checks."

"Yeah, I do still have to shop, but I'm too pooped. I'm going home."

"Are you seeing your new man tonight?" Nancy grinned and arched her brow.

"Probably," Lark said and stepped outside the door. She pulled her coat tighter around her. It was chilly and a breeze made it even colder. "Lord, I hope this storm blows over fast. We don't have time for delayed deliveries."

"How long have you and Charlie known each other, anyway?"

"We've been friends for about twenty years. I moved in with my Gran when I was eight, after my parents died. Charlie and I experienced our first hot kiss together the summer we were fifteen years old." Lark pulled her keys out of her purse and stopped to put on her gloves. "Nance, he's a really good guy."

"Yeah, I vaguely remember all that business with his mom and dad. I don't really know him though."

"It's hard to explain. I think Charlie really wanted to deck Thomas when he hit me the other night, but he didn't. Charlie did threaten Thomas. The thing though that makes it mean so much to me is that he defended me. He did that a lot when we were kids. There were some bullies that used to pick on me because I was an orphan, even though I wasn't, because I've always had Gran. Charlie would come to my rescue and made me feel better. This week, with Thomas, he did it again. Here's hoping I don't scare him off."

"Sweetie, you won't scare him. Is he coming to the dance on Saturday?"

"We haven't talked about it too much. I think so, but I'll mention it to him again."

They walked to their two cars and said goodnight.

Lark walked into the house and her mouth instantly watered. The kitchen smelled wonderful. "Gran, I'm home," she said and hung up her coat.

"Hi, honey. I'm in here," Gran called from the pantry.

"Lord, it smells good in here. What's for dinner?" She walked to the oven and looked in the window.

"I'm making a roast. Tomorrow and Thursday I'll be making the pies for the dance. We'll need to have leftovers if we want to eat anything. I won't have time to cook." She came out of the pantry and held a bag of beans.

"Are you going to make red bean pie, Gran?" Lark smiled.

"Very funny. I want to soak these overnight and make Charlie red beans and rice to get him through lunches for the next few days." She looked at Lark. "Sweetheart, put your coat back on and go over to Charlie's. That ding-dong wouldn't accept my dinner invitation and was being silly. He said he'd mooched too much food off us since he got back. You can tell him that he hurt my feelings." Gran pouted, but smiled.

Lark felt excitement fill her heart, which started to beat fast. She hugged Gran, then turned to the door and grabbed her coat on the way out.

It was cold on the short walk and the wind had picked up. She looked up at the sky and only saw clouds. There wasn't a star or moon to be seen. She walked up to his front door and could hear Breaker on the other side, woofing. She blew on her hands to try to warm them up and knocked.

Charlie opened the door. He wore a navy blue cable knit sweater and jeans. Lark looked at him and sighed.

"You don't have to knock," he said and opened the door all the way.

She smiled. "You are without a doubt the sexiest man on the planet," she said, as she walked into the hallway.

He took her hand and pulled her farther into the warm house. "Lord, your hands are frozen." He lifted his sweater and put her hands underneath onto his chest. "That wakes me up." He laughed. His hands moved around her waist and pulled her into a hug. "Hello, sweetheart, did you have a good day?" He leaned over and gave her a quick kiss.

Lark started to laugh. "My, my, but you are very domestic this evening."

He ran his hands over her hair and laced his fingers behind her neck. "I'm just doing normal for the minute. I wanted to see how it sounded and felt. It was either that or strip you bare in the doorway." He leaned over and brushed her lips with his.

She looked up at him and kissed him back. "Stripping bare is definitely on the agenda for tonight.

Gran says to put your shoes on and come for dinner. You know better than to argue with her."

Charlie leaned close to her and almost put his lips on hers. Lark could feel his warm breath and wanted to melt.

"I know better than to upset the Metcalfe women. I learned that lesson a long time ago and will never, ever do it again. Can I have one of those erection-causing kisses you give, before I put on my shoes?" Charlie whispered near her cheek. "I've gotten used to sitting at the table with a stiffy."

She felt his tongue graze her bottom lip and laughed. "Ducky, you're killing me. You can have whatever you want." She moved her hands under his sweater and stood on her toes. She placed her thumbs over his nipples and circled them. She saw him close his eyes and heard a low moan come from his throat. She placed her lips on his and they gently touched tongues. She let her teeth scrape over his tongue and moved her head back. "We better stop or we won't leave."

His hand found her butt and squeezed it. She flinched and her eyebrows creased.

"What was that?" he asked and looked into her eyes. "You just jumped when I pinched your butt cheek. You did it the other night when we walked Breaker and I put my hand in your pocket."

Lark realized she felt nervous and knew there was no reason to feel that way with Charlie. He would never hurt her. "It's nothing. I'm just a little weird about my rear end. Just ignore it."

"No, sweetheart. Is it something we need to talk about?" He put his hand up on her the side of her face and looked quite serious.

"It's nothing, Ducky. We better get going. Gran will be upset if her roast gets dried out." She smiled and kissed him.

"You're right. I'll get my shoes on." He let her go, grabbed his boots and sat at the kitchen table to put them on.

Lark watched him unlace the shoes and slide them on. While he tightened the laces and tied them up, Breaker came up along side of her and nudged her knee. She bent over to rub his ears and laughed. "You know what Ducky?"

He looked up at her. "Tell me."

"I want to come over there and straddle your lap so bad." She opened the front door and stepped into his yard. She bent over, picked up some snow and held it to her cheeks.

Charlie put on his coat and came out the door with Breaker on his heels. "Lark, are you okay?" he asked.

"Yes, I'm fine. I think I just discovered the true meaning of *hot flash*." She threw the snow down and wiped her face with her coat sleeve. "You're scorching hot, babe."

He took her hand and they started to walk up the drive. "Lou, I was only putting on my boots. How is that hot?"

"The way you manipulated the laces with your fingers, it reminded me of the way you touched me last night. Ducky, you have great fingers." She smiled up at him.

"Wait a minute. See, I'd understand *hot dick* or *hot butt*, but fingers? Hot fingers, really?"

Lark turned around and walked backwards. She wanted to look at him. "Yeah, hot fingers. The way you slid them into me and how I got to suck on them, was so incredible. I love your fingers, babe."

Charlie looked at his hand, and then at her. "I'll have to remember you like that."

"I'm going to have a terrible time trying to sit still during dinner. Maybe I should sit across the table from you. It might be too tempting if we sit side by side," she said, softly.

They reached the door of Gran's house. Charlie put his hands around her waist and carried her away from the door to the side of the house where no one could see them. He set her down, took her hand in his and kissed and licked her palm and wrist. He then moved her hand down to the front of his pants and placed it over the zipper. "Talk about killing, you are doing crazy things to me, woman."

Lark could feel his erection twitch below the fabric. Then she pressed down a little and traced where she knew the tender spot would be, Charlie made a moaning sound and his eyes crossed. He opened his eyes; his hand shot out, grabbed her behind the neck and pulled her close.

Lark felt his mouth cover hers and his tongue dove in and devoured her. It amazed her how quickly he caught on to the subtle movements that could make her heart melt and left her breathless. He put his hands on either side of her face and licked and nibbled her lips.

"God, Charlie. I think you practiced on more women than you admitted. You're so good at this." She whispered.

"I told you, babe. Playboy magazine was my sex manual for several years." He covered her mouth again. "You're going to make me come in my pants, Lark. We should probably stop, again."

She leaned back out of breath. "You're right; Gran would kill us if we were late to dinner."

"We can't rush the dinner either. I know we could both down our meals in under five minutes, but we can't. We have to be tough. It will be hard, but," he traced his thumb over her bottom lip. "God, I never want to let you go." He pulled her off her feet into a hug.

Lark wrapped her arms around his neck and held onto him. "Then don't let go, Ducky."

He looked down at her. "Lou, move in with me. I don't want to sleep another night alone and I want to wake up with you every day." He tightened his hold.

"Are you serious?" She slid down to her feet and looked up at him.

"I've never been so serious in my life."

"You don't think we'd be rushing things a little?"

"I've been dreaming of this for thirteen years. So, no, I don't think were moving too fast." He frowned. "Am I pushing you too fast? I don't want to do that."

She smiled up at him and touched his chin. "No, you're not pushing. Gran is going to have a stroke."

"Does that mean yes?" he asked.

"It means yes. I've been waiting thirteen years, too." She grinned. "Let's go tell Gran."

They moved arm in arm back to the door where Breaker sat with a smile on his muzzle. His tail started to wag as they approached. He followed them and shuffled up to Gran. He nudged her knee until she started to scratch his ears.

She looked up at Lark and Charlie. "You two have the reddest cheeks I've ever seen. You're either coming down with something, or it's really cold outside."

They looked at each other and back at Gran. "It is really cold, Gran. It's freezing, big snow storm moving in, brrr..." Charlie said and rubbed his arms.

Gran gave him the bent eye. "You're over acting Charlie Stone. Sit down. Dinners ready to go."

While they served the meal and passed plates around, Lark looked at him and smiled. "Gran, Charlie and I have some news for you." She looked at her grandmother.

Gran set the bowl of potatoes down and waited patiently.

"I'm going to move in with Charlie. We're going to live together. I'll be just next door. I don't want to get too far away from you," Lark said and waited for Gran's reaction.

"Sweetheart, really?"

Lark nodded.

"Well, that's wonderful." Gran smiled at them.

"You don't mind?" Lark asked, surprised.

"Oh sure, I want you to hate me forever for holding you back. Lark, you're twenty-eight years old and don't need my permission. I'm very happy for both of you. I think you have needed each other for a very long time. I'm tickled pink."

Charlie smiled at Lark. "Your Gran is completely cool."

She nodded. "Don't I know it?"

Chapter Twenty-One

During dinner Lark told them about the goings-on at the warehouse and about the anonymous investor who, for some unknown reason, wanted to take over the business.

Gran told Lark she was pretty calm about it. She thought she should be worried. Lark explained that there was no reason to get worked up just yet. Ryan Barton was doing a great job and she felt very confident that everything would turn out fine.

After they finished dinner, she and Charlie helped Gran get the dishes done and everything put away. Lark went upstairs to pack a few things into a bag to take next door.

Charlie grabbed her bag and said he wanted to take Breaker for a walk. He'd told Lark, he thought she and Gran should have a moment alone, which she appreciated. Gran got a little teary, but hugged her granddaughter and said she couldn't be happier. She told Lark that Charlie was a good man and he would always protect her.

****

When Charlie returned to the house, he got a bowl of food out for Breaker and set it on the floor. "All right, boy. You get to stay down here for a while and protect things. I'll call you when you can come up, okay?" he said and looked down at the wolf.

Breaker munched his food and Charlie felt the wolf ignored him. He did look up from his bowl, licked his wolf lips and went back to the food.

Charlie shook his head and started up the stairs. He wanted to make sure the bed was made and he hadn't left any clothes or socks lying around. He didn't want Lark to think he was a messy kind of guy.

He stopped half way up and leaned against the wall. He thought how his world completely changed in the last week. Before he came back to Canon City, he'd never thought it would be possible to find Lark again. He smiled and felt warmth spread in him from head to toe. He also thought it was funny he'd never wanted to live in this house again, but he and Lark were making new and better memories. It might not be so bad here.

He laughed and continued up to the bedroom. When he turned on the light, his laughter stopped and he stood in the doorway, stunned. He'd never seen anything so beautiful in his life.

Lark was on her side on the bed, naked from head to toe. She apparently took off her clothes the minute she got back. The top sheet just covered her breasts and her gorgeous legs were stretched out on top.

His mouth snapped shut as he slowly entered the room and closed the door behind him. Their eyes locked and he stopped at the foot of the bed. Lark rolled onto her back which pulled the sheet off her breasts. He could see her nipples were puckered and they rose and fell as she breathed. It was a heavenly sight.

Charlie thought he may have broken the speed of sound when he pulled his clothes off fast. He crawled onto the bed and stopped at her knees. His eyes roamed down her body and he pulled the sheet the rest of the way off. His eyes moved back up to her chest and he lightly touched the bruise.

"I didn't ask this morning how your bruises felt. That was bad of me," he said and picked up her hand, kissing the bruise around her wrist. He licked her palm and continued to nibble her fingers.

Lark sat up and put her hand on his chest. "They're fine, but I didn't really think about them much. My brain was a little pre-occupied with how handsome you are."

Charlie ran his hand threw her hair. "Why don't you lie down on your stomach? I want to get to know every part of your body and give you the pleasure you gave me in the shower. I want to start with your beautiful back and maybe give you a massage..." He saw Lark frown.

****

Lark's hand snapped back and she scooted away from Charlie. The fear crashed in on her so fast, she found it hard to breath. The past reared its ugly head and made her chest go tight and her stomach knotted.

"Lou, what's wrong?" He reached for her, but she pushed his hands away.

"This is all...maybe we did rush," she whispered. "I'm not sure I can...wrong, this isn't right."

She moved her legs over the side of the bed and leaned over. She pulled a pair of sweats out of her bag and started to put them on.

"I need to go home." Lark knew exactly why she was suddenly so scared and angry. Memories of all those horrible nights with Thomas, and one night in particular, raced through her head and she felt she needed to get out of this room.

Charlie's hand touched her arm and her whole body tensed.

"Lou, are you still going to move in here with me? What did I do?" he asked. She could hear tension in his voice and his hand moved up her back.

She pulled her arm away from him and slid her sweatshirt over her head. She pulled the pants up and stood. She got a pair of socks out of her bag and put them on. "Nothing. You did nothing. I have to go." She stood up straight and grabbed her bag. As she opened the door, Breaker barged into the room and she moved around him to get out. The voices and laughter in her head got louder and she found it hard to get any air into her lungs. She heard Charlie move in the bedroom and when she was halfway down the stairs, his voice pierced through the noise and made her stop.

"Lou, wait a minute. What did I do? Tell me, please," he begged.

She turned on the riser and looked up at him. She wanted to explain to him what Thomas had done to her, but couldn't open her mouth. "You didn't do anything, Charlie." She put her hand in her hair and thought she might scream. A couple of months ago she thought she'd gotten rid of this feeling, but it still haunted her and she didn't want to think about it anymore. She didn't want to keep having anxiety attacks. She didn't want to live in fear anymore.

Charlie took a step down and she turned and went down the steps and into the kitchen. She dropped her bag and bent over to put on her boots. When she stood up, she felt his hands on her shoulders. His nice warm hands should have made her feel better, but they caused her to jump. She tripped over her bag and started to go down, but Charlie wrapped his arm around her waist and held her up.

"Sweetheart, please, God don't run from me. Please, tell me what I did wrong," he said very quietly.

She looked at him over her shoulder and saw the man who said he loved her. He was so gentle with her and gave her the first ever orgasm of her life. She saw the man who'd trusted her enough to let her take his shaft into her mouth and suck him off. She saw the man she'd cared for and loved for thirteen or more years. The man she knew in her heart she trusted more than anyone else on the planet, but couldn't get her head to remember that trust.

She put her hand on his arm at her waist and felt her throat tighten. She looked away from him and tears ran down her cheeks.

"Lark, babe, what did that fuckhead do to you?" She heard him ask. She put her hand over her mouth to keep from sobbing and squeezed her eyes shut.

She felt him turn her around and put her arm around his neck. He lifted her legs and carried her to the couch in the living room and gently lowered her to the cushion. He went down on his knees and held her tight. Lark couldn't get her emotions under control and the tears she'd held onto for six months continued to stream out of her eyes. She felt his arms loosen and he stood up. He went to the fire place and began to build a log pile. Lark watched him through the blur of tears as he crumbled papers into the logs.

"You put your jeans on," she said and wiped her eyes on the sleeve of her sweat shirt.

He looked over at her and smiled. "I would have followed you out into the snow. You know that, right?"

She nodded and leaned over to take her boots off. He struck a long match and got the paper lit under the logs. He closed the glass screen and stood up, looking at her. Lark saw a ton of confusion on his face and hated herself for hurting him.

"Lark, I think we need to talk. I'm going to run up and get my shirt and socks. Please, don't leave."

"You're right, we do need to talk. I won't leave," she said and pulled her feet up onto the couch. She put her knees under her chin.

When Charlie came back down he wore a flannel shirt. He brought a roll of toilet paper and a bottle of water to her. She thanked him and blew her nose. He sat at the other end of the couch and leaned his elbows on his knees. He tented his hands under his chin and looked at her.

Lark opened the bottle of water and took a sip. She watched the flames build up in the fire place. The tears slowed a little, but still rolled down her cheeks.

"Charlie, I want you to understand that you've done nothing wrong. I'm sorry I freaked, but...well, I have some memory baggage that woke up at the wrong time. I need to get rid of it...I've thought about maybe getting help after the New Year." She let out a breath and put her feet on the floor and crossed her legs. She stared at the flames. "Thomas always had weird ideas in the bedroom. It seemed to make him feel in control and elevated his ego about himself if he could somehow degrade me. He loved it if I started to cry." She unrolled a few sheets of TP and wiped her eyes, again.

"About six months ago, I was up in Denver and Thomas asked if I'd be interested in going to a club. When I asked him what kind of music would be played, he laughed at me and decided it would be better to surprise me." Lark stood up and walked to the fireplace. She couldn't look at Charlie if she was going to get through this story. She didn't want him to see how stupid she felt and she didn't want to see his disappointment with her.

"So, the next time I was in Denver, he said we were going out. We drove to this really weird mansion up in the hills outside of the city limits. I don't even know who owned the place, but it became apparent Thomas spent some evenings there before. The valet and waiters all addressed him by his name and it was no music club."

She walked over to the window and looked out at the snow as it fell from the sky. "We went into this main room where a bar was set up and I knew right away I didn't want to be there. There were several people attending this party and the women all wore some kind of slinky outfits, if they had on any clothes at all. I didn't even really think the attire was wrong until I saw a couple of nude women down on their knees, sucking men's dicks. There was a table by one of the windows with a woman tied to it and a man was taking her from the rear. There was a gag in her mouth and a terrified look on her face." In the pane of glass she could see the whole scene as it played out. She lost her voice for a moment and remembered that horrible night.

She took in a breath and put her fist on the window. "I asked Thomas to take me home and he said just have one drink and then we'd leave." She shook her head and put her hand flat on the glass. She felt the cold on her fingers and willed it to flow into her body, she was so embarrassed.

"I know now I should have walked out, but it would have been a long walk home and I figured if I stayed away from these people, I'd be okay. The woman that lay tied to the table was dragged into another room. I started to hear screams and what sounded like a whip snapping. I made up my mind that I'd walk the twelve miles back to Denver and could maybe find a convenience store or gas station to call a cab. And then my knees started to feel like mush. I'd been drugged. Thomas arranged something to be put into my drink. I wasn't completely knocked out, but loopy enough to be compliant. I don't really remember everything that happened, but at one point I felt alert enough and..." her voice cracked. *Just get it over with*, she thought and squeezed her eyes shut again. "I was strapped to this table on my stomach and my hands were tied or handcuffed behind my back. Someone stripped my clothes off. People walked around the table and someone kept saying to be sure to draw a *back door* number. I had a vague notion what it meant, but was still groggy. I looked to my left and right and on either side were two other women. Both seemed dead to the world. I guess because I was semi-alert and started to scream, I became more interesting to the party goers. Hands started to touch me and...at one point, I was being...taken in the rear and I heard Thomas talking. When I looked up he stood by my head and wore a smirk on his face."

She pressed her lips together and tried not to cry, but tears rolled down her cheeks. "Strange hands touched me and...and..." She put her hands up on the window and leaned her head forward. "I don't know how many men had me that night. I woke up at some time and Thomas was driving us back to the condo. When I demanded he tell me what happened, he said I'd had too much to drink. He never would tell me the truth and told me it must have been a dream. What a joke that was. I could barely walk. I managed to get home to Canon City the next day and saw my doctor that week. I told him pretty much everything I remembered from that night. He said there was so much bruising, he felt certain something happened. The doctor put me through a boatload of tests for STD's and I finished them last month. The blood tests on that first visit showed traces of one of those date rape drugs. The other tests came out normal, so I was fortunate in that way. I haven't let Thomas near me since it happened. Every time he's tried to touch me, it's made my skin crawl and I want to puke."

She felt Charlie's warm hands on her shoulders and looked up to see his reflection in the window. "Don't be sorry for me, Charlie. You didn't know. Now you've heard my deep dark secret. I beg you not to say anything to Gran. She can't know about this, ever. I'll understand if you want to rethink my living here with you. I lied to you in a way, when I said I'd only been with two men," her voice faded.

"Lark, no. I have nothing to rethink, except now I wish I'd beat the shit out of that fuckhead on Sunday." He turned her around and put his hand under her chin.

She looked up at him with tears still trailing down her face. "I knew that night I would never marry him. I was too afraid of him to say anything and thought as the big day got closer, I could find an excuse to either put it off or break up with him."

"Did you ever think about filing a report for being raped with the police?"

"I did think about it, but I've been too embarrassed. I also thought if it got out in the local paper, what it would do to my business. I know too many people in this town and I didn't want to face weird looks at the grocery or on the streets. It was lame, I know, but I didn't want anyone to know. Besides my doctor, you're the only person I've told."

"I swear if he comes anywhere near you, I may just kill him." Charlie put his forehead against hers.

"No, Charlie. As nice as it sounds, you can't beat the shit out of Thomas or kill him. You'd wind up in the state prison and I would probably go completely insane."

He pulled her into his arms and wrapped her in a tight hug. Lark didn't want to cry anymore, but found she'd been storing this up for too long and everything came out for several minutes. She buried her face in the flannel on his chest.

"Once when I was on the road, I felt really depressed and alone. You know, I felt sorry for myself. I started to think maybe there would be some fun if I got drunk and met some woman to have a one night stand with. There were a couple of other drivers that I knew in the same town that night. They were going to a steakhouse for dinner and invited me to go along. I really needed to think about something other than myself so I went with them. The waitress was taking drink orders and I ordered a vodka martini straight up with twist. I'd never tasted one and saw some character in a movie order it," Charlie said.

He kissed her forehead and led her to the couch where they sat down. Lark leaned on his chest and decided to let him tell his story.

"I had two of those drinks with dinner and when the guys ordered another round, I thought I could deal with another martini. I drank the thing and started to feel not quite right. I guess my stomach wasn't happy with me, because I ended up throwing up dinner and had the worst headache of my life the next morning." He laughed. "I learned my lesson that night. I couldn't see anything good coming from getting drunk. I'll never understand my dad's addiction. I didn't like it at all."

They sat quietly for a while and Lark looked up at him. "I'm sorry, I've ruined our evening."

"No way, babe," he said and put his arms around her shoulders. "We both have bad memories from the past. You've known mine for years and now I know yours. We'll be all right and maybe understand a little better when one of us goes crazy about some things."

"There is just one thing, Ducky. When you blocked me in the hallway the other day and I freaked, I knew you weren't going to hurt me, but all those things..."

He put his fingers over her lips. "I understand what happened better now and I won't crowd you like that again. I also understand why you're touchy about your backside. I love it, but won't push you. When you trust me completely to touch your butt, we'll still discuss it first."

Lark sniffed and laughed a little. "I've noticed when you're upset your language gets a little colorful."

"Yeah, sorry about that. There are certain words needed in some situations."

"I agree. I've been known to let F-bombs fly from time to time."

Charlie looked at her and brushed tears from her cheeks. "I don't believe that for a minute. Sweetheart, let's start our evening all over. I don't know about you, but I'm tired. I think our activities last night and this morning used up some of my go power."

"I'm tired, too."

He nodded. "Okay, what if we go upstairs and get ready for bed. We'll get comfortable under the covers and talk for a while. Maybe we might snuggle a little, but not drive each other nuts until tomorrow after we've had a good night's rest."

"That's a good idea. Charlie." She looked up at him. "You're sure you still want me. After what I told you..."

He put his lips on hers and gently kissed her. "Lou, I'll always want you. I want you here with me forever."

Chapter Twenty-Two

They talked late into the night, lying next to each other. Charlie held her in his arms and felt scared to death she might run away. He only dozed a little during the night and listened to her breathe. At one point, she'd woken up suddenly and he felt her body tense. She'd made a growling noise, mumbled something and fell back to sleep.

When the gray morning light came in through the window, they spooned on their sides. Charlie held her to his chest and thought he either resembled a sausage casing or an octopus. Both arms were around her and one of his legs was between hers.

He could tell she was awake and felt her push her back in tighter with his chest. He lifted his hand and moved her hair out of her face.

"Hey, sweetheart," he said.

"Hey," she whispered.

"Did you sleep okay?"

"Off and on and there were some weird dreams." She rolled over, put her hand on his ribs and rested her head on his arm.

Charlie kissed her forehead and saw she didn't have her eyes open. "Do you have to work today?"

She finally looked up at him. "Yeah, just two more days and then things will quiet down until Valentine's Day. What time is it?"

He lifted his head and looked at the clock on his night stand. "About seven-thirty."

"I should get up soon." She touched his lips. "Ducky, we're okay, right?"

He could see fear in her eyes and wanted to erase it once and for all. "Lou, we need to get something straight. I'm not going anywhere. I'm sorry, but you're going to have to put up with me leaving clothes on the floor and coffee cups around. Now that we've slept together for the millionth time and enjoyed sex, it's a done deal. I'm not backing out."

She smiled. "Good."

"You're not backing out either, right?"

"No. I'm in for the duration."

"What time will you be home tonight?"

"Around six o'clock, I should think. Nancy and I talked about doing a marathon night, but nothing came of it. I'm still exhausted and want to just live today. I need to work hard not to let the past continue to sneak up on me. The anxiety makes me tired."

"Good. Maybe we can convince Gran to watch a movie or something."

"She'll be worn out from making pies all day. Why do you want to watch a movie?"

"I don't get to watch too much TV. It's nice to see a movie or something else every now and then. I also don't get to eat microwave popcorn very often. I know it's bad, but I do love the stuff."

"If you get the popcorn with no butter and lightly salted, it's not so bad for you."

"Eww...that sounds awful. You have to get the kind with extra-butter. It's the only way to eat popcorn."

"It shouldn't be any problem with Gran, if we want to take over the TV. She spends too much time watching the weather reports right now. Is that what you want to do tonight?"

"We could, or maybe I could take you out for dinner, but if you are thinking of something else, I'm sure I wouldn't argue with you." He moved in and kissed her lips. "Can I shower with you again this morning?"

"It's too tempting and I do have to go to work." She closed her eyes and pulled nearer to him.

"Is that a *no*?

"Let me think on it for a few minutes."

He realized she'd fallen back to sleep and decided not to disturb her. He was still shaky as to whether they could work things out. He held her and hoped they could get past the bad memories and enjoy a good life together.

She woke up an hour later and went to the shower alone. Charlie went downstairs to get coffee started and feed Breaker. He heard the shower shut off and a few minutes later her hair dryer started to buzz. It was snowing outside and looked cold.

After the wolf scarfed down his breakfast, Charlie let him out the door and watched the crazy mutt chase snowflakes around the yard. He loved that wolf and the pure pleasure the animal showed doing something so simple. He heard Lark come down the stairs and turn into the living room.

"Hey, do you want some coffee?" he asked.

"Yes, please."

He poured a cup and carried them both into the other room. He handed her one and sat next to her on the couch. He put his hand through her hair.

"Thank you." She took a sip and set it on the table. She started to put on her boots.

"Your hair's still damp and it looks cold outside." He rubbed her neck.

"It will be okay. Gran always yelled at me about catching pneumonia, but it hasn't happened yet." She shoved her foot into her boot.

"Do you have a minute before you head out?"

"For you, yes, of course." She finished her boots, picked up the cup, and turned to face him.

Charlie put his hand on her knee and she laced her fingers into his. "Sweetheart, since all that happened last night and what we talked about, I feel like there's a bit of a wall between us."

"You're right. It's the elephant in the room." She looked at him. "I have to get back to ground zero. After that night, six months ago, it took me a few weeks to not blame men for everything wrong in the world. I know in my heart, Charlie, that you're not one of those men. It's just really hard..."

"To get your head wrapped around it. I know about that," he finished her thought.

"It was such a simple thing you said and I don't know why I went off my nut. Maybe I do need to talk to a therapist."

"You know, when I was in juvie and met with that counselor, one of my main fears was that I'd turn into my dad. I was really scared to think I'd become a drunk and beat up someone. When I got out, I pretty much overcame that, but it still worries me sometimes. It's one of the reasons I'd rather drink your Gran's hot chocolate than anything with alcohol in it."

"It will be a long while before I drink anything again - except coffee. This is really good," she said and took another sip.

"Promise me one thing, Lou."

She nodded.

"If I ever do anything out of line, you'll let me know immediately." He put his pinkie up and she hooked hers around his finger.

"It's a deal, Ducky. I love you. I have always loved you. I was so stupid letting things with Thomas continue on for so long," she said.

Charlie saw tears in her eyes and put his hand on her cheek. "You weren't stupid. You want to know what is really dumb? About a year ago, I thought about coming back, but I had too many trips scheduled to make across country and put it off. If I'd only come back, I could have kept..."

Lark shook her head. "No, Charlie, you must not think that. You couldn't have known. There is no reason on earth for you to feel you could have changed things. Please, don't think that." She leaned over and kissed his lips. "You're here now and we're going to be together. I love you so much."

Charlie heard the words and his heart felt ready to explode in his chest. "I love you, too. You've taken me over, Lou, and I can't even begin to think about the possibility of losing you again. I can't."

She put her hand into his hair and kissed him again. "It's not going to happen. We're good, babe." She sat back and smiled at him. "On that note, I better get moving before I start sobbing my head off again."

"How about I help you get the chains put on the Bronco?" he said.

"What? Why?" Lark looked confused.

"It looks like it snowed all night. There's a good seven or eight inches and it's still coming down." Charlie stood up and held his hand out to her.

Lark took it and they walked to the window she'd stood by last night. "Wow, it's beautiful and, yes, to your offer to help with the chains. That would be great."

They bundled up and stomped their way to the house next door. Before they started the chains, they checked in on Gran and found her busy rolling out pie crusts on a large board that covered the kitchen table. Flour was thrown about and Gran laughed when Charlie asked if wearing flour on her cheeks was a new fashion statement.

Lark grabbed her purse and keys and they went back out and spent about thirty minutes getting the wheels on the Bronco chained up. When they'd finished, Lark got into the driver's seat and Charlie told her to drive carefully. He turned from the SUV and headed towards the back door of Gran's, when he was suddenly hit in the back of the head with a snowball. He turned around and saw Lark look at him.

"What?" he asked and held his arms out.

She scrunched her nose. "Can I have one kiss to carry me through the day?"

He wiped the snow off his shoulders and out of his hair. He'd been thinking of giving her a kiss, but didn't want to be too pushy with her. Since she suggested it, though, he felt more relaxed and hurried to the Bronco.

"Well, okay, if you insist." He leaned into the car and placed his lips on hers. He only planned to give her a light kiss, but felt her tongue glance over his bottom lip and moved in for something with more zing. When she responded to him, a lightness surrounded his heart and he knew they would be all right. He moved his gloved hand over her hair and pulled back to look in her eyes. "Will that be enough for the day?"

"Yep, but I'll want more of those tonight, for definite." She smiled and pulled her seat belt down to get strapped in. "Love you. See you tonight."

"Love you, too, babe." Charlie closed the door and watched her drive out to the road.

****

Lark got to work safely and spent the morning in her office. She checked orders and accounts. There hadn't been any word from Ryan Barton yet, but she felt confident he'd contact them by the end of the day.

After she ate lunch, she went down onto the floor and helped the packaging folks get boxes put together. There were still a ton of orders to get ready to ship and it made her proud of the employees when they offered to stay extra hours that night and the next. They wanted to get as many of the shipments out as they could. She needed to tell Nancy what a terrific group of people worked for them.

At around three o'clock in the afternoon, Nancy appeared out of nowhere with a distressed look on her face. "I need to talk to you," she said to Lark.

"Okay, talk," Lark answered and finished taping off a box.

"Not here, let's go upstairs." Nancy turned and started toward the stairs.

Lark put the tape down, followed her up the stairs and into the offices. She saw Nancy look at Alicia and then turn into her office.

She closed the door and turned to her friend. "What's going on?"

"Ryan just called. He found out who the anonymous buyer is," Nancy said and seemed to hold her breath.

"So, who is it?" Lark asked.

"You're not going to like it."

"Nancy, please, just tell me." Lark suddenly felt a knot form in her stomach and didn't like where this was going.

"It's Thomas. He apparently talked to the National people into looking at our loan. He's already put the money into an account to buy it once the deal is finished with Canon City Savings."

Lark let the words sink into her brain. "Shit." She sat down in a chair by Nancy's desk. Her brain scrambled all over the place, but Lark knew only one thing for certain. She was pissed and it would only get worse. She saw Nancy's lips move, but her blood thundered through her veins and she couldn't hear the words.

She stood up and headed to the door. Nancy caught her arm. "What can we do?"

"I want answers and there's only one person who can give them to me." Lark walked out the door and went into her office. She grabbed her purse out of a drawer and took her coat off the back of her chair.

"Where are you going, Lark?" Nancy stood in the doorway.

She looked at her friend and business partner. "Denver."

"No, that's nuts. The roads are terrible and that storm is still moving through. We're supposed to get another foot of snow tonight and the wind's going to kick up. Lark, don't even think it."

Lark put her coat on and zipped it up. She took her keys out of her purse. "I'll be okay. Charlie put the chains on this morning, so I should be all right on the road. I'm sure the highway department has cleared I-25. Don't worry, I'll take it easy." She walked through the door, passed Nancy and stopped. "You know, Charlie said last night he wished he'd beaten the shit out of

Thomas on Sunday when he hit me. I should have taken him up on it."

"Lark, be careful, please. I don't want to owe a quarter of a million and have to find a new partner in the same week." Nancy followed her down the stairs.

"We made it okay last week and didn't even have the chains on." Lark went down the stairs and out the exit door. In the parking lot, she looked up at the sky on her way to the Bronco. "Dear Lord, just get me there in one piece. We'll decide what happens on the road home after I take a tire iron to Thomas."

Chapter Twenty-Three

It generally took two hours to get to Denver from Canon City, but with the weather, it was about three and a half hours for Lark. The roads were cleared, but it continued to snow and the wind gusts blew snow back onto the highway. She took it easy and startled herself when she discovered she was going fifty miles per hour. She eased off the gas and tried to keep the Bronco steady between thirty and forty. It was after six o'clock in the evening when she pulled into the driveway at the condominium she and Thomas shared. She wondered how he'd feel when she demanded the whole amount of the down payment she'd put into the place.

She saw his car in the parking lot and pulled in next to it. *He's home early*, she thought and got out of the Bronco. She stood next to the open door for a moment and remembered why she was there. Little tendrils of fear moved into her stomach and she didn't want to go into this scared. She wanted to stand up to him and find out what game he played. She decided to leave her purse in the Bronco, put her keys in her pocket when she had second thoughts and leaned over the seat to grab her purse. She dug around and found the small can of hairspray she'd put in there some time ago. Shaking the can, she could hear fluid inside and thought if he got out of line she could spray it in his eyes and get away. She also found her boot knife and put them both into her other pocket.

She locked the car door, slammed it shut and walked toward the condo. She went up the steps to the front door and put the key in the lock. She turned it and let out a breath.

The front hallway was lit, but the living room looked dark, as did the kitchen. She slowly made her way down the hall and stopped at the table where they usually put their keys in a bowl and left the mail. His keys were there and a pile of mail. She looked through it and pulled out a couple of envelopes with her name on them. She saw one addressed to him from the National Savings and Loan and decided to take it, too. She stuffed them into the back of her pants. *Great, I'll be arrested for mail theft*, she thought.

She went into the living room, turned on a lamp and looked around the room. There was only one thing she wanted from this place. She knew exactly where it was and would get it. *It* was a jewelry box that belonged to her mother. Inside it was her mother's engagement ring and she wanted that back. Thomas could do what he wanted with the rest of her stuff.

"Thomas, where the fuck are you?" she shouted. She'd decided on the drive up that she would use a lot of colorful language. Thomas hated that and she hoped it would make his high blood pressure go even higher.

She heard a noise come from the bedroom and the door flew open. Thomas was putting on a robe as he walked out into the living room.

"Lark, I didn't expect to see you until Saturday. You must have had quite a drive up this afternoon. You look done in." He moved toward her with his hands out.

She took a couple of steps back and put an easy chair between them. "Why?"

He frowned and looked confused. "Why what, dear? Why do you look done in? How would I know?"

"Why are you trying to buy out my loan for my business?"

"Ah, I see." He crossed his arms and shifted his feet apart. "How else was I going to convince you to move to Denver? You wouldn't even discuss leaving Canon City. I never have understood why you wanted to stay there. It's a nothing town. No theater, no decent restaurants..."

"No clubs?"

He ignored her comment. "I've decided to buy you and Nancy out and close the doors. I will ruin your business and you will agree to move here to Denver."

"I'll fight you on this. My attorney is at this moment making arrangements to derail your train. We're done, Thomas. If you want to keep thinking you'll take over the business, you're deluded."

"Thomas, come on, baby. I'm waiting for you and it's getting cold," a female voice called from the bedroom.

Lark frowned and pushed past him to the door. When she opened it, she felt completely stunned to see a blonde woman lying naked on the bed. She'd been handcuffed to the bed posts and her legs were spread wide open. Lark saw some of Thomas's favorite toys spread out between her legs.

"I don't even want to know about this," she said and turned to the dresser. She opened the top drawer and uncovered her jewelry box. She took it out and started back to the door.

"Who are you?" the woman asked.

"Shut up, Tina," Thomas snarled and blocked the doorway.

"I suppose you've cheated on me all along." Lark shook her head and smirked at Thomas.

"You leave me alone all too often, my dear. What did you expect? I'm a virile man and I have my needs."

Lark smiled at Tina. "I'm the ex-fiancée. I should warn you, he likes to drug his women and share them with other men." She started to turn, slipped her hand into her pocket and then stopped. "Oh, and he likes to hit women. That's how I got this bruise on my chin. Watch out honey. He's got a nasty right hand slap." She opened the jewelry box and took out the ring Thomas gave to her when he proposed. Setting it on the dresser, she snapped the box shut and put her hand back in her pocket.

When she was five feet from him and realized he wasn't going to move, she looked him in the eyes. "Get out of the way, asshole. We have nothing to discuss. My attorney will be in touch."

"You're certainly not thinking about going back out in that weather. Why don't you stay and we could have some fun." He looked over her shoulder at the woman lying on the bed. "Tina is much more adventurous than you are and you could learn a trick or two from her."

"Now I'm going to puke. You might find it of interest, Thomas, that Charlie Stone made love to me two nights ago. It was the best I've ever had and he even gave me three orgasms. I'll say it again; he gave me, unlike you who never gave me any kind of orgasm. I sucked his cock until he shot his semen into my throat. It was pure heaven," she said and could tell she'd hit a nerve. Thomas looked like he was winding up to hit her. She took the hairspray out of her pocket and shot it at his face.

"Dammit, you bitch. What have you done?" he shouted and doubled over.

Lark saw a hole that she could get through, but stopped next to him. "Be glad it wasn't mace. Thomas, you're a supreme fuckhead and I hope you get what you deserve."

She stormed out of the condo, and left the front door open. When she reached the parking lot, she ran through the snow to her car. Her hand shook and it took a second to get the key in the lock, but when she was inside with the doors locked, she felt safe. She looked out the windshield and noticed that the snow came down double time.

***

Lark watched the road with an eagle eye. Because the snow was coming down harder and the radio said the wind had kicked up to sixty miles per hour gusts, it was going to take even longer to get home. She held the Bronco steady at thirty miles per hour. The road was covered in white and it became next to impossible to see the lines, except when she went under the over passes, where there was clear black road for about ten feet.

She tried not to think of the scene she'd witnessed at the condo, but, like a dog with a favorite bone, she found she continued to think about it. A part of her was furious with Thomas and his scheming to takeover of her business. The part that really pissed her off though was the hurt she felt that he'd cheated on her. It was a feeling that would go away with time, but it made her wonder how long he'd cheated and why she didn't see the signs?

Since she cut him off from touching her for the last six months, was Tina the only one he'd been having sex with or were there others? She felt like such an idiot for the amount of time she'd wasted by staying with him.

She decided she'd have to think about all this later and tried to block the subject from her mind. She forced herself to concentrate on the drive and realized the weather approached white out conditions. She knew she wasn't too far from an exit to a truck stop. She slowed down to fifteen miles per hour and tried to read the road markers or signs covered up by blowing snow.

Lark heard something thunk under the front of the right side of her SUV and then bumped over something else. The Bronco started to slide toward the break down lane and she thought the snow piled up along the road by the highway crews would stop the sideways movement. When she hit the snow, her wheels slid on some ice and spun her vehicle around. The momentum pushed it through the snow and the Bronco moved off the road into a ditch. It flipped over and landed on the driver's side. The airbag popped out and hit her in the face and chest. Her head slammed on the driver's side window and she felt herself losing consciousness.

Chapter Twenty-Four

Aurora Metcalfe put on her coat after eight o'clock and carefully made her way over to Charlies. She knocked on the door and waited. The porch light came on and he opened the door with Breaker by his side.

"Are you crazy, Gran? You could have blown away like Mary Poppins or broken something." He opened the door and let her into the house. "Let me take your coat," he offered.

"Charlie, I'm worried. Lark should be home by now. I've tried and tried to call her, but it keeps going to her voicemail."

"When did you last talk to her?" Charlie asked as he hung up her coat.

"This morning when you two came in and she got ready for work. I've been baking all day." She followed him into the kitchen where he offered her a chair.

"Is there anyone you can call at the warehouse who might know when she left?" He held up the coffee pot. "Would you like a cup?"

"A cup of coffee would be great and Charlie Stone you're a genius. I should have thought to call

Nancy." She popped open her cell phone and dialed a number.

Charlie poured the coffee. She looked up at him and thanked him. He remained silent and seemed to listen to her side of the phone call.

"Hi, this is Aurora Metcalfe. Who's this?" A little voice on the other end told her his name. "Oh, hi Jacob. Is your Mom there?" She took a sip of the coffee. "Hi Nancy, do you have any idea when Lark left the warehouse?" she asked.

"She left about three o'clock. It wasn't good Aurora. We found out that Thomas is the one trying to take over the business. She was pissed and left for Denver."

Aurora looked up at Charlie. "She did what? Why on earth did...What?"

"I think she planned to give him a piece of her mind. I told her not to go. The roads are getting really bad. Jim just got in from work and it took him twice as long to get home." Nancy said and sounded as worried as Aurora felt.

She saw Charlie lean against the counter and cross his arms. She continued to look at him and felt her stomach twist.

"Oh, Lord. She must have been very angry." Aurora looked at her watch.

"If she left at three o'clock, it could have taken her three to four hours to get to Denver. It depends on if she met up with Thomas or not, but if she was there for only a half hour or so, she probably wouldn't be back yet."

"It would depend on the roads. Nance, if you hear from her will you give me a call? We'll let you know if we hear anything. Thank you." She ended the call. "Charlie, now I'm really worried. Lark and Nancy found out today that Thomas is the one trying to buy their loan. Lark got very angry and took off to confront him in Denver."

She watched Charlie look out the kitchen window and grab the edge of the counter. "Gran, call the highway patrol and ask them to keep an eye out for her. Do you know Thomas's phone number?"

"Yes, but I'm not going to call him. The jerk would probably lie to us one way or the other." She looked at her phone and hit zero for the operator. "Yes, I need the Colorado Highway

Patrol in Pueblo...yes, thank you." She turned to Charlie. "The operator is connecting me," she said.

Charlie started to put on his coat and gloves. "Gran, I'm going to chain up my rig, just in case." He went out the door and the freezing wind blew into the house.

She went to the window with her phone up to her ear and heard a voice answer. "Yes, thank you. I want to file a report. My granddaughter is somewhere on Highway 25 and hasn't called. I know your people are very busy tonight. I just want them to keep an eye out for her."

She watched Charlie pull the chains out of a bin on the back of the truck. The wind blew through his hair and she thought he must be freezing out there. He got up into the truck and she saw the lights come on and she could hear the engine start. He jumped out of the truck and started to get the chains in place.

"What is her name and what type of vehicle is she driving?" a voice asked.

"Her name is Lark Metcalfe; she drives a red Ford Bronco. The license number is EYD 883."

"What number can we call if we find her?" the woman on the other end said.

Aurora admired the precision and speed with which Charlie got the tires chained. He seemed to know the best and most efficient way to get the job done. Although she was worried sick about Lark, she felt very proud of him.

She heard her cell phone ring in her hands and hurried to get it turned back on. She thought the highway patrol might have found Lark. She looked at the message screen and saw it was Lark.

"Sweetheart, are you all right? Where are you?"

"Hey Gran. I was really dumb and drove to Denver to..."

"We know about what Thomas is doing. I talked to Nancy when you didn't come home. Where are you now?"

"My car slid off the road and I'm stuck in a ditch. I was just north of exit 104. I thought I'd pull in at the truck stop and wait out the storm, but I didn't get there. I didn't want to worry you and tried to call the highway patrol, but their lines are busy."

"Lark, are you okay?" Aurora went to the back door and put her hand on the knob.

"I think so. I'm wearing my flannel lined pants and have blankets."

She opened the door and stepped onto the porch. "Charlie!" she shouted as loud as she could. She shouted a couple more times and then Breaker ran out of the house straight a Charlie. The wolf nipped at his leg. It caused Charlie to turn around. Aurora motioned for him to come in and went back into the house.

****

Charlie put the T-bar on the back of the truck and walked back to the house. Breaker raced ahead of him and blew through the door. *Crazy wolf*, Charlie thought.

"Honey, Charlie's getting his truck ready to go. Here he is." Gran handed him the phone. "I'm going next door to get a thermos. I'll be right back."

He put the phone up to his ear. "Baby, are you okay?"

"Don't tell Gran, but I bumped my head and got run over by my airbag. I don't think anything is broken."

"Where are you?"

"I was southbound on I-25. I'm somewhere between exits 105 and 104. I'm off the road, but I don't think I was that far from 104."

"Is the Bronco running?"

"I can get the lights on and the heat, but the engine won't turn over and it's lying on its side. I don't know why I even tried to start it. I'm not going anywhere. I think that side of it is toast."

"Sweetheart, Gran called the highway patrol to keep an eye out. I've got the chains almost put on my truck. Keep the phone close. I will find you."

"Ducky, are you sure? It's really bad out here."

"I've driven in worse and I love you too much to let you freeze your butt off out there. Do you have a flashlight?"

"You're going to make me cry. Yes, I have a flashlight."

"Hunker down, Lou. Keep the phone on and stay as warm as you can. I'll be there in an hour or so."

"Charlie, be careful. It was near white out when I slid off the road."

"I'll call you when I leave here."

Gran came in the back door and carried a thermos and a thermal bag. "I'm going to put some coffee in the thermos and I got some of the pot roast and potatoes in the thermal. It should keep it warm."

"I'm almost finished with the chains. Will you keep an eye on Breaker?"

"Of course."

"Gran, can I take your phone? I don't have one yet."

"Yes, certainly." She handed it back to him.

"I'll need a quick how-to lesson when I finish the tires. The only thing I'll need to know is how to reach Lark."

Chapter Twenty-Five

Within half an hour, Charlie pulled the truck onto the highway and headed east to Pueblo. He'd called Lark to let her know he was on his way. It usually took thirty minutes to get to Pueblo, but tonight it would be longer. The roads were bad. The highway crews were doing their best to clear them, but the wind kept blowing the snow back onto the road. An hour and a half later, Charlie took the entrance to I-25 north and watched the road signs. He wanted exit 105 so he could turn around and head south.

****

Lark sat on the passenger door of the Bronco with a blanket wrapped around her. The window under her butt was cracked, but with another blanked piled on top of it, she didn't feel the cold. The SUV protected her from the wind, but unless she turned the heat on periodically, the inside got very cold.

She'd cried after she'd talked to Charlie. He risked so much to come out in this weather to find her and she couldn't wait to see him. This whole mess taught her several very important lessons that she would hold onto forever. She realized she loved Charlie more than anything and wanted to spend the rest of her life giving him everything. He was patient and kind to her and laughed at himself easily. She also learned that no matter how mad she was, she should stay off the road in a snowstorm.

Lark only hoped she didn't freeze to death before she could tell Charlie everything in her heart. She giggled a little when she thought if she did freeze, she would have to come back to haunt him, which then struck her as a morose thought and she stopped that train right then.

****

Once Charlie got turned around at exit 105 and headed south, he pulled into the emergency lane with his flashers on and picked up Gran's phone. He hit the Send button and listened to it ring.

"Hi Gran," Lark answered.

"It's me, babe. I just got turned at exit 105 and I'm facing south on I-25. Can you get up to a window facing the road?"

"The car's on its side, Ducky. I think I can stand up. Let me see if I can get the window...ah, shit."

"What happened?" He could hear something bang on the phone line.

"The auto window works. I just got a snow shower on the head." She laughed.

Charlie smiled and was glad to hear her laugh. "I'm going to start blowing my air horn. Let me know when you hear it."

He let the gears out and started to move slowly forward. After he'd shoot the horn off, he'd count to ten and repeat it. He'd gone about half a mile when Lark told him she could hear it.

"How loud?"

"It sounds like you're in the distance."

He continued to move the truck forward and blew the horn again. "Is it louder?"

"Yes."

"What about now?"

"Yep, it's louder."

"Sweetie, grab your flashlight and blink it through the window." He tried to see something along the road and not run himself into the ditch. He hit the horn again.

"That was louder, Ducky. I can hear your truck, too."

"I can see you, babe. I'll be there in two seconds." He put the truck into park and left the hazard lights blinking. He jumped out and made his way through the snow to her SUV. It was half buried and he didn't think he could get her out of the bottom. He brushed the snow off the rear window which wouldn't open. The latch seemed to be jammed. He looked around the area and found a thick tree limb. He tested it to see if it was strong and then threw it up onto the side of the Bronco.

He moved to the under carriage and used it to maneuver himself up to the side of the SUV. He looked in the open window and saw Lark look up at him. "Hey there, Lou, fancy meeting you here." He smiled. "I'm going to see if I can get the door open. Can you move to the backseat?"

"Yeah, I think so."

He watched her get into the back and when she was out of the way, he bent over the door and grabbed the handle. He used all his strength to pull it up and propped the branch he'd found on the side of the truck. He lowered the door onto it and made sure it would hold the door open.

He brushed some of the snow away from the opening and looked in again. "Babe, are you ready to go home?" He saw her smile up at him and move back to the front seat. "The weather is still pretty crappy. It might be best to stop at exit 104 and see what it looks like in the morning. Have you got everything you need?" She nodded. He leaned down and put his hand through the door for her to grab. "Come to me, my pretty."

He could hear her laugh and could see her use the seats to step up. He pulled her half way out and then grabbed the back of her pants to get her the rest of the way out.

"Thank you, Charlie, but I think you gave me a wedgie."

He helped her stand up. "Yeah, we'll get that fixed shortly." He showed her the best way down and once she was on the ground, he shut the door and jumped down. He put his arm around her and helped her get to the road. They made their way to his truck and he got her situated into the seat. He stood on the step and helped her remove her boots.

"Are your feet dry?" He rubbed her feet.

"Yes," she said and her teeth chattered.

"Where's the bump on your head?" She pointed to the side of her forehead. He gently put his fingers on it and saw the lump. "You'll have another bruise, but it doesn't look too bad. Did you lose consciousness?" She shook her head. "Okay, crawl in back to the sleeper. There are blankets and a sleeping bag back there to help you warm up."

She nodded and turned around to get into the back. Charlie stepped back to the ground and closed the door.

When he got the truck back onto the road, he let out a breath. He felt very lucky to find her. "It's a good thing the Bronco is red. I might have missed it if you'd gotten a lighter color," he said.

"It will be easy to find in the spring when the snow melts."

"Naw, we'll have to get a tow truck with a trailer. It looks like you blew a tire in the front and the axle and shock absorbers are gone. I'll take care of it tomorrow or Friday when the weather clears." She didn't respond and Charlie tried to see her in the rearview mirror. "Lou, are you okay back there? Are you getting warmed up?"

"Yeah, I'm okay."

"We're almost to the truck stop. Gran sent some coffee with me and food." He followed the exit and found his way to the truck stop. He pulled into a parking spot and set the brake. "I'll be right back, babe. I have to go and pee. Gran said to call her landline when we were safe." He looked over his seat and saw Lark snuggled down under the blankets. "I've been thinking about the bump on your head. Do you really feel okay or should I try to get you to the hospital?"

"No." She pulled the blanket down off her face. "I'm all right, really. I'll call Gran."

Charlie ran into the truck stop and found the men's-room. He didn't want to leave Lark alone for long and hurried. He went back out to the truck. It was still snowing, but the wind seemed to be dying down some. He opened the door and stepped up into the truck. He looked into the back, again, and saw Lark sitting up with her chin on her knees. She had a sheet of paper in her hand and was staring straight ahead.

He sat sideways on his seat and leaned against the door. He reached back to her and touched her shoulder. "Hey, are you in there?"

She smiled a little. "Yeah, I'm in here." She folded up the letter and put it in her purse. "Did I mention that I go off my nut from time to time and drive into blizzards?"

"No, you didn't tell me about that."

"Gran yelled at me and I think I'll hear more when we get home." She looked at him. "Are you mad at me?"

"No, I'm not mad so much as wondering what you were thinking."

"I thought I could get up to Denver and back in a reasonable amount of time. I hoped to be home before the storm got really bad. I didn't plan to drive into a ditch."

Charlie laughed and watched as she leaned against the side of the truck. She stretched her legs out and closed her eyes. She moved slowly to get her coat off and he leaned over to help pull the sleeve down.

"How come you leave the engine running, Ducky?"

"It keeps the cab warm and it's easier to get moving in the morning. If you shut it off, it can take a half hour to wake up."

She opened her eyes and looked at him, again. "Charlie, everything is completely finished with

Thomas...well, almost completely. Did I mention I'm a mail thief?"

He sat up and felt his brows crease. "When did you become a mail thief?"

"Today. I was at the condo and there was a pile of mail waiting for me. I noticed Thomas left his mail on the same table and looked through it. I found a letter from the National Savings and Loan and stuffed it into the back of my pants with my mail. I just had to take it."

"Why?"

"I think my attorney will find it interesting. It says nothing will happen until after the first of the year with them buying up the loan. Ryan said it was all moot anyway. There's a clause that keeps Canon City from selling the loan without giving us sixty days notice." She shrugged. "It should work out, I think." She folded her hands in her lap.

"You don't sound convinced."

"I just have to be patient and see what happens." She closed her eyes again.

"Was he there at the condo?" Charlie asked, quietly. He'd debated asking this question, but now wanted to know.

"Yes. He had a naked woman named Tina handcuffed to the bed."

"What?"

"All of his toys were spread out between her legs and ready to go." She shivered and brought her knees back up. "I don't even want to think about it. I asked him why he was trying to buy the loan. He said he was going to close the business so I'd move to Denver. He acted rude. In fact, when I told him I'd had the best sex of my life with you two days ago, I thought that he might hit me, again." She shrugged and looked at him. "I don't know what his plan was, so I sprayed hairspray in his eyes. I know for a fact it burns like hell. I don't know what I ever saw in that man."

Charlie laughed and then said, "Remind me never to take you on. Hairspray? That's great."

"Ducky, why are you so far away from me?"

He stopped laughing and held his hand out to her. "I didn't want to crowd you, sweetheart."

"You can crowd me anytime, anywhere, twenty-four/seven. I love it when I can feel your warm body next to mine."

Charlie moved between the seats and sat on the edge of the sleeper mattress. He took his coat off and threw it back into the front. "Lark, I don't ever want to handcuff you to furniture. I've worn them and I'd never do that to you. The bondage thing just isn't of any interest to me."

She took his hand. "I'm glad to hear it. That game isn't really my cup of tea, either." She leaned forward and put her hands around his neck. She traced his lips with her finger. "Ducky, I really love your kisses. They make my heart pound and I lose my breath." She kissed his chin.

"I don't know if you're aware of this, but I seem to have a crazy illness." He put his hands around her and saw her frown. "The minute you're near me, or if I touch you, I'm instantly hard. It's the strangest thing, because it only happens with you."

She put her hand on the inside of his thigh and moved it up. She brushed his lips. "Thank you for saving me tonight." She moved her hand on his shaft and he sighed. "Can I see if I can help your illness?" she asked.

Charlie sucked in his breath as her fingers applied a bit of pressure to his penis. "Are you warmed up enough?" He saw her nod and smile. "I...I better close the blinds." He put his lips on her and nibbled her tongue.

"What blinds?" she asked and pulled her head back with a curious look on her face.

"This truck has really great options." He moved back to the front and started to pull the blinds down on the windows. "Privacy is a must if you sleep in the buff."

Lark slid her sweater off when the front window was covered. He saw it fly over the seat and turned to see her pull her turtle neck off. His body warmed as she sat looking up at him in her lacy bra. Charlie pulled his shirt and thermal undershirt off and put it in the seat and started to undo his pants. He couldn't take his eyes off Lark. She was the most beautiful woman he'd ever seen. He saw the bruise on her chest and moved toward her. He stood over her and lightly touched the blue green mark.

He sat on the edge of the sleeper and put his hand on her cheek. "Lou, I swear to you on all I hold dear, I will never hurt you like this."

Lark put her hand over his. "I know. I really do know that. In my heart and in my head I'm so sure of you. I missed you so much when you were gone and I'm so happy you're back."

Charlie pulled her into his arms and felt her hands on his back. He put his hand into her hair and kissed her neck. "God, I love you," he whispered.

"Ducky?" She looked up at him. "I know I'm a slut, but it's gotten warm in here and I think we have too many clothes on."

"You're my slut and you read my mind."

They both shed the rest of their clothes and Charlie snuggled under the blankets with her. They kissed and touched each other's body over and over. They laughed and lost their breath. They spooned and loved one another.

Chapter Twenty-Six

The next morning Lark woke up and realized the sun shone brightly. She smiled and woke Charlie up. They dressed and went into the truck stop restrooms to get cleaned up. They enjoyed a nice breakfast in the coffee shop and she loved to watch him from across the table. When they finished they decided to head home.

It took Charlie a couple of tries to get the truck out of the parking lot. Lark was the happiest she'd been in a very long time.

"Ducky, while you're driving will it bother you if I stare at your incredibly handsome self?" She turned sideways and put her feet up on the edge of his seat.

"It's a beautiful morning out there, Lou. I'm sure there are prettier things to look at than me," he said and steered the truck onto the highway.

"I don't agree. The most gorgeous hunk is right here in the driver's seat." She smiled and arched her eyebrow. "Would you mind if I got a little serious for a minute?"

"For you, my love, anything."

"First, and most important, thank you for coming to my rescue last night in that horrible weather. You've always been my hero and it makes me love you more." She put her feet down between the seats. "While I waited for you in the Bronco, I had some time to think about what Thomas was up to yesterday - and six months ago. I remember the location of that mansion." She looked at him. "I'm going to talk to my attorney today, and ask him if it's too late to file a complaint."

"Do you mean against Thomas?"

"I'd more than love to see him pay, but it would probably turn into a 'he said, she said' situation."

"Yeah, I think you're right on that one."

"I'll talk to Ryan. Maybe I could do something without being identified that could close that *club*. That mansion needs to be torn down and burned."

"I agree and you've got my support all the way. Whatever you decide to do, babe, I'll be right there with you." He reached his hand across the cab to her.

She put her hand in his. "Do you know what?" She saw him glance at her and shake his head. "I want to go back to that mansion and cut off some dicks. Do you think that would be rude and maybe just a little bit psycho?" She smiled at him.

Charlie looked at her with faked shock on his face. "Your true colors are showing, my darling. Can I watch?" He laughed. "The next time you decide to take off in a blizzard, please, let me know," Charlie said.

"Oh my Lord, we were supposed to have dinner and a movie last night. I completely forgot. I'm sorry, babe." Lark heard him laugh, again. "What?"

"Lou, I had a really great dinner last night. We can watch the movie anytime. Weren't you there?"

Lark snickered. "Yes, I was there and enjoyed every minute. You are fantastic under the blankets, Ducky." She felt warmth move into her cheeks and couldn't believe she'd blushed.

"Are you okay? Your face has gone all red." Charlie grinned at her.

"You are a devil sometimes, Charlie Stone. It makes me love you even more than five minutes ago."

"Are we still being serious?" he asked.

She nodded. "Sure."

"Do you know when I first started to really love you?"

"No."

"We were maybe twelve or thirteen. It was during the summer and we were sitting by the river watching the rafters take off. You asked me how I'd really gotten the black eye I had. I told you about my dad hitting me and talked for over an hour. You never interrupted me once and just listened. I knew you heard everything I said and it really meant a lot to me then. It still does."

"Do you know when I first started falling in love with you?" She smiled and popped her lips. She saw him shake his head. "I was thirteen and Bobbie What's-his-face was teasing me about being an orphan and said all kinds of crude remarks. You bloodied his nose and became my hero. It was the first time I thought, *Ducky is going to be my boyfriend someday.*"

"Am I your boyfriend now?" He grinned and watched the road.

"You bet your butt, and I like it." She laughed.

The drive took a little longer than they thought it would. As they neared Canon City, sanding trucks ahead of them caused the traffic to slow down.

It was after eleven o'clock when they pulled into Charlie's driveway. Lark looked over at Gran's driveway and saw there were four other cars parked there.

"Looks as though Gran's got company." Charlie set the brake.

"Yeah, one of the cars belongs to Nancy. I don't recognize the others."

Charlie turned the truck off and jumped out. He ran to the other side and opened the door. Lark took his offered hand and stepped down out of the truck. They walked arm in arm next door and the minute Lark opened the door, they were attacked by Breaker. The wolf put his paws on Charlie's chest and licked his face.

Lark saw Gran come in from the living room and head straight for her. They hugged and when Gran pulled back, she looked directly at Lark.

"If you ever do that again, I will ground you for life," Gran whispered.

Lark nodded. "Right. Got it. I promise to never do that again." They smiled at each other. "What's going on here? Why is Nancy here?"

"About an hour ago, there was a knock on the door. Mike Strom is here with his son and they brought their attorney. I called Nancy and she got in touch with Ryan Barton. They turned up about half an hour ago and have already eaten one of my pies for the dance. They wanted to wait for you to get home," she continued in a whisper.

When Lark and Charlie entered the living room the men stood and Mike Strom walked up to her. He was tall and gray-haired and Lark always thought he was attractive for an older man. He was aging very well.

"Hello, Miss Metcalfe. Your grandmother said you'd been in an accident last night. I hope you're all right." He shook her hand and covered it with his other hand.

"I'm fine. My SUV slid into a ditch on I-25. It was a good thing I was going so slow," she said and then they made introductions all around.

Mike shook hands with Charlie and then his son Zack stepped up to him. "Didn't we go to school together?" he asked Charlie.

"Yes, we did, from kindergarten on to middle school. You were always picking on Lark and I believe we had a few fights over it."

Zack laughed. "That was you? Man, you got tall."

They all sat down and Mike took over the room. "Lark, I'm sorry I didn't call you sooner. We were up at Jasper and had a terrible time with phones. I got your messages on Monday and looked into the loan immediately." He glanced at his son with a frown. "I want to apologize for the actions of my son and the loan department at the savings and loan. If they'd read the contract completely, they would have seen the clause which says loans will not be moved, sold or otherwise without my permission. The loan for Mile High Bread will not be sold to those assholes up in Denver."

Lark and Nancy looked at one another and smiled. "Thank you very much, Mike," Lark said.

"Ladies, I hope all of this hasn't caused you too much distress. My attorney, Mr. Singleton" - he motioned at the man who sat across from them - "drew up a new contract which he's been discussing with Mr. Barton. It makes it clear that nothing like this will ever happen again. He's given a copy to Mr. Barton, who will advise you on the details. Your business is very important to Canon City and you know how determined

I am to see local businesses stay put. I would hate to lose your grandmothers Apple Crumb Cake mix to one of those mass dealers back east." He looked at Gran. "Aurora, it's the best cake I've ever eaten in Colorado."

They talked for a little longer and it was easy to see that Zack felt uncomfortable. He confessed that he'd met Thomas at a business meeting in Denver a few months ago, and the idea started there. He, too, apologized, but looked as though he wasn't all that sorry. Lark thought Charlie was right when he said Zack was a dick.

Everyone stood up and prepared to leave. Lark looked at Nancy and smiled. "That was an easier finish than I thought it would be."

"Yeah, Mike Strom will be my hero for a while." Nancy leaned toward her. "I've always had a crush on him," she whispered.

"Can you say *daddy figure*?" Lark laughed with her partner. "I'm so sorry this happened Nance. I should have dumped Thomas a long time ago."

"It wasn't your fault. There's no need for you to be sorry. It was just a little hiccup."

"I love your attitude, partner."

She felt Charlie's hands on her waist and looked up at him.

"That seemed to go well," he said.

"Yes, it did. We haven't been properly introduced. You must be Charlie." Nancy smiled at him and they shook hands. "Will we see you at the dance on Friday?"

"I'm very pleased to meet you, Nancy. Yep, I'm not much of a dancer, but I plan to be there."

Lark saw Ryan head for the back door. "I'll be right back." She moved out of Charlie's hold and caught up with the attorney in the kitchen.

She spoke quietly and gave him a brief rundown of what happened to her six months before. She didn't go into all of the details, but still felt embarrassed by her stupidity. It only took a few minutes. Ryan took his coat off the hook and turned around to her.

****

Charlie saw Lark steer the attorney into the kitchen and talk to him privately. He knew exactly what she was telling him and felt amazed she could confront the issue so well. He stood with Gran and then Zack walked over to start a conversation. Charlie didn't pay much attention to him.

He watched Lark as she did most of the talking. She'd grasped her hands in front of her and he could tell by the way she held herself that she wasn't comfortable. The attorney took a pad of paper out of his pocket and made some notes and nodded every now and then.

Finally, the attorney took his coat off the hook and headed out the back door with Lark following. Charlie left Gran and Zack and walked to the door to look out the window. He saw Lark still talking and periodically stop to let the other guy put in a word.

The man put his hand on hers, said something and then got into his car. Lark turned to the house and hugged her chest.

Charlie opened the door for her and she walked directly into his arms.

"Brrr, it's cold out there. I should have put on a coat." She moved in closer.

He wrapped his arms around her tight. "Are you okay?"

"Yeah." She looked up at him. "Ryan's going to call the district attorney in Denver and an attorney here in Canon City who has more experience with this kind of case."

"Your guy can't handle it?"

"He specializes in business law. He admitted this was out of his realm of practice, which is pretty humble for an attorney. They can have pretty big egos sometimes."

"That's good that he could admit it." Charlie saw Gran purse her lips at them. "Sweetheart, Gran just gave me the evil eye. I think we need to go be more sociable."

"Damn, I wanted you to screw my lights out right here and now, just like we did last night at the truck stop, but, okay. I'll behave."

They laughed and walked back into the living room.

Chapter Twenty-Seven

Friday, the day of the big dance, finally arrived. The weather remained calm since the storm on Wednesday and it warmed up to thirty degrees. The news programs from Denver were all excited since the area of Pueblo and Canon City got way above their yearly average of snow.

Lark heard several times at the warehouse that people hadn't seen such a storm since 1982, but Gran said the worst storm she remembered was in March of 1961. That was the year Lark's father was born and Gran remembered it as a nerve-wracking night, but wouldn't go into details. Lark threw her hands up and figured they could all discuss the weather at the dance.

On Friday morning, Ryan called Lark and gave her the name of the female attorney in Denver to talk to about the attack. She left a message for the woman who called her back mid-morning. Lark tried to stay calm, but it felt really difficult to discuss what happened with a total stranger. The attorney said she was pleased Lark decided to come forward about that night. She'd received calls from several other new clients who told similar stories from other nights at the mansion. There were a mountain of complaints about the activities and the district attorney was compiling information to build a case. She asked if Lark would come up to Denver after the New Year and give a deposition. Lark agreed immediately and spoke with the woman's secretary to schedule the appointment.

The plan for Mile High Bread was to close at three o'clock so the employees could head home and get ready for the evening's festivities. Although most of the employees were not members of the Methodist Church, it was a community gathering and the doors were open to everyone. Year after year, the dance seemed to get bigger and bigger.

Lark headed home in a rental car after three o'clock and pulled into the driveway. She needed to get changed and take Gran and her pies over to the church to set up. She noticed Charlie's truck was not parked in his driveway and wondered where he'd gone off to in the big rig. She decided to wait until after Christmas to tell Gran about the attack six months ago. She didn't want to spoil her holidays.

She walked into the house and took her coat and boots off. She saw the pies all boxed up on the kitchen table and could hear Gran's footsteps on the floor above. She went up the stairs and knocked on Gran's door. She opened it and peeked in.

"Hey Gran, I'm home."

"Hi sweetheart," Gran said from the foot of her bed where she sat putting on a pair of pantyhose.

"Did Charlie say where he was going today?"

"No. He did say he would meet us at the community center. Lord, I don't know why I decided to wear a dress." She continued with the pantyhose struggle. "Slacks would be so much simpler."

"Gran, you say that every year and then turn out to be the prettiest woman there." Lark looked at her watch. "I better get changed."

As she walked to her room her cell phone rang. She looked at the incoming call and all it showed was *Private number*. "Hello?" she answered tentatively.

"Hey babe. Guess what? I have a cell phone now. I've joined the twenty-first century," Charlie said.

"That's great. I'll have to get the number programmed in. Where are you?"

"I got a tow company to come and get your car out of the ditch this morning. They took it to the Ford dealership in Pueblo, who will be giving you a call about the damages. I don't know, Lou, it looked pretty bad on the driver's side. You may want to think about another car."

"Charlie, thank you so much for doing that. If I have to get a new one, so be it. I did like that Bronco though. So, where are you now?"

"I thought I should find something better than jeans and a flannel shirt to wear to tonight's shindig.

I've been all over the place looking for a suit, but can't settle on anything. I should be at the church by six o'clock, though."

"You could just wear your jeans and a flannel shirt, Ducky. There will be others dressed down."

"I don't have a good pair of jeans though; they're all faded or have holes in places."

"Yes, but they do accentuate your assets nicely."

Charlie laughed. "You're teasing me, miss, and you know what happens when I start thinking about your assets and stuff."

"Sorry, I'll behave. See you later."

"Bye. Love you."

"Love you, too." She snapped her phone closed and smiled. She held the phone to her lips and thought how much she liked telling Charlie she loved him. It sounded so right.

She looked into her open closet and sighed. It beckoned her and she walked up to the clothes. The red turtleneck dress she'd bought for this night looked at her and she took it out. She held it under her chin, turned to her full-length mirror and realized she didn't like it all that much. It came down below her knees and she didn't want to wear her black suede boots. She threw the dress onto her bed and went through the closet hanger by hanger.

In a dry cleaner's bag, at the end she found a dress she hadn't worn in a couple of years. It was a simple black dress with a scoop neck and lace on the back. It came just above her knee. It was form-fitting and she hoped she could still fit into it. It was sleeveless and she didn't want to freeze. The bruise on her neck and wrist would show, but not too much. She found a dark red bolero jacket, also at the end of the closet. It would cover the lace in back and her arms, so she'd be a little warm. If it got too hot she could take it off. She hoped it still fit, too. She pulled a pair of three inch black pumps out and got to work.

She touched up her make-up and put her hair up in a twist. She decided not to wear a bra, not wanting straps showing through the lace, and put on elastic topped stockings and lace panties. She probably would freeze her butt off, but she rarely felt sexy and wanted Charlie to find her very desirable tonight. She laughed when she thought she would have to tease him about the lace panties.

She took her long wool coat out of the closet, grabbed her shoes and purse and headed down the stairs to put on her boots.

"My Lord, if you don't look snazzy. I thought you bought a new dress for tonight? Are you sure you won't be too cold?" Gran asked from the kitchen.

"No, it gets warm in the community center when people start to dance. I'll probably take the jacket off. And the new dress looks too matronly. I want to turn heads tonight." She slipped her boots and coat on.

"I can think of one gentleman who will find you very alluring tonight," Gran said and laughed.

"That's the whole point, Gran. I'll get the pies in and then we should be ready to go."

They loaded the boxes into the trunk of the car and headed out for the church.

"I miss the Bronco, sweetheart. There was more room," Gran said.

"Yeah, I feel like I'm driving with my butt on the road, this one rides so low. Charlie got the Bronco to the dealership in Pueblo. They're supposed to let me know if it's fixable."

"It may be time to get a new one. Sometimes they never get the damage fixed quite right and they don't run well again."

"That's what Charlie said." Lark smiled at her grandmother.

They got to the community center by five o'clock and started setting up. Lark changed from her boots to her heels and immediately wished she'd left her boots on. Trying to shift tables in three inch pumps was difficult.

Lark volunteered every year to help with the beer and wine table. After she got Gran situated with her pies, plates and plastic forks spread out, she walked over and greeted the owners of the brewery. They'd upped the prices by a quarter for sales this year, which was fine. All the proceeds made by the tables were donated to the Children's Auxiliary at the community center. Lark felt good about donating her time.

As people started to arrive, Lark took every opportunity to look for Charlie. At six-thirty, when she hadn't seen him, she thought about calling him, but a line of customers formed and there was no time. She kept feeling like she was being watched and would glance around the room, but didn't think anyone was looking at her.

Mr. Bicken's walked up to her side of the beer table and smiled. "I'd like a glass of the wheat brew that you served me last year."

"Hey, Mr. B. One glass of hefeweizen coming right up," she said and started to pour the beer.

"Is Charlie coming out tonight, Lark? I wanted to let him know that Fox is doing just fine." He took the beer from her and passed a twenty dollar bill across. "Keep the change, sweetie."

"Thank you, Mr. B. Yeah, he's supposed to be here by now, but I haven't seen him yet. I'll have him find you as soon as he arrives. He'll be glad to hear about Fox. That's great." She took another order and Mr. Bicken's moved over to the table by Gran and his wife.

The music started at eight o'clock and as people began to dance, the lines slowed down and she was able to check on Gran. Most of the pies were devoured and she only had one whole pie and two in pieces left. Lark looked over at Mrs. Bickens cookie table and saw she was getting low on edibles, too. Mrs. Hager's cakes and salads were cleaned out.

Lark started to feel the room warm up, so she slipped her jacket off and held it while she walked over to Gran's table. She was a little bugged that Charlie hadn't shown up yet. She wanted to get a dance or two in with him.

"It looks like you and Mrs. Bickens are going to run out and I think Jay's mom is done with her cakes and salads. Which one of the pies got eaten up first?" she asked Gran.

"Oh, the pumpkin went like hotcakes. It's too bad I only made four. I could have made a killing for the auxiliary."

"Gran, have you seen Charlie?" She continued to look around the room and put her jacket on the back of her grandmother's chair.

"Yeah, sweetheart. He's right over there." Gran pointed and then served a piece of mincemeat pie to a buyer.

When Gran finished with her customer, Lark took her arm. "I don't see him, Gran."

"He's right over there, leaning against the wall and talking to Jay Hager. Didn't you all go to school together?"

Lark didn't answer Gran. She scanned along the wall and found Jay. He was talking to some tall man and she continued to look down the wall. Her head snapped back and she looked at the tall man. He stared at her and when Lark realized it was Charlie, air caught in her throat and she almost lost her balance.

He'd gotten his hair cut to a nice, neat length and combed in a feathery style. She could see his ears. He'd shaved off the five o'clock shadow he always wore. He wore a dark gray jacket with a black turtleneck and dark gray wool slacks. He looked so incredibly handsome; Lark thought she might cry. He smiled at her and she could feel her heart pound in her chest.

She felt Gran's hand on her arm and looked at her in total shock.

"Sweetheart, he's been standing over there for close to an hour and a half. He hasn't taken his eyes off you once." Gran arched her eyebrow.

"What?" Lark looked back and he wasn't there anymore. "Where...he...I...where'd he go?" she stuttered and looked around the room for him again.

"Ladies and gentlemen, if I could have your attention for just a moment," the DJ said into a hand-held microphone. He'd stopped the music and made some announcements.

Lark barely heard anything he said. She wanted to find Charlie again and thought he might be playing a game with her tonight.

"First of all, I want to welcome every one of you to the Christmas Festival for the Children's Auxiliary. It's hard to believe a whole year has flown by and we're gathered again tonight for a very good cause. Thank goodness the storm hit two nights ago, instead of tonight. Aurora Metcalfe and Bernice Bickens would have been in a pickle with all those wonderful pies and cookies."

Lark heard scattered laughter as she moved through the crowd, looking left and right for Charlie.

"The pre-sales figures at this time are over five-hundred dollars and several of the ranchers and businesses in the area have promised to match the final amount, so I don't want to see any crumbs left tonight. I know for a fact Mr. Taylor still has ribs on the barbeque out back and there are still other delicious fixings around. So please give all you can. Now, I don't normally do this, but a gentleman wanted to know if he could ask a lady a very important question. Since I'm a romantic at heart, I agreed."

Lark turned to the riser where the DJ was set up for the evening and saw him hand the microphone to Charlie. She froze in her steps.

Charlie smiled at the crowd. Lark saw his eye catch hers and her heart pounded harder in her chest.

"Hi everybody, I'm not a very good speaker so I'll get to the point," Charlie began and then cleared his throat. "My name is Charlie Stone and I was born and raised here in Canon City. For reasons I won't go into, but, I'm sure, some of you remember, I went away for awhile. When I was a kid, I lived next to a neighbor who was my best friend in the whole world. Lark Metcalfe and I went on picnics; we saved Canon City from alien invaders more than a few times and cleaned out her grandmother's freezer on a regular schedule. It was usually the Fudgesicles that went first."

There was some laughter and a few people looked at Lark. She suddenly felt warmer and crossed her arms over her chest. She became mesmerized by Charlie and couldn't move her feet when she saw him look back at her.

"Lark and Aurora Metcalfe saved me several times and taught me many important life lessons. The most important being to not turn your back on the place you've always called home and those who love you and make you feel safe." He put his hand in his pocket and pulled out a small box. "Lark, I've loved you for going on forever, first as a sister and then as a soul mate. With all these friends and family as witnesses, I want to ask you to marry me." She heard his voice crack. "Please, will you consider being my wife?"

The crowd held its breath and turned to Lark. Some of the ladies sniffed and dabbed their eyes. They watched her expectantly.

She felt tears began to trickle down her cheeks and was stunned. She watched Charlie hand the microphone back to the DJ and step off the riser. The crowd parted and let him through. He stopped about ten feet from her.

She took a breath and tried to say *yes*, but couldn't get her voice to work. She cleared her throat and wiped her face. She moved a step closer to him and smiled. "Charlie Stone," she said, loudly. "I would be proud to be your wife."

The crowd clapped and Charlie took a step closer to her and opened the box. She didn't even see the ring. All she wanted to look at was him. She felt him slide the ring onto her finger, but still couldn't take her eyes off him. She put her arms around his neck and felt his hands on her back. They held each other and then she realized the DJ started to play a slow song.

She looked up at him still stunned and unsure of what to say.

"Babe, will you dance with me?"

She nodded as he pulled her close and they started to sway. "Why didn't you tell me about getting your hair cut?" she asked.

Charlie looked down at her and bounced his head back and forth. "Well, I sort of wanted to surprise you, but you looked at me about twenty times and I realized you didn't recognize me anymore. I didn't think I looked that different." He pulled her closer and held her hand on his chest.

She touched his cheek. "You shaved, too." She looked up into his eyes and ran her finger along his jaw. "You don't look that different and you do. I think it was your ears that threw me off. I haven't seen them for a very long time. I'm going to miss your long hair to grab onto when we're fooling around."

"You look so beautiful tonight." She felt his hand move to the small of her back. "I don't think I've ever seen you wear your hair up and your legs are killing me."

She moved her hand to his shoulder. "I can sort of tell you like my appearance tonight." She saw his eyebrows pop up. "There's something hard pressing against my stomach." She smiled and laughed.

"It's that illness I told you about," he whispered into her ear and nibbled the lobe.

"I hope medical science never finds a cure." She finally saw the ring on her finger and stopped moving. It was an oval cut diamond in a brushed silver-lace setting. "Oh my God." She looked up at him. "You didn't break into your school savings, did you?"

"Nope, I sold my truck this morning and got a pretty good price for it. After I found an acceptable four-wheel drive Jeep to get me up to school in the fall, I discovered I had enough left over for a really good ring, not just a nice ring. I'll have enough to live on for awhile, too."

"It's really beautiful. I have to show Gran."

As they turned to walk off the dance floor, Lark stopped. She held her breath and wanted to run from the room. Thomas stood on the edge of the dance floor with a crowd of people and smirked at her.

Charlie put his hand on her arm. "Go over to Gran's table, Lou."

She turned and put her hand on his chest. "No. Charlie, he's not worth it. Please, it's still a wonderful evening. I don't want him to wreck this for us."

He looked down at her and she could see a fire blaze in his eyes. She knew he wanted to protect her and beat Thomas for hurting her in the past, but she couldn't let him do it.

When Lark turned back around, she saw Thomas move closer to them. He wore a smug look on his face and Lark felt intensely disgusted by him. A few of the people from the crowd moved in closer as the scene developed.

"I was going to cut in and congratulate you, my dear." He looked at Charlie. "It would seem you've won the slut, Mr. Stone. You'll have to ask her about her sexual choices. It's very interesting."

Lark pulled Charlie back. "Thomas, I don't know why you're here tonight, but I have nothing to say to you." She took Charlie's hand and attempted to move him away.

"It looks as though she might have told you about our little adventure a couple of months ago," Thomas said and a few more people around them turned to stare. "She was very entertaining that night, you know? She begged for the attention and became quite distraught when she wasn't punished for the screaming."

Lark turned back to Thomas and felt her own fury stir in her head. "I'm not sure you want to discuss that here, Thomas. I have an appointment with the Denver district attorney to give a deposition about your adventure and what happened. It seems there have been many complaints made about your *club*." She let go of Charlie's hand and stood her ground. "You always denied it to me, but there are enough people here tonight if you want to admit the truth of your actions, I'm sure they'll be more than happy to help me out with my testimony. Maybe you should start out by telling them how you drugged me. The blood tests that were done that week showed I still had the drug in my system. The district attorney found that of interest and wants copies of the reports."

"Be very careful, my dear. You might be stepping onto an iced over river. If you fall through, there might not be anyone to help you," he hissed at her.

"I don't think so, Thomas, or you wouldn't look so angry." She turned back to Charlie and took his hand. "Come on, babe. He's a loser and not worth wasting a beautiful night."

They started to walk away and she saw Charlie stare at Thomas.

"Mr. Stone, did she tell you she begged to be tied down? She moaned very loudly and experienced multiple orgasms that night. She was quite sated in the morning when we left. Lark asked me when we could return for more."

Lark felt bile rise in the back of her throat. She looked up at Charlie and tilted her head. "I tried to give him an out. Ducky, you told me about all those anger demons you've bottled up for years; I think it's time to let them loose. Remember when I said he wasn't worth it?"

"Yes." Charlie continued to stare at Thomas.

"He's worth it; plug him a good one for me, babe." She stretched up and kissed his lips lightly.

"Right." He looked down at her. "This won't take long." He took off his coat. "Would you hold on to this for me, sweetheart?"

Lark took the coat and watched Charlie walk up to Thomas. He pushed the sleeves on his turtleneck up his arms. They stared at each other. Charlie had a good five inches on the aggressor. Gran came up along-side of her and took her arm.

"So, you're a body guard now, Mr. Stone," Thomas sneered and it wasn't a question, but a statement.

Charlie laughed, but didn't look away from him. "Have you ever played chicken, Tommy?"

"I can't say that I've had the pleasure and my name is Thomas."

"The first man to blink gets a bloody nose, maybe even a broken nose." He slapped his right fist into his hand. "Sheriff Bennett, if I were to clock this guy in the puss, because of the degrading statements he just made about my fiancée, what would the law think about it?"

Lark looked around and saw a circle of people watching the two men face off. A couple of the men moved their women behind them and Jay Hager walked up behind Charlie and crossed his arms. She didn't realize that Sheriff Bennett was one of the people, but saw him put a hand up to his jaw. He was a tall, older man with graying hair and she knew he was quite muscular under his coat.

"Well, Charlie, it would seem this prick has disrespected your woman with lies. I don't know that I'll have much sympathy for him," Sheriff Bennett said.

Thomas looked away from Charlie and stared at the sheriff. Charlie grabbed the lapel of Thomas's coat.

"You shouldn't have blinked, Tommy," he growled and brought his fist up into Thomas's face.

The smack was loud and Thomas went down on one knee, holding his nose. Charlie pulled him up and grabbed onto both sides of Thomas's jacket. Charlie reared back and pounded a fist into the man's gut. He let the creep fall to the floor where Thomas held his stomach and coughed. Charlie grabbed hold of the back collar of his jacket and pulled him back up to his feet. He started to turn Thomas toward the door that led to the parking lot, but Lark saw Sheriff Bennett walk up to him and put his hand on Charlie's wrist.

"Charlie, let me take care of this. I'll be sure he leaves Canon City," the sheriff said.

Charlie let go of the jacket and nodded.

They watched the sheriff escort Thomas out of the building. She saw him turn around and look at her. He smirked through the blood coming from his nose. "This isn't over Lark. You'll be hearing from my attorney," he said and Sheriff Bennett pulled his arm and got him out the door.

Some of the folks who'd watched the scene started to clap. Charlie shrugged and walked up to her. She saw the blaze had simmered down in his eyes and he gently put his hand on her cheek. He moved closer to her and she could feel his warm breath on her lips.

"How about that?" he whispered and put his lips on hers. He pushed his tongue into her mouth and gently stroked around her teeth and cheeks and connected with her tongue.

Warmth flooded her system and her heart pounded in her chest. She realized her core was pulsing and her nipples had grown very hard. "Ducky, you are so hot, right now. Are you okay? Is your hand all right?" she whispered back and smiled at him.

He looked down at his hand and flexed it a couple of times. "Yep, I don't think I broke anything." His lips curled and he leaned over to kiss her, again.

She heard whoops come from the crowd and turned with Charlie to look around them. He bent at the waist and bowed. Lark laughed. He took his coat out of her hands and put it back on. The DJ started the music again.

"Sweetheart, if you wouldn't mind, Gran looks a little dismayed over there and I'd like to ask her for a dance. Maybe I can let her know that we'll fill her in later when we get home," he said.

"Yeah, I'll sugarcoat it a little, but I'll have to let her know what happened."

He touched her lips with his fingers. "I'll be there with you, Lou. You won't have to tell her alone." His eyebrows rose and he put his hand on her cheek. "Now, I think we should plan on leaving soon. I'm very interested to see what you have on under that dress."

"Gran would probably be over-the-moon if you asked her to dance," she said and kissed him again. "And I think I'll give her the keys to the rental. I want to see your new Jeep and, of course, show you what's not on under the dress." She arched her eyebrow.

He kissed her again and whispered, "You are such a tease, and how will I ever tame you?"

"That's funny, I just wondered the same thing about you." She grinned.

He ran his tongue over her bottom lip and then turned. She watched Charlie walk over to Gran. He offered his arm and Gran grinned and took it. They made their way out to the dance floor.

Nancy came over to Lark and linked arms with her. "My oh my, if this hasn't been a crazy week. The business is almost taken over by your ex-fiancé and then was saved by our oh-so-brilliant attorney. You got rid of a loser, but are now engaged to a hottie and, may I say, a very good defender. I'm out of breath. It's hard to keep up."

"You're right, it seems like I blinked and everything changed. Wait, is it okay for me to blink?" Lark said.

"Have you set a date yet?"

"He just asked me, Nance. I think I really want to enjoy this engagement though. He's going to start veterinary school at Fort Collins in the fall. I'm not sure if we'll do a wedding before or after."

"Will you let me do a bridal shower this time?"

"We'll have to discuss it. I'm still not sure it's necessary." Lark held her hand up and showed Nancy the ring.

""You're not going to be grumpy-pants with me again?" She took Larks hand and examined the ring. "This is beautiful."

"Charlie has good taste. And I was not grumpy with you. I just didn't want to get good stuff and then have to share it with Thomas." Lark laughed.

"Point taken. I better go find my significant other. See you Monday." Nancy walked over to the beer section and Lark saw her find her husband.

She looked out at the dance floor and watched the dancers. She saw Charlie come toward her with a look on his face that made her toasty warm. He put his arm around her shoulder and kissed her. He laced his fingers with hers and kissed the back of her hand.

"Where's Gran?"

"She wanted to talk to Mrs. Bicken's about the bake-off and I had to thank Sheriff Bennett for his support. I don't know if you ever knew this, but he was one of the officers who arrested me on that really bad night years ago. He testified at my hearing and convinced the judge that I shouldn't be sent to prison. There were many, many times when he and his partner came to the house because of complaints. He's a good man." He looked at her. "It just hit me. You're going to be Mrs. Stone. How very cool is that?" He smiled at her and kissed the palm of her hand.

"Yes and you will be my husband, at my beck and call. I'll require breakfast in bed every Saturday morning. I will also want you to meet me in the shower on a regular basis." She noticed Charlie's grin get bigger. "So, you liked the shower?"

"Oh yeah. In fact, I'm thinking we may want to invest in a bigger hot water tank. The water gets cold too fast."

"I noticed that, but you did keep me very warm." She laughed. "We could always bring your rubber duck in with us."

"Nope. Sorry, I'm not sharing you with anything. You're mine, toots. You better get used to it."

"It might be a struggle, but I'm sure I will."

"How about you come out on the dance floor and let me feel you up?" Charlie wiggled his eyebrows.

Lark sighed and let him lead her out.

Chapter Twenty-Eight

Lark woke up and felt Charlie's arm move tighter over her stomach. She pushed back to his chest and yawned. "Good morning, Ducky."

"Good morning, Almost Mrs. Stone," he said and kissed her ear.

She looked over her shoulder and saw he was propped up on his elbow. She smiled and twisted around to face him. "Merry Christmas."

"Hey, that's right. Merry Christmas to you." He brought his hand up to her face and traced her lips with a finger. "You know, I love waking up with you so much. When the light starts coming in the window, I have to wake up and watch you sleep. It confirms that I'm not dreaming and we're really together."

She kissed his finger and felt warmth run into her pelvis. "You're the best Christmas present I've ever received, except..." She stopped and got a serious look on her face.

"Except what?"

"Except for that one year. I don't remember how old we were, but you saved up your paper route money and got me that pretty little heart pendant with the fake diamond in it. I wonder what I did with that."

"So, that was your best ever and I'm in second place?" His hand moved down to her hip.

"Don't think of it that way, Ducky. You're very important, too." She grinned and started to laugh.

"Are you teasing me, again, Almost Mrs. Stone?"

"Hee, hee...just a little." She crinkled her nose and pulled up to kiss his lips.

He pushed her onto her back and moved between her legs. He scooted down a little and began to nibble at her breasts. "I may have to keep you in bed all day and see how many times I can make you shout my name."

"Oh, Charlie, I love that idea very much, but you know Gran got up at five o'clock to get the turkey and stuffing into the oven. We can't disappoint her, but maybe we could plan on doing this on New Year's Day. What do you think?" She arched her back as he sucked and lightly bit her nipple.

"It's a date, babe. Do you think today would be a good time to tell Gran we've set the date to get married for Valentine's Day?" He moved his hips and put his hand down between them. He ran his fingers over her warm folds.

Lark moaned and bucked her pelvis up against his hand. "Ducky, I love what your fingers do to me. It's heavenly and yes, we should tell Gran today." He continued to tease her nub until she was wet and ready for him. When he moved the head of his shaft to her opening, she moaned again louder and wrapped her legs around his waist as he entered her channel slowly.

She looked up into his eyes. "Hey, I've got an idea. What if we get Gran to make a huge yellow ducky cake for the wedding reception?"

"Ask me again later, I can't talk anymore, Lou," he said and looked down at her with his eyes half closed.

"Oh, babe." She sucked in a breath as he pushed in all the way. "This is the best Christmas ever, my darling man." She put her hand up into his shorter hair and his mouth moved down to her with a tender kiss.

"I love you, Almost Mrs. Stone," he whispered.

Lark and Charlie carried their bags of gifts over to Gran's. She wanted to skip through the snow and laugh until her lungs hurt, but didn't want to become silly. She'd loved the shower they took together that morning and after they drank a cup of coffee, decided they needed to straighten up and behave. Although, her grandmother claimed she was hip, Lark knew she could also be traditional and didn't want to upset Gran. They walked through the snow to the back door of the only home they'd both ever known. Breaker bounced along with them and bounded in the back door when it was open.

Gran was chopping onions and when she turned around, Lark grinned at her and gave her a hug. "Merry Christmas, Gran."

Charlie hugged them both and kissed Gran's cheek. "I have my two favorite women in my arms. How lucky is that?" he said.

"Oh, Charlie Stone, it's too early in the day for flirty stuff. Get your coats off. Oh my goodness," Gran said and leaned over to pet Breaker. "There's a good boy. How's Breaker this morning?" She moved a can on the counter, popped the lid and tossed a treat to Breaker.

Charlie took the bags from Lark and disappeared into the living room. Lark poured them both a cup of coffee. "Gran, your kitchen always smells so heavenly. I love it." She sipped her coffee and watched as Gran put the chopped onions into a skillet. "Are those for the gravy?"

"Yes, it will be a bit before the turkey's ready to come out of the oven, but I wanted to be all caught up, so we could sit for a while and open our presents."

Lark moved up to her and kissed her cheek. "You're so smart."

"Go sit down. I'll be out in a minute."

Lark picked up the other cup and walked into the living room. Charlie had arranged all their gifts under the tree and Lark wished she had a camera. "Gran, bring your camera. I think we'll have some new pictures to add to the scrapbook."

She saw Charlie look over his shoulder at her and he stood up. He walked over to her and took the cup out of her hand.

"It almost looks too pretty to mess up," he said.

Gran walked up behind them and put her hand around Lark's waist. "This is going to be the best Christmas ever," she said and smiled.

"I said the same exact thing this morning." Lark put her hand on her grandmother's shoulder and gave her a squeeze. "Great minds must run in the family."

"It's in the Levi's, sweetheart," Gran laughed. "Now sit down and let's get down to business."

Chapter Twenty-Nine

Four years later

Charlie held up his cards. "I declare war," he said and put down two of the cards. He held the third card and grinned at Lark.

They put their cards down at the same time. She had a two of hearts and he a king of clubs. He picked up all the cards.

"Hey, wait a minute. I think you stacked the deck," Lark said.

Charlie threw the cards aside, grabbed her around the waist and pulled her between his legs. He tickled her ribs and she laughed.

They'd ridden Fox out to a field for a picnic. It was a lovely location behind the Bickens's ranch. It was May and Lark wanted to see the wildflowers in bloom. Breaker was playing with Fox, both animals bounced around the field. The Larkspur, Columbine and Foxglove were in full bloom and the field was a rainbow of colors.

"Okay, okay, I give. Uncle," Lark said. She still laughed and was out of breath.

Charlie wrapped his arms around her and nuzzled her neck. She hugged him back and looked up at the sky.

"What a gorgeous day. We really got lucky." She leaned against his chest.

"Every day with you is gorgeous, Mrs. Doctor Stone."

"I'm so glad Ryan called with the news about those charges finally being dropped. It only took four years, but, hey, I won't complain."

Charlie chuckled. "I think it's hilarious that it took Thomas so long to realize he didn't have a leg to stand on. It makes me wonder what Sheriff Bennett said during his deposition. My only regret is that I didn't get to knock a couple of his teeth out."

"No regrets, sweetie," she said and held onto his arms. "I'm sure the sheriff told the truth and spoke very highly about your behavior that night. Thomas was very rude and I think it's really hilarious that the list of the members of his club got released to the local paper. I'm sure he has some clients who aren't very happy with all that publicity."

"Do you still want to go and burn the mansion down?" he asked and tightened his hold around her.

"Naw, it's closed. That's all that matters." She twisted around and kissed his lips. "That reminds me." She turned all the way around in his arms to face him. "I have another graduation gift for you."

"Sweetheart, the red Bronco must have cost you a pretty penny."

Lark frowned. "Well, I can't return this one. Lord, it hasn't even arrived and I have to return it? That's just not fair and I don't think I can do that."

Charlie felt his brows come together. "What is it?"

"I don't know."

"Lou, what do you mean you don't know? You ordered it, didn't you?"

She bit her lip. "I didn't really order it, but I can't return it."

Charlie tilted his head. "Are you teasing me?"

"Not at all, my darling." She started to laugh. "It will arrive in six months." She raised her eyebrows.

"Honey, are you pregnant?"

"What if I am?" She grinned and leaned over to kiss him. "Will you still keep me?"

Charlie lost his voice and looked at her with his brows still creased. "Really?" he finally whispered.

"Yes, really."

He put his hand up on her cheek and felt tears form in his eyes. "Yes, I'll keep you. I can't survive without you, babe." He sniffed and cleared his throat. "Do you know if it's a boy or girl?"

"Not yet. I'll have an ultrasound when I'm nineteen weeks. I want him to look like you." She held his hand to her cheek. "He will be tall with incredible blue eyes and knock out all the girls."

"She might look like you."

"No, I want a junior Ducky running around and saving us from alien invaders, just like his daddy did when we were young. We have a few weeks to decide if we want to know ahead of time or wait for the big surprise on delivery day."

"Have you told Gran?"

"Not yet, you had to be the first to know. I thought we could tell her tonight at dinner."

"That sounds good." Charlie stretched out flat on his back and pulled her down with him. "You're going to cut your hours at the women's center, right?"

"Ducky, are you going to get bossy?" She put her chin on his chest.

"No, I just want you to take it easy. I know how you are when you're either volunteering or working at the warehouse. I want you to put your feet up and let me suck your toes." He smiled.

"Okay, I'll admit I agree with you. I need to learn how to sit still." She propped up on her arm and looked down at him. "We'll need to put a nursery together and start buying diapers and stuff like that."

"And, I need to get a job. My externship will only last about six months. Why didn't you tell me sooner?"

"I didn't want you to be distracted when you were studying for your boards. I'm twelve weeks and only found out a month ago, but it's been hard to keep my trap shut."

"When are you due to pop?"

Lark laughed. "Pop? That makes me sound like a toaster. The doctor thinks sometime in December, but we won't know for certain until they do the ultrasound." She played with the buttons on his shirt.

Charlie put his hand behind his head and watched her fingers. "Sweetheart, do you think that is a good idea?" She moved her hand into his shirt and felt his chest.

"The doctor said I could participate in love-making until I didn't feel up to it. And, knowing me, I'm going to feel up to it for the whole pregnancy. My hormones have made me extremely horny."

He sat up and kissed her lips. "That wasn't what I was talking about. We're only about two hundred yards from the Bickens back door and you know how easy it is for me to be turned on."

"Dang, you're right. Maybe we should head home. I'm feeling awfully warm out here." She moved her hand to the front of his pants and cupped his twitching shaft. "And, I almost forgot about your serious illness. I'll just have to take care of it, won't I?"

Charlie leaned over and put his lips lightly on hers. "I love you, Lou."

She reached up and ran her hand through his hair. "I love you, too."

He started to lean back in to give her another, longer kiss, when a wet, sloppy tongue started licking the side of his face. "Ah, Breaker." He put his hand in front of the wolf. "I thought we talked about this. When your mom and I are mashing our faces together, you need to hold back and sit down."

Breaker sat down with a smile on his muzzle and woofed at them.

If you or anyone you know needs assistance from domestic abuse or sexual assault, please contact:

The National Domestic Abuse Hotline at 1-800-799-SAFE (7233)

The National Sexual Assault Hotline at 1-800-656-HOPE

Note from author: My dad was a huge sports fan. He used to joke that if they wore a number and sweat, he'd watch it. I watched the traditional sports, football, baseball, basketball, hockey, golfing and tennis, and the not so traditional sports rugby, soccer and Canadian curling all through my childhood. We'd sit on the couch and cheer somebody.

Lark Metcalfe's middle name needed to be Louise and her nickname from Charlie had to be Lou. Mostly, it was for my Uncle Louie who gave me so many good memories. But, also, it was for Lou Piniella. He was a great baseball player and the manager for our Seattle Mariner's. My dad always thought he was one of the most under-rated players, but found a lot of joy when Sweet Lou came to Seattle to coach our big league team.

This is just to give you an idea where some of the names come from.

Lauren Marie

ABOUT THE AUTHOR
LAUREN MARIE

Lauren Marie lives with her four cats in Western Washington State. Although, she has been focusing her current efforts in the paranormal romance, time-travel and reincarnation genres, she is currently working on continuing the Canon City Series.

When she isn't pounding the keys, she is an amateur paranormal investigator. She formed her own group in 2006 to hunt ghosts and some unusual experiences have put in an appearance in some of her stories.

Lauren likes to receive feedback. If you want to send her likes and dislikes, you can go to the contact us page on the web-site laurenmariebooks.com or write to her at laurenmariebooks@ hotmail.com, themenofhallerlake@hotmail.com. or friend her at facebook.com/laurenmariebooks.